MAFIA KING

L. STEELE

1

Mafia King

Karma

"Morn came and went—and came, and brought no day..."

Tears prick the backs of my eyes. Goddamn Byron. His words creep up on me when I am at my weakest. Not that I am a poetry addict, by any measure, but words are my jam. The one consolation I have is that, when everything else in the world is wrong, I can turn to them, and they'll be there, friendly, steady, waiting with open arms.

And this particular poem had laced my blood, crawled into my gut when I'd first read it. Darkness had folded within me like an insidious snake, that raises its head when I least expect it. Like now, when I look out on the still sleeping city of London, from the grassy slope of Waterlow Park.

Somewhere out there, the Mafia is hunting me, apparently. It's why my sister Summer and her new husband Sinclair Sterling had insisted that I have my own security detail. I had agreed...only to appease them...then given my bodyguard the slip this morning. I had decided to come running here because it's not a place I'd normally go... Not so early in the morning, anyway. They won't think to look for me here. At least, not for a while longer.

I purse my lips, close my eyes. Silence. The rustle of the wind between the leaves. The faint tinkle of the water from the nearby spring.

I could be the last person on this planet, alone, unsung, bound for the grave.

Ugh! Stop. Right there. I drag the back of my hand across my nose. Try it again, focus, get the words out, one after the other, like the steps of my sorry life.

"*Morn came and went—and came, and... and...*" My voice breaks. "Bloody asinine hell." I dig my fingers into the grass and grab a handful and fling it out. Again. From the top.

"*Morn came and went—and came, and—*"

"*...brought no day.*"

A gravelly voice completes my sentence.

I whip my head around. His silhouette fills my line of sight. He's sitting on the same knoll as me, yet I have to crane my neck back to see his profile. The sun is at his back, so I can't make out his features. Can't see his eyes... Can only take in his dark hair, combed back by a ruthless hand that brooked no measure.

My throat dries.

Thick dark hair, shot through with grey at the temples. He wears his age like a badge. I don't know why, but I know his years have not been easy. That he's seen more, indulged in more, reveled in the consequences of his actions, however extreme they might have been. He's not a normal, everyday person, this man. Not a nine-to-fiver, not someone who lives an average life. Definitely not a man who returns home to his wife and home at the end of the day. He is... different, unique, evil... Monstrous. Yes, he is a beast, one who sports the face of a man but who harbors the kind of darkness inside that speaks to me. I gulp.

His face boasts a hooked nose, a thin upper lip, a fleshy lower lip. One that hints at hidden desires, Heat. Lust. The sensuous scrape of that whiskered jaw over my innermost places. Across my inner thigh, reaching toward that core of me that throbs, clenches, melts to feel the stab of his tongue, the thrust of his hardness as he impales me, takes me, makes me his. Goosebumps pop on my skin.

I drag my gaze away from his mouth down to the scar that slashes across his throat. A cold sensation coils in my chest. What or who had hurt him in such a cruel fashion?

"Of this their desolation; and all hearts
Were chill'd into a selfish prayer for light..."

He continues in that rasping guttural tone. Is it the wound that caused that scar that makes his voice so...gravelly... So deep... so...so, hot?

Sweat beads my palms and the hairs on my nape rise. "Who are you?"

He stares ahead as his lips move,

"Forests were set on fire—but hour by hour
They fell and faded—and the crackling trunks
Extinguish'd with a crash—and all was black."

I swallow, moisture gathers in my core. How can I be wet by the mere cadence of this stranger's voice?

I spring up to my feet.

"Sit down," he commands.

His voice is unhurried, lazy even, his spine erect. The cut of his black jacket stretches across the width of his massive shoulders. His hair... I was mistaken—there are threads of dark gold woven between the darkness that pours down to brush the nape of his neck. A strand of hair falls over his brow. As I watch, he raises his hand and brushes it away. Somehow, the gesture lends an air of vulnerability to him. Something so at odds with the rest of his persona that, surely, I am mistaken?

My scalp itches. I take in a breath and my lungs burn. This man... He's sucked up all the oxygen in this open space as if he owns it, the master of all he surveys. The master of me. My death. My life. A shiver ladders along my spine. *Get away, get away now, while you still can.*

I angle my body, ready to spring away from him.

"I won't ask again."

Ask. Command. Force me to do as he wants. He'll have me on my back, bent over, on my side, on my knees, over him, under him. He'll surround me, overwhelm me, pin me down with the force of his personality. His charisma, his larger-than-life essence will crush everything else out of me and I… I'll love it.

"No."

"Yes."

A fact. A statement of intent, spoken aloud. So true. So real. Too real. Too much. Too fast. All of my nightmares…my dreams come to life. Everything I've wanted is here in front of me. I'll die a thousand deaths before he'll be done with me… And then? Will I be reborn? For him. For me. For myself.

I live, first and foremost, to be the woman I was…am meant to be.

"You want to run?"

No.

No.

I nod my head.

He turns his, and all the breath leaves my lungs. Blue eyes—cerulean, dark like the morning skies, deep like the night-time...hidden corners, secrets that I don't dare uncover. He'll destroy me, have my heart, and break it so casually.

My throat burns and a boiling sensation squeezes my chest.

"Go then, my beauty, fly. You have until I count to five. If I catch you, you are mine."

"If you don't?"

"Then I'll come after you, stalk your every living moment, possess your nightmares, and steal you away in the dead of night, and then…"

I draw in a shuddering breath as liquid heat drips from between my legs. "Then?" I whisper.

"Then, I'll ensure you'll never belong to anyone else, you'll never see the light of day again, for your every breath, your every waking second, your thoughts, your actions...and all your words, every single last one, will belong to me." He peels back his lips, and his teeth glint in the first rays of the morning light. "Only me." He straightens to his feet and rises, and rises.

This man... He is massive. A monster who always gets his way. My guts churn. My toes curl. Something primeval inside of me insists I hold my own. I cannot give in to him. Cannot let him win whatever this is. I need to stake my ground, in some form. *Say something. Anything. Show him you're not afraid of this.*

"Why?" I tilt my head back, all the way back. "Why are you doing this?"

He tilts his head, his ears almost canine in the way they are silhouetted against his profile.

"Is it because you can? Is it a...a," I blink, "a debt of some kind?"

He stills.

"My father, this is about how he betrayed the Mafia, right? You're one of them?"

"Lucky guess." His lips twist, "It is about your father, and how he promised you to me. He reneged on his promise, and now, I am here to collect."

"No." I swallow... *No, no, no.*

"Yes." His jaw hardens.

All expression is wiped clean of his face, and I know then, that he speaks the truth. It's always about the past. My sorry shambles of a past... Why does it always catch up with me? *You can run, but you can never hide.*

"Tick-tock, Beauty." He angles his body and his shoulders shut out the sight of the sun, the dawn skies, the horizon, the city in the distance, the rustle of the grass, the trees, the rustle of the leaves. All of it fades and leaves just me and him. Us. *Run.*

"Five." He jerks his chin, straightens the cuffs of his sleeves.

My knees wobble.

"Four."

My pulse rate spikes. I should go. Leave. But my feet are planted in this earth. This piece of land where we first met. What am I, but a speck in the larger scheme of things? To be hurt. To be forgotten. To be taken without an ounce of retribution. To be punished...by him.

"Three." He thrusts out his chest, widens his stance, every muscle in his body relaxed. "Two."

I swallow. The pulse beats at my temples. My blood thrums.

"One."

2

Michael

"Go."

She pivots and races down the slope. Her dark hair streams behind her. Her scent, sexy femininity and silver moonflowers, clings to my nose, then recedes. It's so familiar, that scent.

I had smelled it before, had reveled in it. Had drawn in it into my lungs as she had peeked up at me from under her thick eyelashes. Her green gaze had fixed on mine, her lips parted as she welcomed my kiss. As she had wound her arms about my neck, pushed up those sweet breasts and flattened them against my chest. As she had parted her legs when I had planted my thigh between them. I had seen her before...in my dreams. I stiffen. She can't be the same girl though, can she?

I reach forward, thrust out my chin and sniff the air, but there's only the damp scent of dawn, mixed with the foul tang of exhaust fumes, as she races away from me.

She stumbles and I jump forward, pause when she straightens.

Wait. Wait. Give her a lead. Let her think she has almost escaped, that she's gotten the better of me… As if.

I clench my fists at my sides, force myself to relax. Wait. Wait. She reaches the bottom of the incline, turns. I surge forward. One foot in front of the other. My heels dig into the grassy surface and mud flies up, clings to the hem of my £4000 Italian pants. Like I care? Plenty more where that came from. An entire walk-in closet, full of clothes made to measure, to suit every occasion, with every possible accessory needed by a man in my position to impress…

Everything... Except the one thing that I had coveted from the moment I had laid eyes on her. Sitting there on the grassy slope, unshed tears in her eyes, and reciting… Byron? For hell's sake. Of all the poets in the world, she had to choose the Lord of Darkness.

I huff. All a ploy. Clearly, she knew I was sitting next to her… No, not possible. I had walked toward her and she hadn't stirred. Hadn't been aware. Yeah, I am that good. I've been known to slit a man's throat from ear-to-ear while he was awake and in his full senses. Alive one second, dead the next. That's how it is in my world. You want it, you take it. And I… I want her.

I increase my pace, eat up the distance between myself and the girl… That's all she is. A slip of a thing, a slim blur of motion. Beauty in hiding. A diamond, waiting for me to get my hands on her, polish her, show her what it means to be…

Dead. She is dead. That's why I am here.

A flash of skin, a creamy length of thigh. My groin hardens and my legs wobble. I lurch over a bump in the ground. The hell? I right myself, leap forward, inching closer, closer. She reaches a curve in the path, disappears out of sight.

My heart hammers in my chest. I will not lose her, will not. *Here, Beauty, come to Daddy.* The wind whistles past my ears. I pump my legs, lengthen my strides, turn the corner. There's no one there. Huh?

My heart hammers and the blood pounds at my wrists, my temples; adrenaline thrums in my veins. I slow down, come to a stop. Scan the clearing.

The hairs on my forearms prickle. She's here. Not far, but where?

Where is she? I prowl across to the edge of the clearing, under the tree with its spreading branches.

When I get my hands on you, Beauty, I'll spread your legs like the pages of a poem. Dip into your honeyed sweetness, like a quill pen in ink. Drag my aching shaft across that melting, weeping entrance. My balls throb. My groin tightens. The crack of a branch above shivers across my stretched nerve endings. I swoop forward, hold out my arms, and close my grasp around the trembling, squirming mass of precious humanity. I cradle her close to my chest, heart beating thud-thud-thud, overwhelming any other thought.

Mine. All mine. The hell is wrong with me? She wriggles her little body, and her curves slide across my forearms. My shoulders bunch and my fingers tingle. She kicks out with her legs and arches her back, thrusting her breasts up so her nipples are outlined against the fabric of her sports bra. She dared to come out dressed like that? In that scrap of fabric that barely covers her luscious flesh?

"Let me go." She whips her head toward me and her hair flows around her shoulders, across her face. She blows it out of the way. "You monster, get away from me."

Anger drums at the backs of my eyes and desire tugs at my groin. The scent of her is sheer torture, something I had dreamed of in the wee hours of twilight when dusk turned into night.

She's not real. She's not the woman I think she is. She is my downfall. My sweet poison. The bitter medicine I must partake of to cure the ills that plague my company,

"Fine." I lower my arms and she tumbles to the grass, hits the ground butt first.

"How dare you." She huffs out a breath, her hair messily arranged across her face.

I shove my hands into the pockets of my fitted pants, knees slightly bent, legs apart. Tip my chin down and watch her as she sprawls at my feet.

"You...dropped me?" She makes a sound deep in her throat.

So damn adorable.

"Your wish is my command." I quirk my lips.

"You don't mean it."

"You're right." I lean my weight forward on the balls of my feet and she flinches.

"What…what do you want?"

"You."

She pales. "You want to…to rob me? I have nothing of consequence,

"Oh, but you do, Beauty."

I lean in and every muscle in her body tenses. Good. She's wary. She should be. She should have been alert enough to have run as soon as she sensed my presence. But she hadn't.

I should spare her because she's the woman from my dreams...but I won't. She's a debt I intend to collect. She owes me, and I've delayed what was meant to happen long enough.

I pull the gun from my holster, point it at her.

Her gaze widens and her breath hitches. I expect her to plead with me for her life, but she doesn't. She stares back at me with her huge dilated pupils. She licks her lips and the blood drains to my groin. *Che cazzo!* Why does her lack of fear turn me on so?

"Your phone," I murmur, "take out your phone."

She draws in a breath, then reaches into her pocket and pulls out her phone.

"Call your sister."

"What?"

"Dial your sister, Beauty. Tell her you are going away on a long trip to Sicily with your new male friend."

"What?"

"You heard me." I curl my lips, "Do it, now!'

She blinks, looks like she is about to protest, then her fingers fly over the phone.

Damn, and I had been looking forward to coaxing her into doing my bidding.

She holds her phone to her ear. I can hear the phone ring on the other side, before it goes to voicemail. She glances at me and I jerk my chin. She looks away, takes a deep breath, then speaks in a cheerful voice, "Hi Summer, it's me, Karma. I, ah, have to go away for a bit. This new...ah, friend of mine... He has an extra ticket and he has invited me to Sicily to spend some time with him. I...ah, I don't know when, exactly, I'll be back, but I'll message you and let you know. Take care. Love ya sis, I—"

I snatch the phone from her, disconnect the call, then hold the gun to her temple, "Goodbye, Beauty."

3

Karma

The whoop-whoop-whump grows louder, infiltrates my mind. Darkness, so dark, I'm floating. The back of my head hits something hard. Red and white sparks flare behind my eyeballs. I crack my eyelids open and pain slices through my brain. I groan, and the sound echoes back at me. Sweat beads my neck, my palms. My sports bra is sticking to my back. Booty shorts? Check. My running shoes—I wriggle my feet—I still have them on. What happened? What—? The ringing in my ears whooshes up, engulfs me.

He shot me. The bastard shot me?

A trembling grips me; my arms and legs grow numb. The blood beats in my ears. My pulse rate ratchets up and my guts churn. Bile rushes up my throat and I cough. No, I will not be sick. Not now. I take in a breath, another. Focus, focus on the now, as Ma used to say. She was a hippie, who'd hitched a ride with my businessman father. Then married him and given birth to me and my sister. Bequeathed us quirky nicknames, which had ultimately made it to our passports…talk about fate, huh?

As to why she called me Karma? It was a joke, on me. Bad luck seems to dog my footsteps. How else do you explain this…this situation? Me being kidnapped by…tall, dark and dangerous?

My stomach flutters, my scalp tingles. No, no, I am insane. That brooding gaze, that mean glare? Damn it, what is it about me that I seem to attract the assholes, huh? I fumble around, shove my hand in the pocket of my shorts… No! My phone is gone. Of course, bastard had kept it, and then he had pushed the barrel of his gun into my temple. I had squeezed my eyes shut, the blood roaring in my ears, and then I'd heard the bang. Then nothing. But he hadn't shot me. No he hadn't. If he had, I wouldn't be alive. And I'm pretty sure I am.

I run a mental check across my body... No, I don't seem to be hurt anywhere. Which means, he had pretended to shoot me... Likely, shot into the air next to my head... Asshole. Clearly, he'd done it to frighten me...to get me to comply. What a bastard. My pulse begins to drum. Why? Why did he do that? What is he going to do with me?

Whoomp-whoomp-thump. The hell? I stiffen. The container I am in rocks from side to side…very gently. Not a boat… I am in a… I glance around the enclosed space. There's room for, maybe, one more person, a very small person… My foot grazes something. I feel around with my sneaker. There's something springy—made of rubber. A tire? A car honks, muffled, as if coming from a distance or through a layer of metal. A car. I am in a vehicle? In the trunk, probably.

I snake my fist out and into the curved barrier around me. "Ow!" Pain glances down my arm. "Let me the hell out!"

The vehicle seems to speed up. My heart begins to hammer so fast, I am sure it's going to break out of my ribcage. This is not good... I really shouldn't put so much stress on my heart... I was born with a hole in my heart, which hadn't been discovered until a few years ago. It isn't life-threatening, yet. But it could be, if left untreated. The doctors had warned that I would need a procedure soon, but for the time-being, they had put me on medication to see if it would help.

Meanwhile, I'd been told not to exert myself... Instructions which I hadn't adhered to, of course. It's why my sister Summer is overly-protective of me. It's why I had gone running in the park, and why I have refused to take the medicines; because I hate feeling less than anyone else. I had wanted to prove to myself that I was fine.

Damn it, if I hadn't gone running, he wouldn't have come across me and kidnapped me. OMG, he's kidnapping me. Adrenaline laces my blood. My heart beat instantly spikes. That's not good, not good at all. *Calm down, take another breath, and another.* I manage to calm myself down somewhat.

Where is he taking me? Why did he kidnap me? I have to get the hell out of here. Have to. I join my fists, draw in a breath, then yank them up. Connect with the overhead covering. The loud thunk fills the space. I cry out. Pain slices down my arms and my shoulders hurt. There's a screeching sound, audible even through the layer of metal. I am thrown forward, then back. All movement stops. Hell. I've done it now. I've gotten their attention. Jesus H. Christ, are you somewhere around? I'd never prayed when the nuns had held mass, but damn it, if you are there… Please, please… I bring my knuckles to my mouth, suck on the throbbing flesh. Help me, God.

The cover flies up and light pours over me. I squeeze my eyes shut, then crack them open, just a tad. Wide shoulders, a massive chest that blocks out the daylight. His features are in repose, the sun to his back. I can't see his face, but I know who it is. Him.

"Move over." His hard baritone whips through the space.

"What?"

He swoops out his hand, grabs my shoulder and pushes me back. Then swings a leg over and inside the boot.

The hell?

He sinks down. *No, no, no. He can't be doing this.*

"I am."

He lowers his big body and I scoot back, all the way back in that enclosed space, until my back is flat against the barrier of the car… He sinks down into the space I vacated. If he gets in here with me, we'll be face to face, chest to breasts, thigh to thigh, crotch to— I turn my back on him, as he lowers the last of his bulk into the already cramped space.

"Good thinking." His voice rumbles down my back.

"At least one of us is," I growl, "because, clearly, you're not in your right senses... You—"

The cover of the boot slams down and a tiny light bulb flicks on just above us.

"What the—?" I blink, stare up at the illumination. It's not much, but at least, I can see my nose in front of my face.

"Say thank you, Beauty."

"Go fly a kite."

"You can do better than that."

The vehicle roars forward, slamming me back and into the wall of his body. Every hard, corded, coiled inch of him surrounds me. I gulp. Dense waves of heat sear my back, sink into my blood, snake into the hollow between my thighs. Oh, hell!

Goosebumps flare on my skin; moisture laces my palms, my brow. My throat is so dry that I swear my tongue is stuck to the roof of my mouth. Not good. This is not good.

"Where are you taking me?"

"You're hardly in a position to ask questions."

The hard planes of his chest graze my shoulders. I gulp. Freeze. Every muscle in my body goes rigid. His powerful thighs fit in the V of where I have folded up my legs. He slides his arm under my neck, wraps the other around my waist, and pulls me close.

Something thick and long stabs at the curve of my backside, OMG! Is that...is it...? I squeeze my thighs together, try to scoot away. His grip tightens.

"Stop that," he growls.

As if I am going to jump to his every command. I huff, wriggle forward, but end up brushing my butt against his turgid length.

"See what happens when you don't obey?"

I freeze.

"You can't...do this."

"I already am."

"My sister will be worried when she can't reach me."

"You already called her."

"I...what?" I turn my head, glower at him.

"You told her you were going on a long holiday with a friend."

Oh, right. "She'll never believe that," I huff.

Besides, Summer's so overprotective. She wouldn't just let me take off like that without suspecting something, right?

"She has a new husband, a future... She's not going to miss you for a while."

"How did you...?" I shut my mouth. "You...you stalked me?"

"You aren't that important."

Anger coats my tongue. How dare he insult me? "I mean something, because you didn't kill me..."

"Yet." I hear the amusement in his voice.

Bet all this is just one long walk in the park for him. Which is where he found me. How long had he been following me? Did he know my routine? Is that how he marked out the best time to abduct me? My heart begins to thud. This is not good. This is really happening.

"Why me?" I say in a low tone. "Why did you kidnap me?"

"The eternal question." He yawns. The bastard yawns, as if he's bored with this conversation.

"Tell me," I insist, "what do you want in exchange?"

"What makes you think I am interested in getting anything in exchange?"

"What do you mean?" I glance sideways and up at what I can see of that gorgeous face. Those high cheekbones, the hooked nose, that pouty lower lip of his that was made for sinking my teeth into, swiping my tongue across the seam, as I nibble on that delectable mouth... Gah! My face heats and a pulse flares to life between my legs. "What do you mean, you are not interested in an exchange? You must want something in return."

"I have everything."

"Then why take me?"

"That's what I am trying to figure out."

What the—? I frown, "That makes no sense. You must have had a plan when you decided to steal me away from my everyday life. I mean, people don't just see someone else and decide, on the spur of the moment, 'oh, I want that person, so I am going to kidnap him or her,' you know?"

"No," he shakes his head, "I don't, actually."

I blink, open my mouth and shut it again. "I see." I bob my head. "I understand what you are trying to do here."

He arches an eyebrow, "Pray, do tell."

"You're trying to confuse me with your cryptic words, and you're trying to keep me off balance with your stupid domineering ways."

"You meant controlling ways."

I snarl, "What's the bloody difference anyway?"

"To control means to command, to have mastery over, to—"

"Forget I asked," I mutter.

"You, on the other hand, clearly love to be subjugated."

"No I don't," I snap.

"Sure, you do."

"Not."

"Want me to prove it to you?" He lowers his voice to a hush, and instantly my toes curl. A shiver ripples down my spine. Every cell in my body opens, all my nerve endings go on alert…and my synapses…they seem to fire all at once. *Oh, hell, what is this man doing to me?*

I strain away, try to put distance between us once. He hauls me even closer, throws his leg over both of mine, so I can't move.

I try to draw in a breath and my lungs burn. I am having a nervous breakdown. In the boot of a car, with my kidnapper.

No, no no, this can't be happening. I can't breathe. My heart beats so fast, I am sure it's going to jump out of my ribcage.

"Shh!" His warm breath grazes my cheek. "Relax, I promise I won't harm you."

Says the man who almost shot me. A chuckle bubbles up and my entire body shakes.

"What's so funny?" he rumbles.

"You…" I choke out, "you, asshole. Have you heard yourself? You sound like a psycho bastard—"

Cold metal pushes against the curve of my neck. My breath hitches. My pulse rate ratchets up, even as my limbs tremble.

"Shh." His warm breath raises the hair at my temples. My skin prickles and my scalp feels too tight. I open my mouth, but no words come out. *Is that a knife?* It's a knife. A bloody knife. OMG. How many freakin' weapons does this man carry on him, anyway?

He drags the tip of the blade down the side of my throat. The tip pricks my skin. Not enough to hurt, just enough for me to go still. My breath hitches and a trembling grips me. Even as my core clenches. What the hell is wrong with me? Do I find the idea of him holding a weapon against my skin such a turn on? Am I such a sucker for punishment? One who hankers for something darker, deeper, more violent that the usual overtures than a normal woman would enjoy.

"Now, Beauty, don't freak out on me, not after that very promising start."

He removes the knife. I sense him move away as he tucks the knife back from wherever he'd pulled it out, then he grips my chin. He forces my head toward him and my gaze meets his.

Those blue eyes are piercing, a beacon in the darkness. My light at the end of the tunnel. *What? No.* Anger squeezes my guts and fear bubbles up, a tangy, bitter taste on my tongue.

I open my mouth to scream, but he's already there. He lowers his chin, slants his lips over mine.

4

Michael

Heat, sweetness. The taste of her, like strawberries and sunshine, punches me in the gut. My head spins. I need her, want her. I pull her up until she crashes into my chest, her body twisted against mine. I slide my leg, between hers, apply pressure until her body curves further.

Bend for me, Beauty. Break for me. Open. I swipe my tongue across the seam of her lips and her mouth parts further. I swoop in, because…that's my second nature. I take what I want. Use weakness to my advantage. Rush in to consolidate my position when I have the upper hand. I flatten my palm over the flatness of her belly, graze my fingers over the core of her. She moans low in her throat, the sound so soft I'd have missed it, except I've plastered her to me. Her every breath, her every inhale, the trembling that sweeps up her spine… It's mine. I tilt my head, deepen the kiss even further. Thrust my tongue inside the honeyed spring of her mouth and drink from her. Suck on her tongue and a whine bleeds from her. I swallow it.

Bring my fingers up to cup her breast and she arches her spine. Pushes her flesh into the hollow of my palm. I pinch her nipple and her entire body bucks. Against me. Into me. Her hair slaps against my chin, coils around my neck, binding me to her, tugging at me, connecting us... *No.* I tear my lips from her mouth and she tips up her chin, reaches up, seeking my touch, my essence, what only I can give her.

"Beauty?" I clear my throat.

She peers at me from between the fringe of her eyelashes, pupils blown from the pleasure I'd drawn from her. She blinks; her lips part, swollen from my ministrations.

"Wanna shag?" I allow my lips to curl in a smirk. Rake my gaze down her flushed cheeks, her heaving chest. "You're a bit on the heavy side for me, but you'll do for a quickie."

Her cheeks redden; a spark lights in her eyes. *There, you are.*

"Fuck you."

"If you insist."

She pulls away from me, and I loosen my grip. Not that she's going anywhere, considering we were trapped here in the confines of this car for a little while longer. Why the hell did I crawl in here with her? A temporary loss of sanity, that's what it was. I'd heard her beat her fists against the car and...knew it would attract attention. Didn't want that. Couldn't bring her up front so... I'd done the logical thing. I'd climbed in.

"Get away from me, you obnoxious jerk."

"I'm sure you're aware that's not possible, considering." I jerk my chin towards the space around us.

"And who's fault is that?"

"Yours."

"What?"

"If you hadn't quoted Byron, you wouldn't be here."

"Yeah, I would be dead." She glowers.

"Right on your first guess." I nod. "Impressive you recognized that."

"So, what's your plan?"

"Plan?" I frown.

"You know, the hell are you thinking, transporting me to God knows where? Why didn't you kill me like you should have?"

"I'm the one asking the questions, *piccolina*."

"Your Italian insults suck, you know that?"

I blow out a breath. "You English think a word in any other language is an insult."

"Wasn't it."

"Nope."

"Then?"

"It doesn't matter."

"What about what you called me earlier?"

"What?"

"Beauty. You called me Beauty."

"You are fucking annoying. I liked you better with my tongue in your mouth." I lower my head and she arches away. She tugs at my grasp. I release her chin and she faces forward.

"Don't kiss me again."

"You liked it, hmm?"

"No."

"Don't lie."

"I'm not.

"Wanna bet. I am more than happy to go another round." I allow my lips to curve, "It's as good a way as any to pass the time."

I coil a strand of her hair around my fingers, bring it to my nose. Cinnamon and sugar, with a dash of hot spice. My mouth waters, and I release the silken length.

"So, what do you say?"

"Go to hell."

"Been there, and I'm not in a hurry to repeat the experience."

"Do you have a rejoinder for every insult?" She huffs.

"Do you always mouth off your captors?"

"I've never been kidnapped before.'

"I've never…" my voice trails off. I don't lie, ever. And the fact is, she's not the first I have abducted. She's the first whose life I've spared, and hell… Why? Why would I do that? Just a few mumbled words and boom… I'm the bitch in this equation. Nope. No way. I need to take control of this situation. Of whatever it is that stretches between us. Need to snap this connection.

"Never been at a loss of words before, huh?" Triumph tinges her tone, and warmth curls in my chest.

My heart begins to thud, my pulse rate ratchets up, and even before the words are out of my mouth, I know I am going to regret it… But fuck that. I am Italian enough to not mess with forces beyond my comprehension. When I had set out this morning to take her life, I hadn't realized that it would be mine I was forfeiting. Too little, too late. I am helpless, and I have to take the next step. Else we'll both be left hanging between the devil and a dark place, and to hell with that. I'll make the decision and be damned. Pay the consequences; no choices. This is it. It has to be this way. There is no other option.

"I've never had to choke a woman into complying before."

"What the hell?" She yells, whips her head around.

I wrap an arm around her neck then grab the bicep of my other arm.

She struggles, kicks out, manages to free a leg and sinks her knee into my thigh. Pain laces my nerve endings, lengthens my cock even further. Don't judge. My tastes have always been on the edge…and this... This has pushed them past a point of no return.

I manage to slide my other hand behind her head, apply pressure to the sides of her neck and she goes limp.

"Sleep, Beauty."

Her breathing deepens.

"Good girl." I cradle her close, whisper my knuckles over her cheek. "When you awake, it will be the start."

Karma

Whispers, the scrape of something smooth against the back of my thighs. I rub my cheek against the silky-hard sensations. The masculine scent of testosterone, musky, like leather with a hint of woodsmoke. Fresh snow on fallen earth. The cold rush of a winter's wind. The snap and crackle of a fireplace. Warmth creeps up my fingers, my toes. I turn toward it, snuggle in against the hard unrelenting surface. Thud-thud-thud-thud; the beats sink into my blood. My sex clenches in perfect rhythm. Him. He is near. He had crawled into the back of the car with me, had wound his big body around mine and he'd choked me until I'd fainted. I crack open my eyelids and the world swims in my line of sight.

"How dare you?" I cough. "You knocked me out, you obnoxious jackalope."

"Sleep hasn't improved your disposition, huh?" A lean arm appears in front of me, holding a glass of water. "Drink."

I purse my lips, gulp, glare from the glass of water to his handsome, gorgeous, ugly-mean features.

"Do it or I'll pour it down your throat myself." His tone is soft but he doesn't fool me. Bastard would do it, too. I reach for the glass. The water slides between my parched lips. I drain it. My swollen tongue thanks me, and the drumming behind my temples seems to recede. I lower the glass, take stock of my surroundings. I'm in a leather chair, and a seatbelt is strapped across my lap. I also have my running clothes on. I glance down and find my feet are still clad in my sneakers. The low hum of engines, hushed voices soaked up by thick carpeting, and the kind of luxury only the filthy rich or the filthy—period—can buy, reaches me.

"We're on a plane?"

I glance up at the face of my kidnapper. He sits in the chair opposite me. Elbows on the armrests, fingers steepled together in front of him, his legs are spread apart, powerful thighs stretching the soft fabric of his tailor-made pants, and between them, the unmistakable bulge of— I jerk my chin up, meet his gaze. "Private jet, huh? I guess crime really does pay well. How did you acquire it? Did you kill the owner?"

"Tortured him, actually. By the time I was done with him, there was no blood left in his sorry-ass body."

I blanche.

He laughs and I can't tell if it's because it's true or he just likes the look on my face and wants to torment me.

"Do you want more water?"

Maybe both. *Jerk.*

"What I want..." I tighten my grip on the glass, "is to smash your face in." I pull my arm back and hurl the glass at him. It catches him at the side of the temple, then falls to the carpet with a soft thud. Blood blooms from the gash, a trickle of scarlet that rolls down his temple, over the razor-sharp, high cheekbone.

There's a sudden movement, then the barrel of gun is pushed against my temple. "Want me to kill her, Michael?" A hard male voice sounds from somewhere to the side and above me. I swallow; my pulse begins to race.

Michael rubs his chin as he considers me.

The barrel of the gun digs deeper into my temple. I wince, but don't take my gaze off the asshole opposite.

Finally, Michael tilts his head. "Not yet," he rumbles, and I stiffen.

The cold metal disappears from my skin, and I am not ashamed to say that the tension drains from my body.

"Oh, and Antonio?"

Antonio tilts his head.

"No one gets to pull a gun on her, except me. No one hurts her, but me." His lips curl.

I set my jaw and his grin widens. "Now leave us," he growls and Antonio retreats to the far end of the cabin. Shit, now we are alone. Maybe it would be better if Antonio were still here. So what, if he held a gun to my temple? I'd rather face a weapon head-on, than the shark-faced, Mafia asshole who eyes me like I am the tastiest morsel ever. I tip up my chin, grip the handles of my seat, "If that was meant to frighten me—"

"Shut up."

My breath hitches.

"Don't talk to me like—"

He swoops forward so fast that the blood from his temple splashes onto my dress. "I mean it, Beauty. Keep those pretty lips zipped or I'll stuff your mouth, and it won't be with your favorite cupcake."

My shoulder muscles lock, my core puckers. I squeeze my thighs together to stop the insidious moisture that drip-drip-drips from my treacherous core.

"Unless." He taps his fingertips together, peruses my features. "Unless that's what you want?"

No.

"Maybe that's why you've been barking at me, scratching at me, demanding my attention, making it difficult for me to concentrate on anything but your face, your legs, the hard nipples of your breasts that tremble in anticipation of my touch, hmm?"

Of course, not. What the hell is he talking about?

"Is this what gets you off?" I drop my gaze to his crotch, where his bulge has grown noticeably bigger in the last few seconds. "Lording it over those helpless in front of you, those weaker than you? Does that make you feel more macho? Does it feed your manliness, you obnoxious bastard?"

"No, but this will."

He grabs the hardness between his legs and squeezes it. I flinch. My toes curl. I should look away from how he cups the thick girth between those powerful thighs. My throat closes, my ribcage tightens, and moisture pools at my core.

"Down."

"What?" I jerk my chin up.

He nods towards the space between his legs.

"No."

"You have two choices."

Oh?

"You get down on your knees and blow me or..."

Or?

"I get down on my knees, pull your legs apart and eat you out. And then I let you blow me."

I squeeze my thighs together. *No way.* If he touches me now, he'll know how…how wet I am. And I shouldn't be. I hate him; hate him for how he pulls a response from me, by just being…himself. I blink.

What I see with him is what I get, and that's refreshing. In a way, he's more decent than any other man I've encountered in my life. The hell am I thinking about?

"Which one's it going to be, my Beauty?"

"I'm not your anything," I snarl.

"Wrong, you're my captive."

I chuckle. "You don't say?"

"Choose fast and choose wisely, for this sets the course of our future relationship."

"Relationship?" I glower. "You are more deluded than what I first thought."

"No more than what your father was."

"The son shall not bear the iniquity of the father..." I stutter. A quote from the Bible? That's the best I could do? Guess I was paying more attention than I realized to the daily, evening readings by the nuns. God bless their souls, they'd done their best for us. If it weren't for them... I wouldn't be alive.

I wouldn't be here, facing down this absolute brute who, clearly, will not listen to reason, so why am I even trying?

"And the daughter? What is the daughter going to do, hmm?" The blood drips down his cheek and onto his shirt, smearing it scarlet.

"This daughter sure doesn't owe her old man a single ounce of respect. What I do, I do out of choice." I set my jaw.

"Which is...?

I draw in a breath, then unhook the seatbelt from around me and drop down to my knees.

5

Karma

Whispers, the scrape of something smooth against the back of my thighs. I rub my cheek against the silky-hard sensations. The masculine scent of testosterone, musky, like leather with a hint of woodsmoke. Fresh snow on fallen earth. The cold rush of a winter's wind. The snap and crackle of a fireplace. Warmth creeps up my fingers, my toes. I turn toward it, snuggle in against the hard unrelenting surface. Thud-thud-thud-thud; the beats sink into my blood. My core clenches in perfect rhythm. Him. He is near. He had crawled into the back of the car with me, had wound his big body around mine and he'd choked me until I'd fainted. I crack open my eyelids and the world swims in my line of sight.

"How dare you?" I cough. "You knocked me out, you obnoxious jackaloupe."

"Sleep hasn't improved your disposition, huh?" A lean arm appcars in front of me, holding a glass of water. "Drink."

I purse my lips, gulp, glare from the glass of water to his handsome, gorgeous, ugly-mean features.

"Do it or I'll pour it down your throat myself." His tone is soft but he doesn't fool me. Bastard would do it, too. I reach for the glass. The water slides between my parched lips. I drain it. My swollen tongue thanks me, and the drumming behind my temples seems to recede. I lower the glass, take stock of my surroundings. I'm in a leather chair, and a seatbelt is strapped across my lap. I also have my running clothes on. I glance down and find my feet are still clad in my sneakers. The low hum of engines, hushed voices soaked up by thick carpeting, and the kind of luxury only the filthy rich or the filthy—period—can buy, reaches me.

"We're on a plane?"

I glance up at the face of my kidnapper. He sits in the chair opposite me. Elbows on the armrests, fingers steepled together in front of him, his legs are spread apart, powerful thighs stretching the soft fabric of his tailor-made pants, and between them, the unmistakable bulge of— I jerk my chin up, meet his gaze. "Private jet, huh? I guess crime really does pay well. How did you acquire it? Did you kill the owner?"

"Tortured him, actually. By the time I was done with him, there was no blood left in his sorry-ass body."

I blanche.

He laughs and I can't tell if it's because it's true or he just likes the look on my face and wants to torment me.

"Do you want more water?"

Maybe both. *Jerk.*

"What I want..." I tighten my grip on the glass, "is to smash your face in." I pull my arm back and hurl the glass at him. It catches him at the side of the temple, then falls to the carpet with a soft thud. Blood blooms from the gash, a trickle of scarlet that rolls down his temple, over the razor-sharp, high cheekbone.

There's a sudden movement, then the barrel of gun is pushed against my temple. "Want me to kill her, Michael?" A hard male voice sounds from somewhere to the side and above me. I swallow; my pulse begins to race.

Michael rubs his chin as he considers me.

The barrel of the gun digs deeper into my temple. I wince, but don't take my gaze off the asshole opposite.

Finally, Michael tilts his head. "Not yet," he rumbles, and I stiffen.

The cold metal disappears from my skin, and I am not ashamed to say that the tension drains from my body.

"Oh, and Antonio?"

Antonio tilts his head.

"No one gets to pull a gun on her, except me. No one hurts her, but me." His lips curl.

I set my jaw and his grin widens. "Now leave us," he growls and Antonio retreats to the far end of the cabin. Shit, now we are alone. Maybe it would be better if Antonio were still here. So what, if he held a gun to my temple? I'd rather face a weapon head-on, than the shark-faced, Mafia asshole who eyes me like I am the tastiest morsel ever. I tip up my chin, grip the handles of my seat, "If that was meant to frighten me—"

"Shut up."

My breath hitches.

"Don't talk to me like—"

He swoops forward so fast that the blood from his temple splashes onto my dress. "I mean it, Beauty. Keep those pretty lips zipped or I'll stuff your mouth, and it won't be with your favorite cupcake."

My shoulder muscles lock, my core puckers. I squeeze my thighs together to stop the insidious moisture that drip-drip-drips from my treacherous core.

"Unless." He taps his fingertips together, peruses my features. "Unless that's what you want?"

No.

"Maybe that's why you've been barking at me, scratching at me, demanding my attention, making it difficult for me to concentrate on anything but your face, your legs, the hard nipples of your breasts that tremble in anticipation of my touch, hmm?"

Of course, not. What the hell is he talking about?

"Is this what gets you off?" I drop my gaze to his crotch, where his bulge has grown noticeably bigger in the last few seconds. "Lording it over those helpless in front of you, those weaker than you? Does that make you feel more macho? Does it feed your manliness, you obnoxious bastard?"

"No, but this will."

He grabs the hardness between his legs and squeezes it. I flinch. My toes curl. I should look away from how he cups the thick girth between those powerful thighs. My throat closes, my ribcage tightens, and moisture pools at my core.

"Down."

"What?" I jerk my chin up.

He nods towards the space between his legs.

"No."

"You have two choices."

Oh?

"You get down on your knees and blow me or..."

Or?

"I get down on my knees, pull your legs apart and eat you out. And then I let you blow me."

I squeeze my thighs together. *No way.* If he touches me now, he'll know how…how wet I am. And I shouldn't be. I hate him; hate him for how he pulls a response from me, by just being…himself. I blink. What I see with him is what I get, and that's refreshing. In a way, he's more decent than any other man I've encountered in my life. The hell am I thinking about?

"Which one's it going to be, my Beauty?"

"I'm not your anything," I snarl.

"Wrong, you're my captive."

I chuckle. "You don't say?"

"Choose fast and choose wisely, for this sets the course of our future relationship."

"Relationship?" I glower. "You are more deluded than what I first thought."

"No more than what your father was."

"The son shall not bear the iniquity of the father…" I stutter. A quote from the Bible? That's the best I could do? Guess I was paying more attention than I realized to the daily, evening readings by the nuns. God bless their souls, they'd done their best for us. If it weren't for them… I wouldn't be alive.

I wouldn't be here, facing down this absolute brute who, clearly, will not listen to reason, so why am I even trying?

"And the daughter? What is the daughter going to do, hmm?" The blood drips down his cheek and onto his shirt, smearing it scarlet.

"This daughter sure doesn't owe her old man a single ounce of respect. What I do, I do out of choice." I set my jaw.

"Which is…?

I draw in a breath, then unhook the seatbelt from around me and drop down to my knees.

6

Michael

She peers up at me from under her lashes. Her dark hair about her shoulders, her cheeks flushed, she chews on her lower lip and all the blood rushes to my groin. As if I weren't hard enough already. I drag my arm to the side, force my fingers to relax.

"Tick-Tock, Beauty."

She makes a sound deep in her throat, one I am already coming to recognize. That almost subvocal note half-way between a snarl and frustration. My dick lengthens further. At this rate, I am going to jizz myself in my pants, and before she's even touched that part of my body. *Focus, focus.* I draw in a breath, pull back my shoulders.

"Perhaps I should take the lead—"

"No." She scuttles forward, undoes my belt, then seizes the zipper on my pants and lowers it, along with my briefs. My dick springs free.

"Oh." Her mouth forms a circle; her pale lips shorn of lipstick beckon. My balls tighten. My fingers tingle. I'd told her to blow me; doesn't mean I am going to let her control the proceedings.

"Drop your head, take me down your throat."

She swallows.

"Do it."

She folds her fingers around the base of my shaft and sparks explode behind my eyeballs. This was a mistake. I shouldn't have told her to do this. I am revealing too much of myself, in just how my body responds to her.

I grab the armrests, dig my fingers in.

"That all you got?"

She tips her chin up and her green eyes spark fire. Something hot stabs at my chest. This woman, she's a fighter. A survivor, like me. Who will break first? Me or her? It has to be her. It will be her, if it's the last thing I do.

"Maybe you're scared, huh? Maybe you're just like your old man, all talk, no—" She lowers her chin, licks my dick from base to head. Lust slams into my groin.

She swirls her pink tongue around the swollen appendage, licks off the precum oozing from the slit. I hold her gaze, lower my chin. One side of my mouth curls and a deep red stains the creamy skin of her neck. Fascinating. I could spend hours...days exploring every millimeter of that gorgeous expanse of womanhood, wring orgasm after orgasm from her, play her body like it's a finely-tuned musical instrument...

But I want more. I need her open and thirsting for what only I can give her. I have to own her, body and soul, until her every emotion is mine to read. Her every thought is mine to foresee. Her every wish...mine...only mine to grant. If I so deem it.

Hmm. A fierce sensation fans to life deep in my groin. I track it as it spreads up my spine, to my extremities, until it seems to envelope every inch of my body. What would it take for this woman to give up all her secrets to me...willingly? That would be a first. A different challenge. Something I've been searching for...for quite a while.

I widen my legs even more, pump my hips forward. My swollen

shaft slaps her across her lips. She flinches. I glare at her and she pales. I tilt my head. She stiffens her shoulders, squeezes the base of my cock. Then she opens her mouth, drops her chin and takes me down her throat…in one go.

The fuck? It's clearly not her first blowjob… And I had thought, what? That she was innocent? No way. I had been fooled by her youth, her feistiness. Well, no more. It works better this way, for both of us. I don't have to feel guilty for what I am going to put her through, hmm?

She sucks in her cheeks, and I feel the pull all the way down to my balls.

She pulls back, saliva drooling down her chin, dragging the rough edge of her tongue across the underside of my shaft. The pulse thrums to life at my wrists, my temples, even at the backs of my eyelids. Goddam her. She pauses, with her lips framing my cock, and my balls draw up. I can't hold out any more. Damn her.

I swoop down, dig my fingers into her hair. I tug and her neck arches. I wrap my other hand around her neck. She swallows. Every hesitant vibration strums over my palm, sinks into my blood. My heart begins to thud. This is too carnal, too real. This isn't how I intended it to be. I thought I was in control? I was wrong. As long as she is near me, I'll never be able to manage my reactions. I pull her back until my dick slips from her mouth with a wet sound that has me instantly twitching again. Hell. I release her.

She sits back on her knees. A tear trickles from the corner of her eyes. I reach forward to swipe it away, and she flinches. Anger squeezes my guts. I tuck myself back in, zip my pants.

She blinks.

"Go," I jerk my chin toward the seat.

"But." She scowls at me.

"Do it, before I change my mind."

She scrambles back and sinks into her seat, snaps her seatbelt back on. What an obedient little girl. Was she as willing to please whoever she had administered blowjobs to earlier? I squeeze my fingers at my sides. The blood throbs in my veins. Why am I so angry at the thought of her with any other man? I had no claim over her…yet. I need to keep it that way. I need to find a way to keep my distance until I have decided what to do with her.

I spring up to my feet, stalk away from her.

"Michael?"

I freeze, turn on her. "You haven't earned the right to call me by my name."

She huffs. "So, what should I call you? Asshole?"

"Lord or Master will do well enough."

"Okay, Lord Asshole it is, unless you prefer Master Asshole?"

I chuckle, then firm my lips. "You have a sense of humor. Good. You are going to need it over the next few days."

She pales, then squares her shoulders, "If you think you are going to scare me into doing what you want, you have another think coming, buster." Her green eyes flare with a hidden fire. Color smears her cheeks. She's truly magnificent. And I need to get my head examined for finding her so attractive.

She's the woman from your dreams, you asshole. You've been looking for her. And now I found her...and all she is, is a debt I intend to reclaim.

I curl my lips, then turn and stalk away, hellbent on finding a way to take care of the raging hardness that tents my pants.

"Wait," she calls out.

Now what? I glare at her over my shoulder.

She twists her fingers in front of her. "Why did you…stop?"

I tilt my head, "Didn't you want me to?"

"N…no, that's not what I meant. I thought that…"

"I wanted you?"

She stiffens, then jerks her chin.

"You thought wrong. I wanted to see how willing you'd be to fulfill my wishes. Seems you are ready and able to do my bidding… Too willing. It's not enough of a challenge." I yawn. "I don't play with little girls, Beauty."

Her face pales. "I'm nineteen, you prick."

And I'm a full twenty years older than her. I'd known it, of course, when I had taken her… But having her throw her age in my face…makes the age gap even more of a reality. Of course, twenty years is nothing in the Mafia world. There are other Capo's who've married girls thirty years their junior. They swear by the fact that a younger wife keeps them young at heart, too. Only, I hadn't ever thought I'd be one of them. Hell, knowing the age gap hadn't stopped me from being attracted to her from the moment I saw her. Besides, she's here as an asset. All I have to do is use her as I see fit to consolidate my plans. That's all this is—a means to an end. There is no reason to attach any other significance to it.

I shake my head. "What you are, is pathetic."

"You didn't think so when you kidnapped me." She snaps her teeth at me. Cute. I almost smile, then school my features into a semblance of seriousness.

"I kidnapped you because you owe me."

"My father owes you."

"Same thing."

"It's not the same thing." She draws herself up to her full height.

"Frankly I found the entire experience boring."

Her chin wobbles. *Fuck, I hurt her.* But that was the idea, right? It's why I took her in the first place. So she can pay for the sins of her father. I squeeze my hands at my side, then look her in the eye, "Figured I'd find a woman, a real woman, to take care of my needs. Know what I mean?"

She pales.

A hot sensation stabs at my chest. I glance away, then up as the stewardess approaches me. I snap my fingers and her eyes light up. "On your knees; you know what to do."

Karma

Why that arrogant, emotionally unstable prick. He wouldn't. No way. Michael props his hands on his waist and widens his stance. His jacket pulls tightly across his butt and I gulp. This man? He is the epitome of a wet dream. *Look away, look away now.* I lean forward and my breathing heightens. The stewardess sinks to her knees. I can see her framed by the inverted V of Michael's legs and it should be voyeuristic, should make me feel dirty to watch her pleasure him. And it does. And that is part of the appeal.

I swallow hard and slickness coats the space between my thighs. The planes of his broad back flex, then I hear her gasp. His shoulders flex, his arm moves in a forward motion. No doubt, he's grabbed her head, then pulled her forward so he can feed his cock to her. That's the alphahole for you. There's no way she is in control here. No doubt it's him who's *taking* the blowjob from her.

She must have her mouth open as she swallows him, takes that dark, hot, throbbing length down her throat. As I just had. And he'd hated it, when I'd done that. But with her? His shoulders blades pull back and his entire body tenses.

I bend lower, watch as her body jerks, and again. She's moving her lips across his hard length, taking him in, sucking, licking… The sound of slurping fills the air and my mouth waters. This is insane. The dark taste of him coats my palate, the edgy scent of testosterone lingers in my nostrils. I wriggle around in the seat, but can't find a comfortable position. Dig my sneaker clad feet into the carpeted floor, grasp the armrests, watch as his thigh muscles clench.

Her body jerks faster, no doubt as he uses her mouth. As he crams his dick between her lips. I hear the sounds of gagging and my belly flip-flops. I squeeze my thighs together as he thrusts his hips forward. His butt muscles tighten, then he throws back his head and a groan fills the air.

I glance around the space but none of the other men—there are five men other than Michael on the plane; how had I not noticed that before? That's how wrapped up in him I've been—and none of them are paying attention to the spectacle unfolding. Does he do this often? Get the stewardess to jerk him off? Every time he gets on the plane, maybe? He'll whistle and she'll come running? Something hot stabs in my chest. *Bitch.* Not her, but me, for wanting…what? To be her… No, it's not that. I want his attention.

A gasp leaves my lips. I want to have his full and complete focus, to be the cynosure of all that smoldering, melting scrutiny. To have his fingers dig into my skin, my breasts, my aching core. *The hell is wrong with me?* I straighten, force myself to watch as his muscles coil with tension. His spine is straight, his feet planted on the floor as if he owns the goddam space... Which he does... And every molecule of air in this infernal enclosed area has been sucked in by the heat generated by the sexual hunger that flows from him. Unrequited.

He'd wanted me. Despite what he'd said earlier, he'd enjoyed what I'd done to him. Perhaps, too much?

Had I scared him away? A low chuckle catches in my throat. Am I being delusional? Me, the woman who had practiced blowjobs by watching them on porn hub...and the erotic novels I've been reading since I turned fifteen. Don't judge. A direct consequence of being surrounded by nuns—God bless their souls. I loved each and every one of them, but their singular preoccupation with sacrifice and sin—the two words that had etched themselves in my mind—had perversely driven me to seek out the forbidden. Well, as much as a teenage girl had been able to access, that is. God bless the internet.

I tilt my head, squeeze my thighs together, scrutinize his movements as he swoops up his free hand to press it to the curved ceiling overhead, then renews his pleasure seeking, as he yanks her head back and forth, at least I assume so from the sucking, mewling noises that emerge from their direction. My heart begins to race and my fingers tingle. I shouldn't...shouldn't. *What the hell!* I press the hell of my hand into my core and grind down, just as Michael speeds up.

His entire body goes solid, a vertical column of desire that swells and flows, and I can't take my gaze off those solid, tight hips of his.

As he thrusts forward, backward...forward. My hips catch the rhythm, as I push up and into the heel of my hand, then back. I mirror that frantic rush up the slope toward that distant horizon, where the silver lining of the sun shines against the clouds, the wind blows hard, shoves the darkness away. And for a second, I am there, right there with him, soaring up, up. A low growl rips from his chest, his butt clenches, his thighs tighten, stretching the material of his pants, his elbow seizes, then he groans. And I splatter right there in my panties.

I throw my head back, my eyes half-closed, panting. A bead of sweat slides down the valley between my breasts. *Jesus, what's wrong with me? Why did I find the sight of him using another woman to pleasure himself so…hot?*

I lower my hand to my side, cross one leg over the other as he pulls out a handkerchief from his pocket and hands it to her. She glances around him to meet my gaze. Her lips curve up, wet, gleaming from the evidence of his cum.

How dare he do this to me?

She licks her lips, then pats them with his handkerchief before shoving the piece of cloth down her breasts. He gave her a part of himself to keep. *Fuck him.* He knew exactly how that would make me feel.

She rises to her feet, turns and saunters away.

He glances over his shoulder at me. "Did you enjoy that, Beauty?"

My nails dig into the cloth at the apex of my thighs. *No. Of course, not.* I glare at him.

One side of his lips turns up. "Remember the feeling, for it's the last time you come without my permission."

7

Karma

Why that arrogant, emotionally unstable prick. He wouldn't. No way. Michael props his hands on his waist and widens his stance. His jacket pulls tightly across his butt and I gulp. This man? He is the epitome of a wet dream. *Look away, look away now.* I lean forward and my breathing heightens. The stewardess sinks to her knees. I can see her framed by the inverted V of Michael's legs and it should be voyeuristic, should make me feel dirty to watch her pleasure him. And it does. And that is part of the appeal.

I swallow hard and slickness coats the space between my thighs. The planes of his broad back flex, then I hear her gasp. His shoulders flex, his arm moves in a forward motion. No doubt, he's grabbed her head, then pulled her forward so he can feed his cock to her. That's the alphahole for you. There's no way she is in control here. No doubt it's him who's *taking* the blowjob from her.

She must have her mouth open as she swallows him, takes that dark, hot, throbbing length down her throat. As I just had. And he'd hated it, when I'd done that. But with her? His shoulders blades pull back and his entire body tenses.

I bend lower, watch as her body jerks, and again. She's moving her lips across his hard length, taking him in, sucking, licking... The sound of slurping fills the air and my mouth waters. This is insane. The dark taste of him coats my palate, the edgy scent of testosterone lingers in my nostrils. I wriggle around in the seat, but can't find a comfortable position. Dig my sneaker clad feet into the carpeted floor, grasp the armrests, watch as his thigh muscles clench.

Her body jerks faster, no doubt as he uses her mouth. As he crams his dick between her lips. I hear the sounds of gagging and my belly flip-flops. I squeeze my thighs together as he thrusts his hips forward. His butt muscles tighten, then he throws back his head and a groan fills the air.

I glance around the space but none of the other men—there are five men other than Michael on the plane; how had I not noticed that before? That's how wrapped up in him I've been—and none of them are paying attention to the spectacle unfolding. Does he do this often? Get the stewardess to jerk him off? Every time he gets on the plane, maybe? He'll whistle and she'll come running? Something hot stabs in my chest. *Bitch.* Not her, but me, for wanting...what? To be her... No, it's not that. I want his attention.

A gasp leaves my lips. I want to have his full and complete focus, to be the cynosure of all that smoldering, melting scrutiny. To have his fingers dig into my skin, my breasts, my aching core. *The hell is wrong with me?* I straighten, force myself to watch as his muscles coil with tension. His spine is straight, his feet planted on the floor as if he owns the goddam space... Which he does... And every molecule of air in this infernal enclosed area has been sucked in by the heat generated by the sexual hunger that flows from him. Unrequited.

He'd wanted me. Despite what he'd said earlier, he'd enjoyed what I'd done to him. Perhaps, too much?

Had I scared him away? A low chuckle catches in my throat. Am I being delusional? Me, the woman who had practiced blowjobs by watching them on porn hub...and the erotic novels I've been reading since I turned fifteen. Don't judge. A direct consequence of being surrounded by nuns—God bless their souls. I loved each and every one of them, but their singular preoccupation with sacrifice and sin—the two words that had etched themselves in my mind—had perversely driven me to seek out the forbidden. Well, as much as a teenage girl had been able to access, that is. God bless the internet.

I tilt my head, squeeze my thighs together, scrutinize his movements as he swoops up his free hand to press it to the curved ceiling overhead, then renews his pleasure seeking, as he yanks her head back and forth, at least I assume so from the sucking, mewling noises that emerge from their direction. My heart begins to race and my fingers tingle. I shouldn't...shouldn't. *What the hell!* I press the heel of my hand into my core and grind down, just as Michael speeds up.

His entire body goes solid, a vertical column of desire that swells and flows, and I can't take my gaze off those solid, tight hips of his.

As he thrusts forward, backward...forward. My hips catch the rhythm, as I push up and into the heel of my hand, then back. I mirror that frantic rush up the slope toward that distant horizon, where the silver lining of the sun shines against the clouds, the wind blows hard, shoves the darkness away. And for a second, I am there, right there with him, soaring up, up. A low growl rips from his chest, his butt clenches, his thighs tighten, stretching the material of his pants, his elbow seizes, then he groans. And I splatter right there in my panties.

I throw my head back, my eyes half-closed, panting. A bead of sweat slides down the valley between my breasts. *Jesus, what's wrong with me? Why did I find the sight of him using another woman to pleasure himself so...hot?*

I lower my hand to my side, cross one leg over the other as he pulls out a handkerchief from his pocket and hands it to her. She glances around him to meet my gaze. Her lips curve up, wet, gleaming from the evidence of his cum.

How dare he do this to me?

She licks her lips, then pats them with his handkerchief before shoving the piece of cloth down her breasts. He gave her a part of himself to keep. *Jerk!* He knew exactly how that would make me feel.

She rises to her feet, turns and saunters away.

He glances over his shoulder at me. "Did you enjoy that, Beauty?"

My nails dig into the cloth at the apex of my thighs. *No. Of course, not.* I glare at him.

One side of his lips turns up. "Remember the feeling, for it's the last time you come without my permission."

8

Michael

"The fuck are you up to, *Stronzo*?"

I don't look up from the screen. The camera is pointed at the bed in the center of the room. More specifically, at the woman sleeping on it. She hasn't moved since we arrived on my island a few hours ago. I'd left it to my men to escort her there. She'd tried to speak with them and they'd ignored her…as they had been instructed. They hadn't looked at her, or met her gaze—they knew the consequences of disobeying my orders. She'd glanced around the room, walked up to the window, which was open… And I knew what she'd see—sheer drop to the ocean below. Her shoulders had sagged, and she'd flounced around, examined every corner of the room, before she'd staggered to the bed and thrown herself on it. She'd fallen asleep in seconds, like the child that she is.

Except, when it had come to sucking my dick…she'd known her way around that particular appendage. Or bringing herself to climax… Should I be insulted that she jacked off to me? I tighten my fingers into fists. It should have been my fingers, my lips, my cock on which she came… If I let her… Which I won't. Not for a while. She'll have to pay for the mistakes she made me commit. Once I figure out exactly what I am going to do with her.

"You lose your tongue along with your ability to think coherently?" Luca prowls into the room.

My brother can be a real fucking pain in the ass at the best of times. And right now, when he is in a foul mood… Which, admittedly, he is entitled to, considering I had broken the one pact we had strictly adhered to since purchasing this island—no women. It's a hideout, which only our closest *famiglia* know about, and a few of our associates…. And strictly on a need-to-know basis.

"Maybe it's your balls that are bothering you?" Luca smirks. "No, now wait, did you replace your brain with your dick? Is that why you brought her…here?"

I draw in a breath, stare at the sleeping figure. She hadn't stirred in the last—I glance at my watch—in the last half an hour. She's okay, right? I lean in closer to the screen. Breathe Beauty, breathe for me. Her chest rises and falls. My shoulders slump. The tension drains, leaving…a strange tightness in my chest.

"No, don't tell me, maybe she has a magic pussy or something?" Luca murmurs, "That why you can't take your gaze off of her?

My left eyelid twitches. *How dare he talk about her in that tone?* And what the hell is wrong with me that I am taking this entire conversation so personally? It's no different from how my siblings and I kid each other all the time.

I push back from the table so fast that my chair screeches against the floor. "Or something," I keep my voice casual.

"You don't fool me, *fratellone*." There's a sly edge to his voice. "Clearly, she means something to you."

"You're right about that."

"I am?"

"She's an asset, one who will help me claim what's rightfully mine."

"The title of the Don?"

"That too." I smirk. It's no secret that I am ambitious, that I want to become the next Boss of Cosa Nostra. But that's assuming our current Don decides, at some point, to retire. Not that I am in a hurry, but every step I take is calculated to get me there. Except her.

She's the wild card. The one that came into my possession by chance, and now I am figuring out the best way to play her.

"That's wise," Luca nods. "Then you wouldn't mind if I—" he nods his chin toward the screen, "tried my luck with her?"

Red tints my vision. Only when my fingers hurt, do I realize that I've crossed the floor and have hauled him up by his collar.

"So, it's like that, huh?" One side of his lips curls, the expression so fucking similar to mine. His gaze narrows, calculating. He glances past me at the screen, then back to my face. "You want me to guess, or you going to come clean about her?"

Her? There is no her. She's a prisoner... She belongs to me and her fate is mine to decide. Period. I release him. He doesn't move. I pivot, walk to the bar in the corner of the room, pour myself a whiskey.

"Want one?" I pour without waiting for his reply. Then walk back and offer it to him.

"She's mine." I declare.

His eyebrows shoot up. "Oh?"

I toss back the drink. It burns its way down my throat. My stomach clenches. My dick hurts. Fuck. This entire sequence of events since I'd heard her voice those fucking words is...a nightmare. Confusing. And that's not something I am used to dealing with. I have to convince myself she means nothing... More importantly, I have to ensure that Luca's attention is focused away from her.

"Mine to leverage," I clarify.

"She's better off if you kill her."

My guts twist. The thought of her not breathing, not sighing, not mouthing off at me, as she's done so often since we met... No, I have to convince him that it doesn't matter either way to me.

"She has her uses," I drawl. "I plan to use her to get the Seven to back off from enquiring after the Mafia."

I prowl back to the bar, pour myself another drink.

"Only..." Luca murmurs and I stiffen, cap the bottle of Macallan.

I raise the glass, wet my lips with the dram. Rich cloves and the taste of ginger spices explodes on my tongue. As lush as figs, as moist as her cunt will surely be. I tighten my fingers around the glass. "Only?" I turn.

"That's not your style. Are you planning something that you're not letting me in on?"

"Would I ever do that?" I tilt my head.

"Only all the time." He chuckles, "We may stop the Seven from coming after us right now, but it's only a matter of time before they resume their efforts."

"What if I find a way to buy us time, on a more permanent basis?"

"What do you mean?"

"What if I secure an alliance with the Seven?"

"They'd never agree to it."

"Not unless they don't have a choice."

"What do you mean?" He tilts his head.

I hold his gaze, and his forehead clears, "Ah, I see." He rolls his shoulders, "You mean to—" he jerks his chin toward the screen.

"I am thinking of it," I murmur slowly.

"Of course, you'd be killing two birds with one stone. Alliances which help further our business are not new." Luca strokes his chin, "But in this case, you'd be sleeping with the enemy, literally."

"Stranger things have happened."

"Not that she is hard on the eyes or anything."

I growl low in my throat and Luca throws up a hand, "Fine, I'll back off. But you know it's risky. What if the Seven don't agree to it? After all, money is a powerful motivation. More important than saving the life of a loved one, sometimes."

"What if I don't give them a choice?"

"You mean wed her and bed her first, and then take her help in winning them over to your side?"

"I mean giving neither of them a choice. She'll do as I say."

"You're assuming that you'll be able to control her."

"What's wrong with that?"

"Don't underestimate women."

"Don't underestimate my way with women."

"Hmm." He purses his lips in that annoying way he's had from when we were little. I am the older one here, and yet, Luca is the one who has a wise head on his shoulders. It's why I use him as a sounding board more than any of my other brothers.

"What?" I scowl, "What's on your mind, *stronzo*?"

"It's risky."

"It's better than killing her, which is what I had in mind when I came upon her."

"What changed your mind?"

Her eyes, her lips, the scent of her skin, the way she looked at me with her bright green eyes, so curious, so full of life that it had sparked a yearning deep inside.

"I need to consolidate my position at the earliest possible time," I murmur.

"Maybe you're attracted to her?"

"I need to send a message to the other four families that we have some strong powers aligned behind us."

"There are easier ways to do that."

"How?"

"You could deploy our men and shoot them."

I laugh, "And start an outright war?" I shake my head, "There's a time for violence and a time for..."

"Romance?"

"An arrangement." I frown.

"With her or with yourself."

"What the fuck are you talking about?" I growl, "Whatever is on your mind, just come out and say it already."

"Just that this seems a very long and contrived way of consolidating our position."

"She's already here with us," I point out. "Half the job is done."

"You're hellbent on this?" He scowls, "There's nothing I can say to change your mind?"

"Why should I?" I widen my stance, "She's the key. Don't you see it? Her sister is married to the fourth richest man in the UK, one who is part of a close-knit circle of powerful men who hold the ability to open up not only the British Isles, but also Silicon Valley."

"So, in one stroke, we not only send out a message to the other families, we also widen our sphere of influence geographically."

One of our father's stipulations: I have to marry and produce an heir before I turn forty in order to secure the role of Don. Else it will open the line of succession as a free-for-all. Anyone from the four other ruling families could challenge me to a fight, and if they won, I'd lose everything I have worked toward. Not that they can't attack me now. The only thing stopping them is the fact that my team and I are too strong. However, like most things, power ebbs and flows. I need to marry and quickly consolidate my position.

A sound comes from the direction of the screen. I turn to it. Beauty yawns, sits up, and the cover falls to her waist. Her breasts, encased in that stretchy sports bra, fills the screen.

"I see you've been keeping close watch on your assets." Luca smirks.

I wave my hand and the screen shuts off.

"Hold on… It was just getting interesting." Luca walks toward the screen, but I plant myself in his path.

"I see." He bares his teeth.

"No, you don't."

"You sweet on her, hmm?" He scratches his jaw.

"Fuck off."

"Your American roots are showing, *cazzo*." He clicks his tongue.

"The fuck I care about that?" I rub the back of my neck. "You're half-American too, or have you forgotten?"

"Tried my best, but it's a stain that doesn't wash off easily, and neither will the mistake you've made by bringing her here."

"Bringing who here?" A new voice sounds. I glance up to find my second brother Massimo, followed by my youngest twin siblings Christian and Alessandro walking into the room.

Antonio, my right-hand man, stands to attention by the open door. He's been told not to let anyone except family inside. Doesn't mean he ever lets his guard down. Since he fell in love with one of the women that we'd saved from being trafficked, and married her—

with my blessing—his loyalty has been unshakeable. Not that he had been anything but faithful before that. But finding his woman had made him even more faithful, something for which I am appreciative. He meets my gaze and I wave him off. He steps back, shuts the door behind him, and I turn to my brothers, "The fuck you guys doing here?"

"Someone's pissed," Christian murmurs.

"Think big brother, here, isn't getting enough?" Alessandro smirks.

"Or maybe he's getting too much and it's not satisfying enough? After all, quality over quantity, and all that," Massimo drawls as he precedes the other two further into the room.

I scowl as the three of them prowl around the space. Christian sinks into a couch, then promptly turns sideways and stretches out. Alessandro lowers his bulk into a chair, and props his feet on the coffee table, "Thought you were supposed to be in London?" He jerks his chin at me.

"I was," I mutter.

"Is it a woman who had you returning so quickly?"

I hold his gaze, don't say anything else.

"Knew it," Christian crows. "It has to be a woman who's put him in such a filthy mood."

"It's not only my mood which is going to be filthy soon," I growl. "What the hell are you three *stronzi* doing here, anyway?"

"You're repeating yourself, *fratellone.*" Massimo smirks.

"Fuck off." I rub the back of my neck.

"Now he's taking refuge in insults." Christian chuckles, "And it was you who'd asked us over for a meeting."

Of course, I had. How could I have forgotten that? I walk over to stand over the three of them. Luca follows me. "Get your foot off the table, Xander," I growl at my youngest brother.

"Seriously?" He grimaces, "What's wrong with where my foot is?"

"Want me to show you?" I pull my knife from my belt, flip it over in my hand. I glare at him, and he grimaces.

"You're such a bore, Mika." Xander lowers his foot to the floor anyway.

"Why did you call us?" Massimo straightens in his seat. "It has to be something serious that had you summoning all of us here."

Goddam it to hell. I can't believe I forgot about that. Shows just how much she's addled my mind that I can't recollect half the orders I've issued in the last few days. I glance between them, "Can't I ask my own brothers to join me? After all, we are a family, aren't we?"

"We met just before you went to London, so I take it there have been developments?" Massimo tips his chin up at me.

"You could say that." I rake my fingers through my hair, then survey them, "I'm getting married."

"Married?" Xander slowly bats his eyelids, then bursts out laughing, "*Che cazzo?*" He snickers, "You sure have a strange sense of humor, Michelangelo."

"I hate that name," I say through gritted teeth, "and what's wrong with my getting married?"

"Everything." He tries to school his features into some semblance of seriousness, then bursts out laughing. Again.

"And here I thought Xander would be the first to get married, considering he's had a lifelong crush on Theresa." Massimo leans forward on the balls of his feet.

"Hey," Xander protests, "I don't have a crush on her."

"Oh, please," Christian scoffs, "whenever you see her you go all googly-eyed."

"Googly-eyed?" Xander sputters, "What does that even mean?"

"Why is it that the two of you still squabble like you are ten?" I rub the back of my neck.

"Guess they never grew up, unlike you, Mika," Massimo smirks, "though I can't help but think that London's polluted air got to you. Maybe that's why you decided to get married?"

"You may have a point, " Christian turns to Massimo. "Think we need to call the doctor to have him checked out?"

"Fuck off, *testa di cazzo,*" I growl.

"Oooh," Christian mock shivers, "I am so afraid."

"I am your Capo, dumbass," I say mildly, "better show me some respect, or I'll be asking for your pinky finger next."

"Sometimes," Luca sighs, "you sound like an actor from a bad Hollywood Mafia movie."

"I don't watch movies."

"More's the pity." He looks me up and down, "If you did, you'd know that your story has the makings of a chick flick."

"A chick flick?"

"A romantic comedy," he clarifies, "where the hero and the heroine meet and are attracted to each other, only to realize—"

"I know what a romantic comedy is," I say dryly.

"Do you now?" Christian pretends to do a double take. "Next you'll be telling me that you are in love."

I laugh, "Good one." I smirk. "I see you've been polishing up your comedic skills."

"And you're going to have to polish up your role as a husband."

"Only until I get an heir." I raise a shoulder.

"Surely, there are fringe benefits," Xander murmurs. "Who's the lucky woman, by the way?"

"Someone none of you know."

"*Fantastico.*" Christian rubs his hands, "Is she so beautiful that you don't want us to meet her before the wedding?"

"Yes, she is, and no, that's not the reason I don't want you to meet her before the big day. It's purely because she is currently unaware that's the plan I have in store for her."

"So, you what, kidnapped her?" He fixes me with his shrewd gaze, "What else are you not telling us, Michael?"

"I am telling you everything you need to know at this stage."

"You know that, as your lawyer, I do need to know everything, if I am supposed to help you on this in the future."

"And what makes you think I will be needing your help on this?"

He laughs, "You and I both know that almost everything you do needs my expert touch to steer it along at some point."

"Don't remind me." I scowl.

"Not that I am not grateful for it."

"You better be." I glower at all three of my younger siblings, "It's why I gave you three roles in which you didn't have to get your hands dirty." Massimo's my lawyer, Christian takes care of our finances, and Alessandro? He's the artist among us. My youngest brother—he's younger than Christian by two minutes, has the softest heart, the face of a fallen angel, and the talent of a Renaissance artist.

The joke among us growing up had been that he should have been called Michaelangelo, not me—the oldest, the most cynical brother, on whom the responsibility falls to keep the family business going. One way or the other, though, all of us have our lives intertwined with the firm. Once you're born into a Mafia family, really, there's no way out, particularly for the males. Even if you are as prodigiously talented as Xander, who paints masterpieces... We use his growing fame in the art world to identify potential new targets we can kidnap and hold for ransom in return, not for money—that would be too crass—but for influence, power, and the ability to infiltrate governments and those in the higher echelons of power. It had long ago ceased to be about wealth. Our focus now is to build up our network, to ensure we have the means to influence governments and heads of organizations.

"And I, for one, am grateful that I don't need to be directly involved with the day-to-day business," Massimo murmurs.

"Enough to back me up in what I am going to say next?"

"Which is?"

"That you support my wedding and the consolidation with the other families that I am aiming for."

"But that's not the only reason you are marrying her, is it?"

Luca and I exchange glances. Massimo has always been quick on the uptake. If it weren't for the fact that he's too smart a lawyer and very good at what he does, which is to ensure that my men don't land in prison, I'd have him more involved in the strategizing and planning of our operations.

It helps that our parents had sent all seven of us—including Seb and Adrian—to the US to receive top-class education. It's what came of having a mother who was American. Although, the way she'd taken to the Mafia way of life, and subsumed herself in the old ways, you'd often forget that she was Texan by birth.

"Well?" Massimo scowls, "What's behind this sudden rush to marry? What kind of alliance are you actually seeking through it?"

"It's something Luca and I talked over before you got here."

"Good thing, then, that I got in here before you spilled all your secrets." A new voice interrupts me. I turn to watch Adrian my half-brother, and only one of the two other people outside of my immediate family whom I trust, walk in. "What did I miss?"

"Nothing," I murmur. "Now, all that's needed is for Sebastian-asshole-Sovrano to join us and—"

"Someone mention my name?" Seb walks into the room and I groan. I walk over to the bar, seize the whiskey bottle and top up my glass.

"Drinking alone, *stronzo*?" Seb prowls over to the bar. He bypasses the bottle on the counter, to walk around to the other side. Then, he bends down, and when he straightens, he holds a bottle of only my most expensive whiskey. He opens it, then snatches a glass and is about to pour when I caution him.

"That will cost you, *testa di cazzo,*" I growl.

"Why? Aren't celebrations in order?" He smirks, "I am just getting started, is all."

Of course, he'd overheard our previous conversation.

"Eavesdropping again, *fratellastro?*" I address him by the Italian word for stepbrother, hoping it will irk him, but this time, he doesn't take the bait.

"The door was open, *fratellastro.*" He smirks.

"Why are you here anyway?" I glower at him.

"Family meeting." He glances around the space, "Surely, you didn't think I would stay away."

"You weren't invited."

"I am here now, aren't I?" He pours liquor into a tumbler, then grabs five more and places them on the table. He proceeds to top them up. With my whiskey. Mine.

A growl rumbles up my chest.

He fills up the glasses, then glances around the assembled faces. "What, no one joining in the festivities?"

Next to me, Luca shifts restlessly. "Seb…" he warns, but I throw up a hand.

"No, let him be. He's right, after all."

"He is?" Luca glances between us, his gaze wary. Seb and I don't agree on much. It's not only because he is the closest in age to me, older than even Luca, while being my stepbrother. My father had had a mistress, a woman much younger than him who had borne him two sons. When she had died in an accident, he had brought Seb and Adrian over to our house. Seb had been five, and Adrian only three when my father had asked my mother to take them in and take care of them. She hadn't refused. Whatever her thoughts were about the situation, she had kept them to herself. But she'd had a big heart, and not once, had she allowed Seb or Adrian to feel like they weren't her own sons. But while Adrian had bonded with us instantly, Seb is...one of us and yet, he isn't. Maybe because he was older than Adrian when he joined us, so it was more difficult for him to adjust to living with us. Or perhaps, he is conscious of the fact that he grew up dependent on us. And then there's the fact that he is my father's bastard son, which means my father will never accept him as the next Don. Something he resents, even as he acknowledges that he couldn't have survived without us.

"You are part of the family, Seb," I murmur. "You always have been."

"Just not good enough to ever have a chance at becoming the Don, though?"

"There is only one Capo," I lower my voice to a hush, "and that's me."

He raises his glass. "To the wedding of the one and only Capo," he says in a voice which sounds sincere. Fucking *stronzo*. Not that he means it.

I move forward and tip some of the alcohol into my glass. The others crowd around the bar as each of them reaches for their own glass and raises it.

"To the Capo," Luca fixes his gaze on mine, "and to the alliance with the Seven."

"The Seven?" Seb turns to me, "That's who your new bride is related to?"

I tilt my head, "Is that a problem?"

He scratches his chin, "Amongst them all, they own most of the UK and parts of Silicon Valley too, I hear." He fixes his gaze on me, "Ambitious, are we?"

"Disbelieving, are we?"

"It's not my life, *fratellone.*" He raises a shoulder. "And I assume this has to do with getting access to enough connections to consolidate your position with the other families?"

Seb really is smart. As intelligent as Massimo, as hungry as Luca, with the rakish charm of Christian and the beauty of Xander…

All of it, rolled into one ambitious, cynical, man who'd do anything to take over as Capo one day. It's what makes Seb so dangerous, and yet also, the one with the most promise. It's why he's the only one of all my family who can stand up to me. Precisely why I trust him the least and kept him as close as I can. The only way to keep track of someone who poses a threat to you is to keep them in your inner circle.

Do I trust Seb? That's an interesting question. I don't think he'd do anything to hurt my family, but given the right motivation and circumstances, could he turn on me?

"So," Christian glances between us, "when do we get to meet your new bride?"

"At the wedding," I murmur

"What?" Xander blinks. "We don't get to meet her before?"

"No."

"Don't you trust us with her?" Massimo drawls.

"Never." I fold my arms across my chest.

"Aww shucks." Seb smirks. "The way you're acting, you'd think you have her hidden away here and want us to get the hell away so you can spend time with her."

I glare at him and a look of understanding dawns on his features, "So you do have her here with you?"

Of course, Seb would have to figure it out. Not that I am hiding anything from them or anything. "And if I do?"

"*'Sto cazzo!*" Seb exclaims. "Why, you old coot, you kidnapped her and brought her here, eh?"

"Fuck off," I growl.

"You did, didn't you?"

I glare at him. Asshat is seriously getting on my nerves.

He places his elbows on the bar, and leans forward, "Was it love at first sight?" He smirks, "You saw her and it was the proverbial *colpo di fulmine*?" He's referring to the thunderbolt that Italians use as a term for describing love at first sight. Like most things, my people are prone to exaggeration. Hence, love at first sight needs to be described literally as being unexpected and as powerful as a lightning strike.

I snort. "Next you'll be telling me that you've experienced it yourself, the way you talk passionately about it."

"Me?" Seb laughs, the sound without mirth, "Would I be standing here if I had?"

I peer into his features, take in the tightness of the skin around his eyes, the slight slump to his shoulders, which is a surprise. I've never seen Seb anything but on the offensive. Apparently, the *testa di cazzo* has his share of secrets. Something I intend to worm out of him someday. Just not right now.

One thing he's right about... I am anxious to meet with my bride-to-be, but not for any of the reasons he thinks. Fucking her is out of the question, at least, until the wedding. On that much, I am clear. There, however, remains the task of breaking the news to her... Something I need to mull over. I need to figure out a way to get her to willingly agree. This entire plan which I had hatched on the spur of the moment is, clearly, more complicated than I expected.

But how hard could it be, anyway, to get her to see things my way, hmm?

I place the glass back on the bar counter, then step back, "I am sure you can see yourselves out."

I shut down the camera, then turn to leave.

Seb chuckles. "So anxious to see your woman?" he calls after me.

"Vaffanculo," I hold up a middle finger above my shoulder, "not that it's any of your business."

"Everything you do is our business," he retorts. "Considering you're the Capo... Capo."

I pause, turn to glare at him over my shoulder, "It's because I am Capo, I am asking you for the first and last time to never talk about her, *capisci*?"

I hold his gaze, and he finally lowers it. Good. Seb may be as alpha as they come, but he knows I am the one in charge. And I intend to be for a long time. If he thinks he can displace me from my hard-won position, he has another think coming. No doubt, one day, he is going to challenge me, too. I know that as well as I know my name... It's why the next move I make is going to be very important, one on which hinges the future of me and my *famiglia*.

"I am leaving, and when I return, I want the lot of you to have cleared out." I glance around the faces of my siblings, "You feel me?"

9

Karma

The domed ceiling far above the bed has an ornate pattern. How old is this building? From the outside, it had a baroque architecture... The kind I've seen in magazines. It was beautiful. Does he own it? He must. Just like he owns the private jet we'd flown in that had landed on the private airstrip on the other side of the island.

He'd stalked off the flight and driven off in a car. His men had directed us to the second car. There had been two more following us as our little procession had made its way here.

Is this the only building on the island? Where is this island, anyway? Somewhere in Italy, given the language his men had been speaking. Michael himself, though, spoke with an odd accent, something between American and Italian.

Michael, huh? As if knowing his name means I know anything about him? He is, clearly, Mafia... If he hadn't given himself away when I had mentioned my father...the proceedings after that had given away his identity. I stand up and stretch.

The hair on the back of my neck prickles. I glance around the room, but there's no one. A shiver runs down my spine. I wrap my arms around my waist, take stock of my surroundings. There's a closet in the corner, an old-fashioned dressing table pushed up against one wall. Beyond that, a door. I walk to it, push it, and step inside a bathroom that's spacious enough to have a clawed bathtub in the center. Beyond that, a large window allows light inside. On the other side is a sink. I walk over, catch my reflection and flinch.

Dirt streaks my face and my hair has bits of… I pull at it—dried leaves? There are towels on a chair nearby. I strip out of my clothes, ignore the bath and walk over to the shower stall at the far corner. The shampoo and the shower gel smell of moonflowers. Whoa! How did he know that this is my preferred scent? I step under the water, which is hot… Thank god.

I let it flow over me, sink into my tired muscles, allow my muscles to unwind. When the hot water runs out. I step out, dry myself, survey my clothes. My sports bra has flecks of blood...his blood. Hmm. I wrap the towel around my torso, cinching it in under my arms. I step out of the bathroom and my breath leaves me.

"What are you doing here?"

Michael turns from the window. The light haloes him, and for a second, the shadows mask the lower part of his face. His blue gaze burns into mine. I flinch. He peruses me from head to toe and his eyes gleam. Then he lowers his eyelashes, jerks his chin toward the bed. A new change of clothes is folded on the bed. "You're welcome." He smirks.

Fuck you, very much. I snarl low in my throat. "How did you…?" I frown, then turn on him. "You were watching me?"

He tilts his head.

"You…you creep."

"You really do need to get more inventive with your insults, Beauty."

"Stop calling me that."

"Stop trying to resist every step of the way, it's…annoying."

"What's annoying is you haunting me, turning up at every corner, insinuating yourself into my life, making it a living hell, taking me away from everything and everyone that—"

"Made you unhappy."

I still. "What are you talking about?"

"You hated your life."

Yes.

"You know nothing about me."

"On the contrary." He drums his fingers on his thigh. "Karma West. Birth name: Karma Rhodes. Born twenty years ago to Charlotte and Adam Rhodes. Mother died when you were a young, leaving you in the care of your father. Who promptly threw himself into his work, then fell into debt. He then abandoned you and your sister to the foster care system, and left the UK to escape the wrath of the Mafia. Your sister made it out of the foster care system when she came of age, then took you on as your legal guardian. Just a few weeks ago, she married Sinclair Sterling, one of the richest men in the UK. You attended their sham wedding... Then drank the night away with your two friends at the pub two streets down from their residence in Primrose Hill. Wanted to go home with a man...but didn't. Along the way, you also dropped out of a graduate course in fine arts at Goldsmiths, where you had received a full scholarship, instead preferring to spend the days at your pop-up shop in Camden Market where you hawk your wares."

"I don't hawk. I share my designs," I snap.

"You mean the clothes you sew?"

"They are dress creations that I fashion," I sniff, "and sell under my independent label."

"What-fucking-ever." He smirks. "That's...when you are not haunting your local pub or dancing to electronica with fellow goths who pretend to understand you. But really, no one does."

"And you do?"

"You have to admit, I know far more about you than anyone else." He rubs his knuckles across his thigh, and I shiver.

No, he doesn't. He has no idea that I have a heart problem or that I'd been seeing a specialist about it before he took me captive... Or that...in a way, I am glad that he took me away from my life because, while my sister Summer means well, she is stifling me with all of that attention. In a way, he set me free. Does he know that? Now, all I have to do is take back the ability to make my own choices. I tilt up my chin, "You've barely scratched the surface of who I am."

"Hmm." He draws his gaze down my features, over my chest, "And what a thing of beauty that is, too."

My nipples grow erect. "Get out."

His smile widens.

"I need to change."

"Go right ahead."

Bastard. Of course, he'd taunt me about that. I march up to the clothes folded on the bed. There's a pale yellow dress, and next to it, underwear—a matching bra and panties set. My cheeks flush. Did he choose my underwear? Nah, he probably had it ordered or something for me, not that I am going to ask him. That will simply reveal just how nervous I am. I take in the comfortable ballet pumps next to the bed on the floor. Not my style, but at least they look comfortable.

His gaze bores into mine and the skin around his eyes tightens. A strange nervousness seems to roll off of him as he flexes his shoulders. He can't be nervous. Can he? Nah, it's my imagination. Alphahole here isn't be afraid of anything…or anyone. All of this is just a ruse to get me naked. If he thinks I am going to shrink away from it…he's…mistaken. I tip up my chin, drop the towel.

His entire body stiffens. A breeze blows in from the window and I shiver. *Look at the clothes. Reach for them. Put them on. Do it. Cover yourself.* I grip my fingers at my side, try to glance away from his perusal, but I can't. He walks over, until he's right in front of me. So big, so tall. I have to tilt my head back, and then further back, to meet his gaze. Blue eyes deepened to an azure steel reflect back every single one of my emotions. Uncertainty. Lust. Desire. His gaze rests on my features, down to my lips. A moan wells up my throat. Down to my nipples which instantly pebble, across my trembling belly, to the slippery core between my thighs.

"Open your legs."

No.

No.

"Yes." He jerks his chin. I shuffle my feet apart. Draw in a breath. Another. Dense clouds of heat spool off of his massive body, and slam into my chest. I pant. His gaze rolls down my thighs to my feet. My toes curl. Then back to my pussy. Liquid heat thrums low in my belly. Blood engorges my nub. Hell. Is it my own audacity that's turning me on as much as the fact that he can't seem to take his gaze off my cunt?

"*Che cazzo,*" he exclaims, "is that what I think it is?"

"What do you think it is?"

"When did you get your clit pierced?"

"None of your bloody business." I'd have had my nipples pierced too, but that would have been too obvious, and if my sister had picked up on it? Gah, Summer would have had a cow about it.

Maybe, once I escape this asshole, and I've told Summer that I am safe, I'll figure out a way to be independent and stand on my own two feet without having to be dependent on anyone else... Then I can pierce any bloody part of my body and I won't have to explain it to anyone.

His lips twist, "You're wrong, Beauty. Everything about you is my business. You're my property now, you understand?"

"I'm a woman, a person, you bastard. I am not a possession."

"Wrong." He yawns. "When you left your life behind, you gave up all rights. Now you'll do everything I tell you to, when I tell you to, how I..." he leans forward on his heels, "tell you to."

"I didn't leave my life behind. You took me," I object.

"Tomayto, tomahto; potayto, potahto."

"Let's call the whole thing off," I retort.

He raises his eyebrow. "As I was saying, you're mine now, and you'll do as I say..."

"No."

"Yes." He nods, "Starting with that." He jerks his chin toward my core.

"What the hell do you mean?" I scowl.

"You need to shave."

I blink. "Excuse me?"

"I'll send someone to help you clean up the hair." He pivots, then begins to walk toward the door. "I prefer it completely bare."

Anger explodes in my chest. My gaze narrows. All of my senses seem to pop. A low cry spills from my lips. I close the distance between us and throw myself at him.

10

Michael

The hair on my forearms rises. All of my senses jangle. I swivel around and catch her around the waist, lift her off of the ground.

"I hate you. I fucking hate you," she snarls, then swings her fists. I duck. I must be losing my touch, for her knuckles graze my jaw, and my dick, which had stood up and saluted her bare bottom the moment she'd bared it, is sure it's found heaven. My groin tightens and my balls ache. I tighten my grip around her. "Stop."

"How dare you insult me…you…you…pig?"

A chuckle trembles up my throat and I swallow it. "Calm down."

"Let go of me."

"No."

She goes still.

"No?"

"Not until your blood pressure drops back to normal."

"The only person I see having a bloody cardiac is you." She brings up her knee. I twist my body to the side, she catches me in the thigh, and damn it, but my cock instantly lengthens. The fuck is wrong with my reactions, that I can't control myself around her?

"Back off, Beauty or you'll regret it."

She makes that noise deep in her throat, that sound of anger and frustration that sends sparks down my spine, engages all of my nerve endings so that all my brain cells seem to shut down, then flare all at once.

"Last. Chance."

"Oh, sod off." She strains in my embrace, and her breasts thrust into my chest, her nipples sharp enough to stab me through my jacket and my shirt.

Fuck. I squeeze my arms, haul her even closer. I'm not copping a feel... Okay...so maybe I am, but can you blame me? This tiny soaked-with-bath-water-and-desire female...is...simply the most delectable piece of femininity that I have ever come across and..

My breath leaves me.

"You didn't just do that," I growl.

"What, you mean this?" She slips her palm between us and squeezes my balls... Again... Fuck. A growl tears from my lips. My thighs spasm and sweat breaks out on my brow. "You're going to regret that, Beauty."

She bares her teeth. "Oh yeah? What are you gonna do? Spank me."

Hmm.

Her gaze widens, her breath hitches, her pupils dilate and...fuck this shit! I am only a man. There's only so much I can take.

I bend my knees, peer into her eyes. "How many?"

"What?"

"How many slaps?"

"Fuck off."

"You choose or I will, and I promise you, the number will not be one you like."

"Bet you won't like this either." She clears her throat and spits. A gob of warm saliva slashes across my lips.

She freezes.

So, do I.

The warmth drips down my chin, and something snaps inside of me. I scoop her up, twist her and throw her over my shoulder. She screams, struggles, and I throw an arm over the back of her thighs, squeeze her close enough for her knees to dig into my side. She beats at my back, down my side. Nice. My muscles warm, lengthen. I reach the bed, seat myself, then drape her across my lap.

"Let me go." She huffs.

"No." I bring my arm down and my palm connects with her butt.

She yells, "You bastard, how dare you!"

"Don't challenge me, baby girl."

"Let me, the fuck go, this moment!" she howls.

"Or?"

"Or I'll scream."

"Is that a promise?" I spank her left butt cheek and she screams. Slap her right and she gasps, sputters. Bring my palm down again on her left and her entire body bucks.

"Fuck you, asshole."

"Not just yet, and I do prefer alphahole."

"You conceited, obnoxious, swollen-headed—"

"Love it when you talk dirty, darling." I take aim, lower my palm across the curve of her ass, right over the reddened palm print I'd left there, and she squeals. And again. And again. My palm tingles, my forearm muscles hurt, and still, I don't stop. *Eight, nine, ten.*

A sob bubbles up from her, "I'll never forgive you for this."

"Good."

"I'll get back at you."

"Hope you're keeping count, hmm?"

Twelve, thirteen, fifteen. She squeals, digs her fists into the bed and growls.

"Had enough?"

"I'll never beg you to stop. Never apologize… Never," she retorts.

I slide my fingers between her swollen lower lips and she hiccups.

"Fuck, Beauty, you are soaking wet," I growl

"From the bath, you idiot." She snarls, "I took a shower not ten minutes ago."

"Let's put that to the test, hmm?" I drag my knuckles down her slit and she moans. Slip a finger inside her slippery channel and she wheezes. "Please."

"Please what?"

"Please stop."

I draw her slickness up her cunt, into the valley between her butt cheeks and she freezes.

"Anyone taken you here, Beauty?"

She makes a low noise at the back of her throat.

"That's what I thought." My groin hardens. The blood begins to thud at my temples.

I press my wet middle finger into her back hole and her butt clenches; her spine arches.

"How does that feel?"

"How do you think, you jerk?" She yells, "I'll push something up your ass and ask you the same question!"

I laugh. I can't help it. The laughter just bursts out.

She turns her face, peers at me from between the strands of hair that fall over her face. "It's not bloody funny."

"You're right." I wipe the smile from my face. "It's boring. I've wasted enough of my time." I stand up and she falls to the ground on her ass.

She mewls, and I hesitate. I should take care of her…make sure I soothe the reddened skin that bears my marks. No. What am I thinking? She is…my captive. An experiment, perhaps, to find out how long I can hold out before my control snaps. She is nothing. Nothing. And I am trying too hard to convince myself.

"Get dressed." I pivot, stalk to the door.

"Michael."

I keep walking.

"Stop."

I reach the door, shove it open.

"Goddamn you, you can't ignore me. You can't keep me here."

I step through.

"Master," she calls out to me.

I pause.

There's silence for a beat.

I turn, glare at her over my shoulder.

She pales, tips her chin up. Brings her arms to her sides so the full beautiful expanse of her body is bared to my gaze.

I peruse her face, the flushed features, the trail of tears down her cheeks. This woman... She is magnificent. Unclothed, naked as nature intended, with that dyed black hair of hers in disarray around her shoulders. She is…dangerous.

I should keep away from her… I should…punish her for how she brought out the base part of me, for how her nearness has unhinged me. I should break her. Only, in this fight between us there will be no winners. There is only way forward… And it leads into darkness. Fuck her, and fuck me for what I am going to have to do to her.

I drum my fingers on my thigh, "I don't have all day, Beauty."

"How long," she squeezes her fingers together in front of her, "how long do you plan on keeping me here?"

"For as long as it takes."

11

Karma

He spanked me. I shift my weight from foot to foot as I stare out of the window. After Michael left, I had taken a quick shower, then ignored the clothes he had left out for me, because... Yeah, as if I am going to obey that prick after what he did to me.

And if you defy him, will he spank you again?

My thighs clench. *Oh, my god, what the hell is wrong with me?* I did not just think that, did not.

I had marched over to the closet, then pulled on the first dress I had come across—this knee-length dress in pink, which I absolutely hate, but whatever. It's something to cover myself up with. There had been enough clothes in the walk-in closet… Most of them seemed new, along with underclothes that were made of the finest laces…and decadently cut.

And all the clothes fit me... no doubt about it, they were to my measurements, how the hell had he managed that? How had he gotten them delivered here so quickly?

I'd run my fingers over the fabric of the dresses in the closet. Everything is exquisite. Even if they have been bought off the shelf they are of the finest quality. The undergarments are as seductive as the outerwear is modest. It's as if he wants me to appear docile to the world, but under my clothes, appear every bit the whore he, no doubt, regards me as. Whore… Yeah, he definitely thinks of me as his possession.

It's why he'd taken me across this knee, then taken his palm to me like I was an errant child and I… I'd loved it. *Damn it.*

I grip the window frame with my fingers. Damn the obnoxious brute of a man. He hadn't hurt me, to be honest. The slaps had stopped just this side of being hard…unlike him. He'd been aroused from the beating he'd given me, too.

My belly trembles. I'd felt his length thrust up and into my sensitive center. The faster he'd beaten me, the more I'd tried not to scream, and the less I'd succeeded…. And the harder he had become under me. It had been… Strangely arousing. How could it be?

I swipe the hair from my eyes. His wide palms had seared me with each contact. His fingers cupping my flesh, leaving drums beats of fire in their wake. I squeeze my thighs together. There's no denying the arousal that coats my core as the images cling to my subconscious mind.

How would it be to have him spank me again, then turn me over and part my thighs and swipe me from backhole to my clit, the way he'd used his fingers earlier? My bottom throbs and my pussy clenches. *No, no, no.* I am not going to let him crawl into my head and play with my fantasies.

The man kidnapped you, held a gun to your forehead, then knocked you out and you… All you can think is how hot he is, how sexy, how completely ovary-exploding that smirk of his is. If he looks at me one more time and drawls some insult… I'm going to lose it.

I'm going to throw myself at him again and lose every last shred of my dignity. I stalk to the center of the room, look around the space. The hair on the back of my neck stiffens. I glance around the space again. It looks like a normal bedroom, but appearances can be deceptive, right? Why can't I get rid of the feeling that I am being watched, even now? I bite the inside of my cheek.

Has he hidden a camera in this room? Would he do that? Is he watching me, even now? I shiver. Wriggle my hips. It's creepy as fuck. But…when had I last been the single-minded focus of someone's attention to this extent? Not my mother or my father, not the nuns at the school that I had attended, not my older sister Summer, who—well, okay, so she fussed over me, worried about me. She is my substitute parent, after all.

But Michael... He is intrigued by me. Maybe that's too complimentary a word… More likely, I am something to pass his time. His newest shiny plaything, to toy with. He looks at me like a boy would a captured butterfly when he has no idea what to do with it. He could imprison me in a bell jar, watch as I flutter my wings and try to escape, or he could pluck my wings out. I shiver.

Ugh, that is not comforting. I rub my fingers over my goosebump ridden arms.

Whoever this man is, he's not kidding around. Every time he's seen me, he's had a plan, an agenda… To put me down. To strip me of all of my dignity, to make me crawl and… I won't. No. No way, am I going to give in to him. The moment I do, I'll lose his interest, and then he'll kill me. I swallow. Or…or worse. *No, don't go there. Focus on the now.* I am here, alive and—the door opens—apparently, I have a visitor.

A woman stands silhouetted in the doorway.

I blink. "Who're you?"

"I'm Cassandra." She smiles, "I am the Capo's housekeeper."

"Capo?" I scowl, "You mean Michael?"

She nods, her dark eyes wide, her face pleasant. She's in her thirties, hair scraped back in a bun that makes her seem older than her years. Her starched black dress comes to below her knees and is shapeless in the way women who don't want to draw attention to themselves tend to dress. She has sensible shoes, which don't detract at all from her shapely, fair legs. In her hands she holds a vanity kit.

"What do you want?" I frown. Okay, so I am being belligerent, but can you blame me? I don't trust anyone in this house.

"I'm here to help you shave your vagina," she murmurs.

"What the hell?" I choke out, "I can't believe that asshole actually went through with this."

She moves toward me and I throw up my hands, "Whoa, hold on, I can shave myself, thank you very much."

She hesitates, "Are you sure? I can help you—"

"No," I snap, "Just...hand over the stuff I need and you can leave."

She blinks, then holds out the vanity kit. "As you wish."

I grab the bag from her. "Is this what you do? Shave the women he brings here?" I snap.

"He hasn't brought any other woman here before."

"Oh!" I gape. O-k-a-y. What the hell does that even mean? Nothing... Don't go attaching meaning to actions where there are none, bitch. Fine. Okay. I blow out a breath. "Whatever," I murmur, then stare at her. "Was there anything else?"

"The Capo asks for your presence at dinner." She half smiles, then beckons "Whenever you are ready, please come down to the dining room on the ground floor."

I toss the kit onto the bed, "I am ready now."

"The Capo insists that you shave first."

"And if I refuse?"

Her eyes widen. "I don't think you want to do that."

My backside throbs. No, of course, I don't want to disobey Lord Alphaholington himself. A snicker catches in my throat. Whatever. It would be nice to be away from this room, even if it is a meal with his obnoxious alphaholeness.

"Fine," I sniff, "I'll be down once I've..." I wave the bag in the air.

She smiles, then turns and heads for the doorway.

"Wait, Cassandra."

She stops.

"Michael kidnapped me, you know. Is he holding you against your will too?"

She turns, fixes me with an inscrutable gaze, "The Capo gave me a job when I needed it most. He saved me and my family."

What the—? Not what I had expected to hear, but makes sense.

The jerkass is smart enough to surround himself with people who owe him. What better way to gain their complete loyalty than my making sure that you provide for them and their families?

She half bows again, "Best not to keep the Capo waiting, signorina."

Turning, she leaves.

An hour later, I leave the room, freshly shaved—and no it's not because I want to please the asshole. It's only because... I feel much cleaner after shaving myself all over. My panties stick to my freshly-shaved pussy as I walk. Shit, the skin there feels so much more sensitive than usual, now that it is exposed. It's hard not to be constantly aware of it. Bet he wanted me to feel this way. That's why he'd insisted that I remove all hair from there. *Jerk.*

I walk down two flights of stairs, then head past double doors that have been flung open. I peek out to see a grassy lawn sloping down. Trees fringe the sides of a path that curves and disappears. In the distance, the wide-open sea beckons.

I keep walking until I stop at another set of double doors. This should be it. I shove open the door, walk in and come to a halt. Michael is standing at the window with two men I have not seen before.

Michael turns to me. He looks me up and down. His nostrils flare and his eyes gleam. Asshole looks almost pleased that I defied his orders. Holy shit. Did he know that I would ignore the clothes he'd laid out and opt for something of my own choosing?

His lips curl and I resist the urge to stamp my foot. Walked right into that one, didn't I? *Sneaky bastard.* I glance away, just as one of the other men turns to me.

My breath catches. Oh, wow, this guy is beautiful. Face like an angel, piercing blue eyes similar to Michael's, but darker in color. High forehead, sharp cheekbones, that same hooked nose. He's as tall as Michael, is dressed similarly in a dark fitted suit that hugs his corded length. His jacket stretches across shoulders that are bulked up as if he lifts weights every day. Light pours over him, catches the golden lights in his dark blonde hair.

The overall effect is that of lightness. Where Michael carries a dark, edgy, dangerous aura, this man...has an electricity that sparks off of him. It seems to light up the space as he walks toward me.

I blink.

He holds out his hand, "Karma?"

I put out my hand to take his when there's a snarl from the direction of the window, "Get away from her."

12

Michael

"Forgive my stepbrother, he can be an impolite motherfucker."

Seb grabs her palm and brings it up to his lips.

The *stronzo* kisses the back of her fingers. I stiffen. How dare he? And after I warned him to stay away from her. I'd told them all to leave, but Seb had stayed back. Next to him, Adrian shuffles his feet.

Clearly, Seb had coerced him to wait, as well. Now, he glances between us, uncomfortable. "Seb," he says in a low voice, "we should leave."

"What's the hurry?" Seb drawls in a tone that ensures that I can hear it.

Clearly, he is testing me. I roll my shoulders, take a step forward. Then stop. It won't do to give away what I feel...*which is...a confusing set of emotions that sits heavy in my gut.*

I take in her face, her gaze alight as she glances up at him. No doubt, her attention is captured by the bastard's beautiful countenance. It's what makes people trust him, that is, until he pulls the rug out from under them.

Seb's smile widens. His gaze dips to her lips, down the slope of her breasts—and I snarl low in my throat.

He laughs. "Why, *principesa,* I believe it's going to be delightful to get to know you."

Anger laces my blood.

"Didn't I tell you to leave?" I growl.

"How could I? Especially after you mentioned that you have a guest. It was but polite to stay on and introduce myself to her. Though I understand, now, why you prefer to keep her to yourself. She is stunning." He peers down at her, and his face alights with a smile, "Your beauty is breathtaking, *principessa.*"

Karma giggles. I glance sideways, watch the blush rise to her cheeks. Anger crawls at my gut. She isn't allowed to respond to any other man, to react to their flirtation, to have them hook her arm in the crook of their elbow and allow them to lead her to the table.

Seb pulls back the chair and she drops into it. He places his hand on the back of her chair and his fingers graze her shoulders. My vision tunnels. I stalk up to them, grab him by the back of his collar and haul him back.

"Whoa!" He swings around, fists raised.

"Leave," I snarl. "Get the fuck off this island and don't come back until I send for you."

His eyebrows furrow; his breathing is ragged, "You should know better than to step up behind a man."

"You should know better than touch what is mine..."

"Interesting choice of words." His smile twists, "I do believe this is the first time I've seen you lose your composure, *fratellastro.*"

"Fuck off." I jerk my chin toward the exit.

"Or what? "

The blood begins to thud at my temples. I step up until we are toe to toe, "You don't want to find out."

A chair scrapes, and she appears between us. "Stop it."

"Stay out of this," I growl without taking my gaze off of the *stronzo* in front of me.

Seb shoots me a glance from under hooded eyebrows. "You threatening me?"

"What do you think?"

She thrusts her face closer, "I think you guys are hangry."

I glower at the man in front of me.

"It happens to men and babies. When they are hungry, they can't think straight, and often, end up fighting. So why don't we sit down and eat, huh?"

Her stomach rumbles, the sound loud in the silence. She giggles, the sound a little nervous. "If I don't eat soon enough, I am going to faint."

"No, you're not." I glance at her sideways.

She turns her face up, "I really am starving."

I frown.

"It's not a ploy or anything. I mean, I'd love to see the two of you beat the shit out of each other, but it's easier on a full stomach, huh?"

The door opens and one of my staff walks in with a tray of food. He stops, glances between us.

"Ah, food." Seb rubs his hands together, "Dinner does seem like a good idea."

"We are going to eat." I turn to Seb, "You, on the other hand..." I jerk my chin toward the exit.

He dips his chin, then turns to Beauty. "Another time, my lady. I look forward to deepening our acquaintance."

Not if I have anything to do with it. I grab his shoulder, shove him toward the exit. Adrian turns to me, "I'm sorry, Michael. Seb can sometimes be a dick."

I tilt my head, "You're a good brother, and an even better made man." I widen my stance, "It's one of the reasons I have tolerated Seb, so far. But his time is running out."

Adrian firms his lips.

"Next time, I won't be so lenient."

Adrian nods. "I'll talk to him," he mutters, "you have my word." He follows Seb out, and the door clicks shut behind him.

I glare at Beauty then jerk my chin toward the table. Her jaw firms but she doesn't say a word. Thank fuck. She marches around and drops into the chair at the center of the table.

I stalk back to my chair opposite her, hold up my arm.

Emanuel places the dishes of food before us.

"*Buon appetito.*"

"*Grazie,* Emanuel." I wave him off.

The scent of garlic and parmigiana fills the air. Opposite me, Beauty stares at the dish, picks up her fork and hesitates.

"It's not seafood."

She shoots me a glance from under her eyelashes. "How did you know that I am allergic to..." Her features tighten. "I don't want to know."

"You're learning quickly."

I twirl strands of spaghetti and bring the fork to my mouth. She watches me as I close my mouth around the fork, wipe it clean. Her pupils dilate and her breathing deepens.

"Like what you see?" I smirk.

She reddens, lowers her gaze to the plate. She cuts the pasta with her knife—a fucking knife—and I stare. She scoops it up with a spoon, and—*Che cazzo!* —I drop my fork on my plate with a clatter.

"What the fuck are you doing?"

"What?" She scowls at me, "What did I do now?"

I glance at the strands of pasta hanging off of her spoon, then back at her face.

"What is it?" Her frown deepens, "You going to tell me, or are you simply going to glare at me like I committed an act of treason?"

"It's worse than that."

"It is?"

I nod. "You cut your spaghetti with a *knife*... Then proceeded to eat it with a *spoon,*" I growl.

"So?"

"So?" I glower, "That's...a fucking crime."

"Umm... *That's* a crime?" Her lips tremble. "You are the Mafia and you call *that* a crime?" She snorts, tries to control herself, then laughs, turns it into a cough, which turns into a real coughing fit. She places her knife and spoon down—finally, fuck—reaches for the glass of water and drinks it.

When she's calmed herself down, and wiped away the tears which had run down her face, she glances at me.

I scowl at her, and she giggles, snorts again. I glare at her. "What the fuck is so funny?"

"N...nothing." She chuckles, then manages to get a hold of herself. "So...you were saying—"

"Nothing," I say through gritted teeth, "if you want to continue to eat your pasta like a philistine, be my guest."

"But I don't." She giggles again, then firms her lips. "No, really Michael, show me how I am supposed to eat pasta."

My glare intensifies and she raises both of her hands, palms face up, "No, I mean it. I want to learn. Promise."

"Hmm." I take in her features, her pink cheeks, her bright eyes, and fuck me, she looks beautiful. No, she always looks beautiful. Now, she looks full of life, happy, relaxed, the way she's always meant to be. My scowl deepens.

The fuck am I thinking along those lines? One shared meal and I am harboring thoughts of what...? Wanting her in my life for a longer period of time? Fuck that. That's not why I brought her here. She's here to fulfill a purpose, that's all.

I pick up my fork. "You are supposed to pull aside a small amount of pasta, maybe two or three strands, twirl it on the plate, then carefully lift the fork." I demonstrate to her, "The big mistake people always make is to try to pick up too much at once. It takes practice to get it right." I twirl a few pasta strands with my fork then nod toward her plate. "Now, your turn."

She looks like she is about to protest, and I shoot her a warning glance, "If you are going to eat Italian food, learn to do it properly."

"Fine, fine," she huffs, "don't get your knickers in a twist."

She twirls some of the pasta around her fork, then reaches for her spoon. *Porca cane!* I make a warning sound at the back of my throat and she glances at me, "Now what?"

I glare at her spoon, then back at her face.

She rolls her eyes, but lowers the spoon back to her plate. She twirls the pasta, then raises the fork with the pasta strands wrapped around the tines. Before she can get it to her mouth, the strands unravel and she lets out a groan of frustration. She looks at me and I nod at her fork.

"*Pazienza*. Try again."

She lets out a sigh before turning her attention back to her fork. This time, she grabs fewer strands of pasta, carefully twirls the fork, and slowly lifts it to her mouth. "Happy, now?" She pretends to be irritated with me, but I can tell she's feeling proud of herself.

"I'll be happier when you taste the food."

She tries the forkful and her expression lights up.

"Good, eh?"

"It's incredible." She scoops up another forkful, following my instructions to the letter, and wipes the tines of the fork clean, then closes her eyes, chews. A moan spills from her mouth. She swallows and my belly tightens; my dick lengthens, tenting my pants. Fuck. Is everything with this woman an orgasmic experience?

She cracks open her eyes and her gaze locks with mine. She reddens, then scowls, "Like what you see?"

My lips quirk and I firm them. So much sass, so much fire. Why does this girl always seem to get to me?

I rake my gaze across her mouth, down the flushed skin of her throat. "Every bit of it," I murmur.

Her blush deepens. "I love eating." She frowns.

And I'd love to eat you. I twirl more pasta onto my fork, bring it to my mouth and close my lips around the fork. "Don't let me keep you from your food."

She swallows, lowers her gaze to her own plate, then digs in with a relish that is fascinating to watch. Her every movement so immersed in taking full enjoyment from the moment. Everything she does, she puts her heart, her passion into it. When was the last time I was that…involved with what I do? Be it my work, my people, the things in my life that I took forward to... When had I begun to take it all for granted? When had I become so cynical that everything had begun to blur into a meaningless mess? A patchwork of black and white and grey, sometimes interlaced with crimson.

Then she'd splashed right into the center, a joyous rainbow. Something... Someone to be savored and held and stroked. Caressed until blood swells her skin, thrums at her fingertips, pours into her veins and engorges her pussy. As I drag my fingers up her curves to her neck, across the creamy expanse of her chest, where I squeeze her nipples, tease them into hard peaks of delight to be nibbled on, sucked on.

Her fork hits the plate with a clatter, and I look up.

She leans back with a sigh. "That was the best meal I've had in…forever."

Good. I take another leisurely mouthful.

"Who is the chef? I'd love to pass on my compliments to him."

"Her," I murmur.

"What?"

"Larissa cooks all of my meals."

"Oh," she tilts her head, "I'd love to meet her."

"You will."

As I place my fork on my plate, there's a knock on the door.

13

Karma

The door opens and Emanuel strides in. He picks up Michael's now empty plate and sets a crystal creamer next to him, then walks over, collects my plate as well.

"*Grazie,* Emanuel," I smile at him.

"Prego, signorina." He walks out just as another women enters the dining room.

She's wearing a chef's apron and a scarf around her neck. Her black dress reaches to just above her knees, and on her feet are six-inch heels. Hangonasecond. Who cooks wearing stilettos? I sit up, stalk her as she walks to the far end of the table. She glances from me to Michael.

Her eyes flare and her lips turn up.

Michael jerks his chin toward the woman, who nods. She takes off her scarf, places it on the table. Then unties the apron and lets it drop on the floor.

Umm, what?

She flips around a chair, steps onto it, then onto the table.

I scowl, "What's she doing?"

Michael doesn't reply. I glance toward him and find that he's watching her progress with a single-minded focus. The kind I thought he'd reserve only for me. My heart begins to thud. It can't be; this can't be happening….

"You…you don't mean to..." My voice sounds too loud. I cringe.

She glides across the table to stand in the space between us.

Michael makes a swirling motion with his finger.

"I… I don't understand." I fold my fingers together in my lap, take a steadying breath. "What's for dessert?"

"She is."

"What?" My pulse thuds at my temples.

She reaches behind her neck and unhooks the clasp of the dress she's wearing. It slides down to the surface of the table and pools around her ankles before she kicks it aside. Underneath, she's completely naked. *Look away, look away.* I trace the line of her spine down to the curve of her smooth ass…her smooth, perfect butt cheeks. She sinks down onto the table on her back, then lowers her head until it touches the table not a few inches away from me. Her legs are toward Michael.

He rises to his feet, raises the small crystal pitcher and leans over her. He tilts the glass container and a trail of white pours out across the tops of her thighs, across her pussy—completely bare, just the way he likes it. He draws the liquid down one leg, up to the arch of her ankle. Then he places it aside.

"Why…why are you doing this?" My voice comes out too thin, too high.

"You defied me, Beauty; you need to be punished for it."

"What do you mean?" I scowl, "How did I defy you?"

He glances at my dress and I draw in a breath. He means the outfit he laid out, the one which I'd ignored. The asshole. I went against his stupid order and now he wants to what? Put me in my place?

He hangs over the other woman, one hand pressed to the table near her hips for support. He dips his finger into the cream then trails it down her inner thigh. The darkness of his skin against the white of the cream is...obscene. My throat closes. I curl my fingers into fists, dig my nails into the palms of my hands and pain shoots up my arms.

He peers up at me from under sooty lashes and I gasp. His nostrils flare; the skin around his lips is stretched tight. His gaze clashes with mine and I can't look away. The band around my chest pulls in further. A burning sensation builds behind my eyes. How dare he touch her that way? How dare he try to pull off this exhibitionism in front of me?

I straighten my shoulders; the skin around his eyes creases. He rakes his gaze down my features, over my lips. He stares at my mouth and holy hell, it's like he's touching me right there. A moan bubbles up and I swallow it back. I clench my thighs together.

"Look at her."

I shake my head.

"Do it." He lowers that deep voice of his to a hush and I shiver. I drop my gaze to where the cream drips down her inner thigh.

He snaps his fingers and I jerk my face toward him. "*Vieni qui.*" He crooks a finger.

A snarl ripples up my throat. How dare he order me around like I am some kind of dog...or a bitch...on leash? Gah!

"Now, Beauty." He lowers his voice to a hush and I shiver. Only when my feet hit the ground do I realize that I am walking toward him. What the hell—?! My body seem to have a mind of its own where this alphahole is concerned. It can't help but obey him when he commands. How dare he be able to wield so much power over me?

I pause in front of him and he smirks. *Jerk.* He dips a finger into the bowl of cream then holds the cream-coated finger out to me. "Open," he growls.

You've gotta be kidding me.

I purse my lips together and he arches an eyebrow.

"Open. Your. Mouth," he orders. "Do it, Beauty."

I part my lips and he slides his finger inside my mouth.

"Suck it off."

No.

"Now."

I curl my tongue around his finger and his breath catches. A hot feeling flares to life in my chest, at the backs of my eyes. He wants me to suck his fingers, huh? Fine. I'll do just as he says, obedient woman that I am. I open my mouth, lean forward and take in his other fingers. His chest heaves. I pull back until his fingertips are poised at the edge of my lips, then move in again. I close my mouth, swallowing his fingers.

His shoulders tense.

I curl my tongue around the underside of his fingers, licking it to the top as I pull out, only to lean forward again. I claim his fingers, let him finger fuck my mouth, my gaze never wavering from his. Wetness pools between my legs, my core clenches, and my toes curl. I wriggle my hips, needing something more to relieve the yawning emptiness between my thighs. I want more. I'm overcome by a yearning for the emptiness between my legs to be filled. By him. *No.* I pull away so fast that I stumble, the popping sound of his fingers leaving my mouth echoing around the room.

His eyebrows draw down, his jaw tics, and he opens his mouth, but I don't wait. No way, am I allowing him to seduce me with his voice, his words, that rich timber of his subvocals which curl around me, coax me, seduce me into doing as he wants.

I pull away, then run around the table.

"Stop."

I keep going.

"Don't leave this room."

Are you fucking kidding me? You think I'm going to stay here and watch as you…you…finger-fuck that woman? As he had just done to my mouth. And I had let him. I had encouraged it. Enjoyed it. My chest heaves and my breath comes in short pants. I twist the handle of the door.

"You are going to regret this."

I'll regret it more if I stay. No way, am I giving in to whatever twisted plan he's set in motion for me. I pull open the door and rush out. Down the corridor, to a large room, cross it, pass a large fireplace, a comfortable leather settee on the other side, to the massive double doors at the far end. I shove open the doors, race across the lawn.

Footsteps sound behind me and I increase my pace. I have to get away from him.

"Karma, don't go any further."

"Fuck you," I glance over my shoulder. He's a few feet behind me. His features are contorted, his gaze narrowed. He's racing toward me so fast he blurs.

He shoves out his hand, "Stop!"

"No way." I turn, spring forward through the undergrowth, and my feet touch air. I throw my hands out and scream.

14

Michael

She disappears over the edge and my heart slams against my rib cage.

I see sparks behind my eyes. No, this can't be happening. I propel my body through the undergrowth, thrust out my arm. My fingers graze her skin and I grab at her wrist. Hold.

She screams, and the sound is torn away by the wind.

"I've got you."

Her body dangles, sways. One of her pumps slips off her foot. She screams again, and the blood thuds at my temples, at my wrists. The weight of her body drags me forward. *No, no, no, I am not going to let her die. No way, am I ready to go over the edge either.* I dig the toes of my shoes into the ground, hook them around a protuberance and come to a halt. Stay there for a beat, another. Sweat streams down my forehead, down my nose. She glances up at me as the moisture trails down to splash onto her cheek.

She blinks, her green eyes dilated with terror, her pupils so large, I can see myself reflected in them.

"I am not letting you go.

"P...promise?" Her chin quivers and her teeth chatter.

"You bet, not until I have exacted my revenge for this stupid stunt."

Her gaze narrows and some of the color returns to her cheeks. There's my Beauty, my Huntress.

"It's your fault I landed here, in the first place."

"Oh?"

A gust of wind blows against us. Her body sways, I skid down further, and she yells, "Don't you fucking let go of me, you motherfucker!"

"Never thought I'd hear you say the words, baby girl."

"Fuck you."

"Time for that later." Pain shoots up my arm. It feels like it is being torn out of the socket. I grit my teeth so hard that pain shoots up my jaw. *Not letting her go. Not letting her go. No.* I shove my other arm out. "Take it."

"No."

"Not the time to act prissy."

"Not until you tell me what this is all about."

"Huh?" *The woman is one hair's breadth away from falling to her death, and here she is, arguing with me?* "The fuck you talking about?"

"You know." She swallows. "I want to know, why?"

"Why?"

"The real reason you saved my life."

"I'll do one better."

She frowns.

"I'll show you at dinner tomorrow."

Her mouth opens and closes. Her other shoe slides off. She whimpers. Color fades from her cheeks again.

"Work with me here, Beauty." I glare at her and she blinks. A tear drop makes it way down her cheek.

"Didn't think you'd be the kind to resort to tears."

"I'm not." She sets her jaw.

"Or that you wanted to die without living fully?"

"Is that what you are doing?" She scowls; her dark hair flows around her shoulders.

"I've only been half alive... Until I met you."

"What?" She blinks.

The fuck am I talking about? "Your arm, give me your arm first."

"Only if you promise to complete that statement."

"Now," I growl, and she winces.

"Do it." I infuse all of my dominance into that phrase. She holds up her other arm. *Thank fuck*. I grab her hand, slide forward a bit further. She screams.

"Trust me," I implore.

"I did and look where that got me."

I grit my teeth, lock my muscles and haul her up...an inch, another. The wind seems to pick up. She bites down on her lower lip.

"I am not letting you die that easily."

I pull her up another inch.

"I'm sure that's not out of any sense of compassion or a conscience. It's not like you have one anyway, right?"

"You done insulting me?" I blink away a drop of sweat.

"Just getting started."

"Good, so am I." My shoulder muscles knot and a burning sensation crawls up my forearms as I drag her up, until her arms are just over the ledge. "When I get you on firm ground—and believe me, I will—I am going to teach you a lesson—one you won't forget."

"You don't scare me."

"Good." I haul her body toward me. "Then you won't mind when I show you exactly what I have in mind for you." She huffs, digs her feet into the curve of the ledge and pushes herself up. I brace myself, bend my legs and pull her over the edge. She falls on her front next to me, her breathing loud. I sit up and haul her into my arms. "I am going to fucking kill you for what you did to me."

She trembles, her shoulders shake. "I... I thought... You said you wanted to save my life to teach me a lesson."

Her features crumple.

"No," I growl. "Not now."

A tear slides down her cheek and my heart stutters. Fuck this. Fuck her. Fuck everything that brought me to this exact moment, when I have my end in plain sight.

"Why do you have to be so fucking annoying?" I growl.

"Why do you have to be so—"

I lower my head, close my lips over hers. I thrust my tongue inside her mouth. A moan swells up from her and I swallow it. I suck from her, draw her breath, bite down on her lower lip, and she shudders. I tilt my head, haul her even closer, wrap my arms around her and yank her to me. Her entire body trembles. Her breasts are flattened against me, and her nipples harden. The blood rushes to my groin. I dig my fingers through her hair and tug her head back. Grip her chin, tilt it up and lower my lips to hers. She throws her arms around my neck and strains in my hold. Another hoarse whine bleeds from her and something inside of me shatters.

I tear my mouth from hers, chest heaving, blood buzzing, my nostrils filled with her scent. Her taste is heavy in my mouth, her melting core drawing me in. She raises her eyelids and those green eyes stare back at me, dilated...this time, with passion. She licks her lips, raises her chin.

"No." I unknot her hands from around me, stagger to my feet and pull her up with me. I head for the house, pulling her along, and her legs seem to give way from under her.

"For fuck's sake." I turn, swing her up in my arms.

"I can walk." Her voice is hoarse; her frame is too light. Anger boils up my spine. Why does she always have to complicate everything? Why is it that everywhere I turn, she is there, turning my world upside down? If she had gone over the ledge, if I had reached her one second later ... My arms tighten around her.

She winces, shoves at me, "You're hurting me."

"Good."

"Why are you upset?"

"I'm not."

"You could have fooled me." She purses her lips.

"You are too much trouble, you know that?" I growl.

She huffs, "Your mistake for having kidnapped me."

"You're right."

"I am?" She scowls up at me.

"Abso-fucking-lutely," I drawl, "I can't wait to get you back to your room so I can get on with the rest of my evening. Larissa is waiting for me."

15

Karma

"You ass, I almost died and now you shove your...your floozie in my face? You're a real piece of work, you know that?" I struggle in his arms and he tightens his grasp.

"Stay still," he orders, "or I might drop you."

Jerk! "Don't you dare," I shove at his shoulder, and my palm encounters the hard muscles of his body. Goosebumps rise on my skin. Shit, why does he draw such a primal response from me?

He continues walking and I glance up at the jut of his chin. For a second there, when he'd kissed me, I was sure I'd been wrong about him. That he isn't the kind of monster I'd thought him to be. He saved my life, didn't he? He'd come after me after that…that show that he'd put on for me. Why did he do that?

"Why wouldn't I?"

"You are scared about how I make you feel?"

His jaw tenses.

"You are worried that you are attracted to me?"

"You?" His lip curls. He stares straight ahead, lengthens his stride. "Is that what you think?"

"Why else would you have left behind that…that…?"

"Beautiful woman, who is actually the kind of female I go for. I promise you, girls with little to no experience are not my type."

"How do you know I have no experience?"

"Are you telling me that you have had experience?"

I tip up my chin, "Are you trying to ask me if I am a virgin?"

"Are you?" He lowers his chin.

I gape. "Seriously, like, is that even a thing anymore?"

He holds my gaze and the blood rushes to my cheeks.

"What?" I scowl. "Didn't think you were the kind to worship at the altar of the hymen."

His gaze intensifies.

"But then you are Mafia, so I guess you forget that the rest of the world has progressed enough to recognize that the hymen is a myth. Many girls aren't born with one, and most lose it thanks to exercise or when we use tampons."

He arches an eyebrow and I feel the blood rush to my face.

"What?" I snap. "Why are you looking at me like that?"

"Answer the question." He lowers his voice to a hush, "Are you, Karma?"

"Yes," I murmur, "I am Karma."

He scowls. "Are you a virgin, Karma?"

"None of your bloody business."

"It is, actually." His arms around me tighten and I gasp as he pulls me closer into his chest. The heat of him seems to increase in intensity. The planes of his chest seem to harden until they dig into the flesh of my arms.

"You're hurting me," I protest.

"Tell me." He growls, "Are you a virgin?"

"No," I snap, and his scowl deepens.

"Are you lying to me, because if you are..."

"No, I am not." I set my jaw. "Why would I lie to you about that anyway?"

"Good," he growls, "because I am tired of your impertinence."

"Impertinence?" I scowl. "I am simply trying to show you just how backward you are in your thinking."

"Take a good look around you. Where do you think you are?"

"Somewhere in Italy, with someone who kidnapped me and brought me here and is holding me captive and not even telling me what he wants from me."

He pauses so suddenly that the breath catches in my chest.

I sense his gaze on my face deepen and glance up, then wish I hadn't. Blue eyes, bottomless and cold. In their depths is something unfeeling, something inhumane, something that causes my muscles to stiffen, my pores to pop. The hair on the nape of my neck rises.

"Wh…what?" I clear my throat. "What is it?" I force out the words through a throat gone dry, "What do you want from me?"

"I told you," he drawls, "your father owed me, I took you in payment."

"And what are you going to do with me?"

His lips twist, and I flinch.

I tilt up my chin, keep my gaze trained on that cruel, beautiful, gorgeous face of my captor. "I mean, other than that…"

"Other than what?"

"Of course, you want that. It's why you brought me here."

"Want what?" His lips curl.

"You know," I scoff.

"No, I don't." He holds my gaze, "Why don't you tell me?"

"Sex," I snap, "you want sex with me."

"That's too easy."

"What do you mean?" I scowl. "Obviously, it's why you took me and brought me here and are now trying to impress me with your wealth, and power and control, and your stupid dominance—"

"You think I am dominant?"

"Unfortunately, while I wish I could say otherwise, I have to concede that much to you."

"At least, you are honest."

"At least, you are…" I search for a suitable adjective. "Not bad looking, for a kidnapper."

He blinks. "I wasn't aware that was a quality one needed to have to suit the role."

"It's important." I bob my head up and down, "Very important. I mean, if you were old and fat and had onion breath…" I shudder, "it would be so much more worse."

"You taking the piss, Drama?"

"It's Karma, you asshole."

"Maybe I'll call you Llama."

"Don't you fucking dare."

"Language…" he says in a mild tone.

"Oh, fuck off." I hunch my shoulders and turn my head away from him. Tears prick the backs of my eyes, and honestly, that's just stupid. Why do I care what he calls me? Hell, he can call me Destiny, for all I care. Not that it is insulting or anything. Actually, I'd take Destiny over Karma anyway, considering the number of times I've been teased for having been called that. It's a stupid name. Why did my mother have to call me by that name. Being a flower child is all well and good, but why couldn't she have called me by some other new age easily pronounceable name instead? And why did she have to die on us, anyway?

I had been a baby when she'd passed on. The only things I remember about her come from the photographs of her that we have. I don't remember anything about her in real life. If it hadn't been for my sister Summer, who became the de facto maternal figure in my life, well, I'd have never had any inkling of what it would be like to have a mother. Thanks to Summer, though, I've always felt loved. She's done a lot for me, my sister.

Surely, she'll be missing me. Despite the messages that this man says he's been sending her from my phone, surely, she'll know that something is wrong and she'll come in search of me? Surely.

I sniffle, and to my horror, a tear makes its way down my cheek. Shit, shit, shit. The last thing I want is to be seen as being weak by this man. I don't want him to see just how defeated I feel right now. That the true horror of my predicament is finally sinking in.

Shit. I have been kidnapped by this monster and he is not letting me leave. I can't even try to jump off a cliff without his somehow snatching me back from the jaws of whatever fate had in store for me. How the hell am I going to find a way out of here? Why the hell had he come after me in the first place?

"Why?" I demand, my voice hoarse. "Why the hell did you have to turn my bloody life upside down?"

"Why did you have to turn my life upside down?"

I blink.

"Wh...what?"

"You heard me." He lowers his face until his lips are right above mine. Until that hooked nose of his bumps mine, until those long thick eyelashes of his kiss mine. "It's you who's turned my plans upside down."

"I... I have?"

He nods, "I was supposed to kill you, not bring you here and spare your life and—"

"Wait, what?" My heart gallops so hard in my chest, I am sure it's going to break through my rib cage. "What do you mean kill me?"

His lips twist, "Off you, shoot you in the head, or did you forget that I did hold the gun to your forehead? If you've forgotten, I don't mind reminding you."

"No," I snap, "I remember."

"Good," he nods, "so you can understand how crazy it seems that I'm standing here, carrying you in my arms, and after saving you from throwing yourself down the side of the cliff into the sea—"

"My foot slipped," I snap. "I would never kill myself."

"Sure didn't seem like that to me."

"Believe me, I love my life. Or rather, I loved it before you came along."

"Did you?" He peers into my face.

"What's that supposed to mean?"

"You may have told yourself that you were happy, but the woman I saw that day on the hillside of the park was lonely and quoting Byron in the hopes of finding a reason to live."

I open my mouth to retort, but he tilts his head, "Am I wrong?"

I glance away.

"Thought not."

He straightens, then heads off, once more, in the direction of the house. He retraces my earlier steps, back across the lawn, through the front door, then up the stairs. He walks down the corridor, enters my room, and lays me down on my bed. I turn away from him, wrap my arms about my waist. The softness of the pillow under my cheek, that masculine scent of his that surrounds me, all of it confirms that I am safe. Safe.

A trembling grips me. Maybe it's the fact that I almost went over the side of the cliff. *OMG, OMG… I almost died. Gah.* My arms and legs feel too weak. A ball of emotion clogs my throat. What the hell? I had been fine this far, so why am I breaking down now? A tear slides down my cheek. *Stop that, you idiot. What's wrong with you? Why are you crying now?*

Say something. Protest again. Ask him to let you go. As if any of that is going to work. Face it, I am here as his captive and I'll stay here until he lets me go… Which is never. Unless he kills me... But he's never gonna release me and I am going to spend the rest of my life in this stupid room, on this stupid island, playing stupid word games with this over-the-top, mean, growly, grumpy, way-too-handsome, egoistical, controlling, arrogant tyrant.

Another tear slides down my cheek and I can't stop shaking. Gah.

The bed dips, and the next second, the heat of his body sears my back.

16

Michael

"What are you doing?" Her voice is shrill. "Why did you get into bed with me?"

Good question. Something I am asking myself, since I'd sworn I wouldn't bed her until we are married. Not something I am going to let her know. Especially since I haven't told her what my plans are for her yet, either. Why am I so hesitant? Since when have I needed a woman, or anyone else for that matter, to be willing before deciding to go through with a plan. Nothing stops me from marrying her without her consent. Hell, nothing stops me from sleeping with her without her consent, either. And ultimately, I am going to marry her, whether she agrees to it or not. So why does it feel so important that she submit to her fate willingly?

Why do I want her to want me? Want her to *want* to marry me? Why do I need her to feel something more than the resentment she so clearly bears for me? Why do I crave her...devotion?

Her body in submission to me, her will in subjugation to mine, her heart in my grasp, her attention on me, her arms and her legs tied back as she spreads herself open to my ministrations; with her pussy in readiness and wet for my penetration, as she gives herself over to me. Willingly, over and over again. As she allows me to fulfill every depraved, filthy craving that has painted my mind from the moment that I first laid eyes on her.

Fuck. The blood drains to my cock. My pants suddenly feel too tight.

I stay there, with the length of my front plastered to the soft curvaceousness that is her body.

Gradually, her trembling stops, and her muscles tense as she grows aware of me. I know the exact moment she feels the arousal that tents my crotch, for she stiffens.

Every part of her goes rigid, her curves tightened in attention. Every single pore in her body seems to be tuned into me, and for a moment, I enjoy that. The fact that she is so tuned into my presence. That she's so hyper-aware of everything, anything that I am going to say and do next.

I close my eyes, draw in a breath, and the lush moonflowers fragrance of her skin reaches me… Laced with that unmistakable, sugary-sweet scent of her arousal. My cock throbs and my groin hardens further. Hell, if I stay here a second more, I am going to turn her on her back, cover her with my weight, hold her down, and close my mouth over hers, Right before I slide down to rest my head on her creamy thigh as I take my time familiarizing myself with that succulent flesh between her legs.

She gulps, the sound heavy in the space. I should move. I should simply get out of here. I should return to Larissa. Better still, I should leave Beauty be as I attend to the rest of my business for the day: the war with the Russian Bratva that is heating up again, the rivalry with the Kane Company that's proving to be a pain in the ass; the upcoming talks with the Five Families and the Don that could, likely, mark the turning point in my career and everything that I've worked for to-date; my errant stepbrother, Seb, whose loyalties I need to test… Hell, the many things that I need to address as the Capo… All of which are crucially important to ensure that things stay on plan. None of which seems as vital as the woman lying in front of me.

I draw a finger down the shape of her hip and she shivers.

I reach the edge of the skirt of her dress, slip a finger under it, and she chafes her thighs together. The scent of her arousal deepens and my mouth goes dry. Jesus. How could she smell so luscious, so juicy, so ready for the picking, like the flesh between her legs needs me, wants me, yearns for me to do whatever I want with her.

"M... Michael." Her voice trembles, "Michael... I have something to tell you?"

"What?"

"I am dirty."

"Excuse me?" I blink, pause in the action of slipping another finger under her skirt, "What do you mean?"

"My clothes, I mean," she murmurs, "they are filthy from that headlong dive I took off the side of the cliff."

"So?"

"So I am making the bedclothes dirty," she explains.

"I'll have it cleaned up."

"Uh, I need to get out of these clothes. They are uncomfortable, and itchy and—"

"Fine." Once she sets her mind on something, nothing can stop her, can it? I roll off the bed, then bend and scoop her up in my arms.

"What are you doing?" She huffs.

"What does it look like?"

"Why do you have to answer every question with a question?"

"Why do you have to ask so many questions?" I sneer.

"What kind of an answer is that?"

"Exactly."

"You're impossible," she cries. If she'd been standing, bet she'd have stamped her little foot.

"You're too easy to tease."

"Were you teasing me?" She snarls.

So cute.

"Not really." A chuckle rolls up my throat and I swallow it down. Bet if I showed her just how amused I am right now, she wouldn't be very happy about it. For that matter, nothing I've done so far has made her happy. Not that I have tried to make her happy or shit like that. Hell, she is my captive, not my guest. Not that I have had any guests here on this island. I haven't had anyone else over, period, except for my close family.

She is the first—other than my very close circle of confidants, who I can count on my fingers—who I've allowed such close access. I pause half way to the bathroom. What does that mean? Do I trust her enough to allow her such proximity to me so quickly? For that matter, from the moment I first saw her, I haven't allowed her too far from me. It's why I'd brought her to this island. So I could observe her without any distractions. What the hell is wrong with me? Why am I acting like a man possessed? Why do I feel so out of sorts? Probably because I haven't fucked her yet...

Okay, assuming that explains the shortness in my breath, the tenseness of my shoulders, the knot that seems to have lodged itself permanently at the base of my spine—let's say that's why I feel so goddamn on edge... It still doesn't explain why I am standing here in the middle of her room, with her in my arms, about to run a bath for her.

"Michael?"

Since when did I get so solicitous? Since when did I...put another's needs before my own? Since when did I...want to fight the world and anyone who'd dare stand between us? Since when did I want to pluck the stars from the skies and lay them at her feet? *Che cazzo,* I am turning into a complete cliché, if there ever was one.

"Michael!"

I draw in a sharp breath.

"Hey, Michael!" She punches my shoulder and I glance down at her upturned face.

What the hell is she doing to me? Since she came into my life, everything really has been turned upside down. It's time to get things back on track. To show her who is the fucking boss here. Which is me, by the way. Not the curvy, tiny sprite who scowls up at me as if everything that had happened today was my fault. Which it was... but that's beside the point.

I will not feel sorry for taunting her with what I'd done to the other woman. I will not feel guilty about the fact that I pushed her to the end of her tether, so she ran out and almost fell over the side of the cliff. If I had lost her... If anything had happened to her—

"Michael, hey, what's wrong?"

"Why the fuck should anything be wrong?"

"You're trembling."

"I am not," I say through gritted teeth.

"Yes, you are."

"No, I am not," I growl, "and you'd best shut the fuck up before I do something that both of us will regret later."

"Oh, you'll do something, will you?" She sets her jaw. "Of all the moronic, bloody, asinine things to say," she snarls and I snap my teeth.

"Enough!"

She stiffens. "Stop talking to me like I am some stupid, brainless twit who you can yank around with a lasso around my neck."

"Then stop acting like one," I retort. "Though, come to think of it," I eye her slender throat, "a collar around your neck may not be a bad idea, actually."

She pales, "Stop trying to frighten me."

"Am I succeeding?"

"No." She blinks rapidly.

"Liar."

"Asshole."

"Alphahole to you, doll." I smirk.

She gapes at me. "You have such a big ego, you know that?"

"Not the only thing that's big, by the way." I head toward the bathroom door as she opens and shuts her mouth.

"Honestly, that was cringeworthy," she complains.

"You disagree?"

"I have no opinion on it, either way."

"Lying again, Beauty?" I lower her to the counter near the sink, then point a finger at her, "Stay." I growl, and she rolls her eyes.

"Like, where would I go? I am on a stupid island, you dummy."

"At least, learn to insult effectively."

"Just callin' it as I see it, buster."

I arch an eyebrow, "If you are going to curse, do so in Italian."

"You offering to teach me?" She tilts her head at me.

I fold my arms across my chest, look her up and down, "You sure you want to learn?"

"I asked, didn't I?"

"Remember, once you start down this path, there's no going back."

"From what?"

"Wanting to not just curse, but taste, bite into, suck on, lick up…" I lean in closer to her, "chew on, slurp, kiss, rub," I bend my knees, peer into her eyes, "fondle, squeeze, pet, fuck—"

"Stop." She slaps her palm over my mouth, "Please, stop."

I allow my lips to curve up, "Scared, Beauty?"

"Never."

"Let's put that to the test, shall we?"

17

Karma

"What...what's that supposed to mean?" My voice quivers. Hell, I hate that. I so don't want to appear weak in front of this man. I bite down on my lower lip and his gaze drops there.

"Scared, Beauty?"

"Of course, not."

"You should be." He bends his elbow behind his back, and when he straightens his arm the light catches a flash of silver in his hand. "Wh...what's that?"

He swoops out his arm and the front of my dress loosens. I glance down to find he's cut through the straps holding up the dress. "What did you do?"

"What does it look like?"

"Do you have to answer every question with a question?"

He arches an eyebrow, then swoops out his hand again. His movements are so fast, they seem like a blur. I blink. He retreats, then surveys his handiwork. I glance down as the dress falls apart.

Oh. He cut enough slashes in the front of the dress for it to literally deflate in on itself. Whoa. I glance up at his face, "Was that supposed to impress?" I murmur, "I mean, all you had to do was ask me to get undressed—"

"What's the fun in that, hmm?"

He hooks his left forefinger in the neckline of my dress and tugs. With a whisper, the entire front of the dress separates. He throws it aside, as the back of the dress falls away, leaving me clad in my bra and panties. I raise my hands to cover myself, then stop. Damn it, I am not going to act like a shrinking violet. I have seen worse. I survived the foster care system, I survived dropping out of Goldsmiths and forging my own creative path. And look where that got me? Sitting in my underwear on the counter of the bathroom of a Mafia Capo in Sicily. Jeez, at least my life is not boring, I have to admit.

I place my arms in my lap, stare up at me, "What now?"

His lips curl. He reaches out, slides the flat edge of his knife under the strap of my bra, tugs. The thin material snaps. He does the same on the other side, then slides the tip of the blade under the strap between my breasts. He twists the blade and the tense material snaps. My bra falls away and cool air assails my heated flesh. My nipples instantly harden and my breasts swell. He doesn't look down at my chest; neither do I.

His gaze intensifies; the darkness in those blue eyes swirls, coils in on itself. He seems both relaxed and on edge. Bored and turned on. Intensely focused, as always, and yet also, strangely, disconnected from everything. This mass of contradictions about him is what attracts me and challenges me and makes me want to do everything possible to get a rise out of him; get under his skin, break his control, watch him as he finally shattered. Or maybe that would be me. What will he do when he finally gives into those emotions that writhe and twist under his skin? Will he hurt me? And why does that thought not scare me?

"That all you got?" I allow my lips to curl. "The big, bad, alphahole Capo who loves to keep his men in check... That all you going to do to me?"

"You don't have any sense of self-preservation, do you?"

I shake my head.

"That makes two of us."

He steps back from the edge of the sink. "On your feet."

I frown and he arches an eyebrow. "Do it," he growls, "now."

I slide down so my feet touch the floor, and my dress and the remnants of my bra fall away. I tip up my chin, hold his gaze. He reaches down, his arm moves, and I don't need to look down to know that he's cut through the straps holding up my panties. The fabric falls away, exposing my pussy to the air. I hold my elbows at my sides, not daring to glance down at myself.

He glances down at my core and his breathing grows ragged. "You shaved."

"Like I had a choice?" I scoff.

"You didn't," he agrees. "Part your legs for me, *Belleza*."

"And if I say no?"

"I'll do it for you." His grin widens, "And trust me, I'll enjoy it, too."

"Bastard." I slide my feet apart, and he thrusts his massive thigh between them, forcing my legs further apart.

The thick muscles feel like a column of iron against my most tender place. My core clenches and my lower belly ties itself in knots. I lock my thighs around the muscle, press my core into the rigid pillar.

His breath catches and his dark pupils seem to grow even blacker. One side of his lips twists, as he raises his knife and places the flat edge against my cheek.

I freeze, watch as he slides the blade under a lock of hair. He flicks his wrist and the strand slices clean through before it drifts to the floor. Heat flushes my skin; my core clenches. My nipples grow impossibly hard, and damn it, I can't understand this crazy response to his screwed-up gesture. I mean, I've always known my tastes are a bit out there. They would have to be to mesh with the goth side of me, the one that is attracted to everything dark and beautiful. Like him.

He flattens the blade against the side of my face, draws it down without breaking skin, down my neck, down to the valley between my breasts.

My nipples continue to tighten, until they are painful points. My breasts seem to swell. Moisture gathers between my legs, and his nostrils flare.

"That turns you on, hmm?"

"Of course, not." My voice cracks and his grin widens.

“If I were to check between your legs, would I find you wet, Beauty?

Yes. Yes. "No." I shake my head.

"You know what?" he says in a conversational tone. "I am tired of you lying to me, sweetheart."

He retracts his hand, flips his knife so he’s holding it with the handle face up, the blade pinched between his fingers. He pulls back his thigh, only to replace it with the handle of the blade.

"Wh…what are you doing?" I squeak.

"What do you think?" He nudges the handle of the blade against my entrance and goosebumps pop on my skin.

"Michael," I whisper, "don’t."

"Tell me you don’t want this, Beauty. Tell me that depraved part of you inside that I’ve sensed does not want to know how it feels to ride a knife handle."

No. No. I nod and his entire body tenses. His jaw tightens, his chest planes seem to harden, and his shoulders seem to grow wider, filling my line of sight.

Heat flushes my skin and my toes curl. I curve my fingers into fists at my sides, hold his gaze as he fits the handle of the knife into my melting slit. He thrusts up and into me and I gasp. My heart begins to race and my pulse pounds at my temples. Why is this very obscene, very kinky action of his such a turn on? It shouldn’t be. I should be repulsed. I should be crying out, asking him to stop. Telling him he can’t insert a weapon into the most delicate part of me. I open my mouth, but the words don’t come out. Instead, I part my legs wider, bend my knees, and push down on the handle. Too much, too thick. My lips part, a groan trembles from my mouth, and I wheeze.

His gaze intensifies and the skin around eyes tightens. "Fuck." He groans, "F-u-ck, Beauty. "

He winds his fingers around the nape of my neck, brings me close enough for my breasts to press into the fabric of his shirt. He urges me to tip my chin up, as he glares into my eyes. His pupils are dilated, the black filling his iris until only a dark blue circle remains around the circumference. A lock of his dark hair falls over his forehead. A strand of grass clings to the thick strands, reminding me of the fall I had taken so very recently. He looks like someone on the verge of coming undone, and somehow, the thought fills me with a gnawing need. The emptiness swells in my belly, crawls up my spine, and I raise my palm, press it into his cheek.

"Michael," I whisper, "fuck me with your knife handle."

Embers spark in his eyes. He bares his teeth, grips the back of my neck even harder, then he pulls the knife handle out, only to slide it back inside. A groan spills from my lips. He dips his head, places his mouth so close to mine, his nose bumps mine, his eyelashes brush mine.

Jesus… This… When he does this. When he watches me with so much intensity that it feels like he's crawling his way inside me, when he peers into my eyes as if he's searching for my hidden depths, as if he means to solve me, decimate me, rip me apart and put me back together in a fashion that makes so much more sense to him, to me.

He pulls out the knife, then slides it up inside me again, deeper, deeper, and my thighs tremble. My breasts swell further. My knees seem to almost give way and I grip his biceps, feeling the rock-hard muscle push back, unyielding to my touch. And it's so damn erotic. The heat of his body around me, the toughness of his body under my palms, the hard length that he's inserted up between my legs—that somehow symbolizes exactly how screwed up this…whatever connection is there between us, is.

He continues to fuck me with the knife handle, and heat crawls up my spine. Sweat breaks out on my forehead, dampens my palms at the point of contact of where I am still holding onto his shirt sleeve covered biceps.

He glances down his nose at my mouth as he weaves the knife

handle in and out of me, in and out. The trembling begins at my toes, sweeps up my thighs, coils in my belly. "Oh," I gasp, "oh, my god."

My eyelids flutter as I tense, my muscles lock in preparation as I hurl faster, closer, to that edge.

"Michael," I gasp, "please...."

"Eyes on me," he snaps and I crack open my eyelids to stare into that blackness that swirls in his eyes. The blue, like chipped ice around the edges, promises me that, even if I manage to conquer his blackness, I'll slip and fall through the icy surface, to an uncertain end, from which I won't return without being changed.

"What are you doing to me?" I whisper as his lips twist.

He pulls out the knife, slides it up and into me one last time, hitting a spot deep inside that I didn't know existed. A moan bleeds from my lips, and he bares his teeth, "Come for me, Beauty. Come all over my knife."

18

Michael

She snaps her head back, her spine curves, her lips part and she shatters. The orgasm sweeps up her body and she tenses, stretches, green eyes a tormented, coiling mass of storm clouds that boil over as she screams. I fit my mouth over hers, absorb the sound as she slumps into me. I pull out the knife, place it on the counter behind her, then tear my mouth from hers and slide to my knees. I lick my tongue up the moisture dripping down her inner thigh, to her damp pussy. I tug on her clit ring and she groans. I slurp at her cunt and she shudders.

"Michael," she chants, "Michael. Michael."

"Mika," I growl against her sweet, scented pussy, "call me Mika."

"Oh, Mika." She grips my hair as I ease my tongue inside her channel. "Mic-ah!" She gasps, tugs on my hair. My scalp tightens and my shoulders go rock hard. I grip the backs of her thighs, yank her closer as I proceed to fuck her with my tongue. In-out-in. I squeeze her asscheeks, position her hips just right as I proceed to eat her out.

"Jesus," she whines, "please, Mika, please—"

I pull my tongue out of her, only to close my mouth around her cunt.

She groans, pushes her hips forward, chasing the release that only I can give her.

"Oh, my god. Oh, my god," she warbles.

I can't stop the rumble that rolls up my chest, as I glance up at her to find her breasts jutting out, nipples pebbled, head flung back and her dark hair flowing down the curve of her back. A goddess, a huntress, a Beauty about to come apart on the tongue of this Beast, the one who is going to show her why she shouldn't trust anyone so easily with her pleasure. I slide my finger in between her buttcheeks, down to her backhole. She tenses, a ripple shudders up her spine. She parts her legs further, allowing me to slide a finger inside her backchannel, as I continue to fuck her with my tongue, in and out, in and out of her.

Her entire body, seems to vibrate with tension as she grabs handfuls of my hair, and presses herself closer to where my I am eating her out. Her back bends, her breasts jiggle as she pants and gasps and throws her head back, and that's when I pull back. I release her, rise to my feet, grab my knife by the blade and freeze. "What the fuck?"

She cracks open her eyelids and blinks, "Wh…what's wrong?"

I stare at the blood that stains the handle of the knife, then glance up at her.

"So, you're not a virgin, huh?"

She lowers her gaze to the knife handle and color leaches from her cheek, "Guess I am not now."

"What the hell, Karma?" I growl, "Why the hell did you lie to me?"

"How did I know that you'd put it to the test so quickly?"

Shit, shit, shit. I squeeze my fingers around the blade and pain slides up my arm. The knife cuts through my fingers; blood drips down my fingers and drips to the floor.

"You…you're bleeding," she whispers.

"Look at me, Karma."

She glances away, shakes her head.

"I swear, look at me or— "

"Or what? You'll make me? Is that it?" She firms her lips. "Look, being a virgin is hardly the kind of thing you want to confess to, okay."

"So you lied to me?"

"I am nineteen and never been with a man." She squares her shoulders. "How the hell do you think that makes me feel?"

"I'll tell you how that makes me feel." I bend my knees, peer into her face, "It makes me want to make sure no one else touches you but me. It makes me want to hide you away and protect you and take care of you and ensure that your innocence belongs to me. It makes me want to— "

"What, marry me?" she says lightly and I stiffen.

She searches my features and the color leaves her face, "Oh, my god! You really think because you took my virginity you should marry me?"

"Yes."

She blinks and her jaw drops. "What the fuck?"

"Language." I scowl, and she merely stares back at me.

"You're kidding, right?"

I straighten and she shakes her head. "You *are* kidding." She laughs uncertainly. "You really have a rotten sense of humor."

"I am not laughing."

She presses her lower lip between her teeth and my dick twitches. She folds her arms about her waist, calling attention to her beautiful tits, the hourglass figure that has her tiny waist, flaring out to meet those fleshy hips, sleek thighs, down to those upturned ankles that beg me to fall at her feet and worship at those gorgeous toes.

Oddio! I really have it bad, if all I can think of is sucking on her toes, before moving my way up her body, pausing only to take a bite of that scrumptious pussy, before I fasten my mouth on those luscious nipples and suck and lap and slurp on them until they are full and heavy and trembling in my grasp.

"I... I don't understand." She murmurs, "Are you serious?"

"Have I ever been anything else but?"

She looks at me, then glances away. "What do you want?"

"I told you already, sweetheart. You are going to marry me."

"And if I refuse?"

I tilt my head.

She opens and shuts her mouth, "Look, you don't have to do that. I mean, virginity is overrated anyway and— "

"Shut up." I bring the handle of the knife to my mouth, and without taking my eyes off of her, I lick the blood—her blood—off the grip."

She draws in a breath, her gaze widens, and her pupils dilate. "Wh...what are you doing?"

"What do you think?" I step back, pass the knife to my other hand, then wipe the blood from the blade—my blood this time—on the sleeve of my shirt. More blood drips from my fingertips from where I'd wrapped it around the blade earlier.

She makes a sound of distress, turns, grabs a towel and reaches for my injured hand. She wraps the towel around it, folds my fingers over it. "There, that should help," she murmurs.

"Why did you lie to me?" I glance down at her bent head, "I would have been gentle with you your first time."

"Maybe I didn't want you to be?" She peers up at me from under her eyelids, and her green eyes are filled with uncertainty, "Look, I couldn't bring myself to confess that, okay? It just felt like I would be handing you an advantage of some kind..." She raises a shoulder.

"So instead, you let me fuck you with a knife handle."

"Kinky, huh?" Her lips twist. "Not that I didn't enjoy it."

That's what I am afraid of. My tastes are far gone enough, and the longer I stay with her, the more I am going to reveal just how depraved I am when it comes to taking my pleasure.

I hadn't intended for things to get this out of hand with her... But something about this woman makes me want to drop all the veneer of civility and bare the animal I am inside to her. I want to scare her, shock her… Fuck the hell out of her. I want to take her pussy and imprint myself inside of her, so she'll never forget what it is to belong to me.

It's precisely why I am going to keep my distance from her. I'll marry her, I'll use her to get to the Seven, and then I'll set her free. Until then, I am going to restrict my interactions with her to the bare minimum. It's the only way I am going to survive this unscathed.

I pivot, head for the door and she calls out, "Wait, Michael."

I pause.

"What you said about marrying me… You… You really mean that?"

I nod.

"You don't have to do it, you know. I mean, just because there is something between us..."

I turn, glare at her over my shoulder, "So you admit, there is something between us?"

"I admit no such thing."

"You just said so."

"I meant…" She draws in a breath, "Okay, yes, so there's some kind of weird chemistry between us. Doesn't mean we have to get married." Her lips draw up in a parody of a smile. She's smart, this woman, and quick-witted and able to think on her feet. Exactly the kind of woman I have been searching for. The kind I want by my side…

Wait, what? I don't need anyone else. I have myself and my siblings. They are all I need to consolidate my position.

Oh, well, I do need her…but only as a means of getting to the Seven. That, and the fact that her father did promise her to me. It would be crazy to not use that to my benefit. So, I will… And then I'll release her.

"Your father promised you to me in return for his life. I am just making sure you honor the debt. Also" I look her up and down, "I took your virginity."

"Oh, please, let's get past that, okay?" She takes a step forward, "And my father may have pledged me to you, but we don't have to fulfill it."

"No?"

She nods, "You and I both know you could do much better than me."

"Is that right?"

"Yes." She folds her arms around her waist. "Don't you want to marry a nice, shy, demure bride who'll do as you tell her to?"

No.

No.

"Yes." I jerk my chin.

"You do?"

"It's how you are going to be by the time I marry you."

"Oh, pfft." She waves her hand in the air, "Have you met me? I am wild, evil-tempered, I swear like a trooper—"

Everything I find fascinating about you.

"I'll never stop standing up to you."

Something I look forward to.

"You'll never be able to tame me."

My cock instantly lengthens. "Is that a challenge?"

"What?" She frowns, "Of course, not. I am merely pointing out why I am so wrong for you."

And yet, why do you feel so right?

"Nice try," I allow my lips to curl, "but it's not working."

"No?"

I shake my head. "Your father gave his word. Now you are going to keep it."

"And if I refuse?"

His grin widens. "I look forward to changing your mind."

19

Karma

Shit, shit, shit. This is not how it's supposed to be. I guess I was holding out some hope that he would let me go eventually. Then, I had made that stupid suggestion, as a joke, and he was supposed to laugh it off, or merely ignore it. Instead, he'd informed me that's his plan. Bloody hell, that's the last thing I want. What sane person would want to marry the person who kidnapped her?

He'd told me my father owed him. And I'd thought…that he'd hold me captive, probably threaten me, maybe contact Summer for some kind of ransom… And, to be honest, there has been a part of me afraid to admit my ultimate fear—that he plans to kill me. Although, he could have done that a long time ago, so maybe not...

Okay, the simmering chemistry between us could have something to do with it. It is hard to ignore. And I'd even thought, perhaps, at some point, I'd give in to that temptation… But marriage? What the hell? Why would my jerk of a father promise me to someone in the

Mafia without telling me? And why did he wait until now to find me?

Shit. I pace the length of my room, back-forth-back.

After Michael had left yesterday, I'd showered, then emerged to find Cassandra waiting for me. She'd changed the bed clothes and had a first aid kit with her. She'd treated the few scratches I'd gotten from my accident, and helped me dress for bed.

Frankly, I had been so affected by what had happened after my fall that that I had all but forgotten about that incident, let alone checked for any scrapes or bumps. It's a miracle I escaped without any serious injury. In fact, it's nothing but a freakin' marvel that he'd managed to get to me in time and haul me back.

As long as he is near me, it seems I'll always be safe. Shit, why am I thinking that way? I wrap my arms about myself. Maybe it has to do with the way he'd held me close and carried me back and gotten into bed with me… I could have sworn he'd felt... Something? Remorse at having pushed me that far? Relief that I was safe? Or maybe it's my imagination playing tricks on me.

One thing is for sure, though. I am *not* going to marry him. Nope, nah, no way.

I have to think of a way out. I walk to the window once more, survey the steep drop to the sea below. The dress I'd pulled out of the closet billows around my knees. This is another creation that fits me, and the quality of the material is soft and, clearly, expensive. Only, it's a pale pink. So not my color.

I curl my fingers around the window sill. How the hell am I going to get away from him? He is never going to let me go. No way, can I break out of this stupid building, and even if I could, we are on an island. I need to find a way to get to the mainland. Need to get to a place with a phone, or with other people, normal people. Surely, someone could help me then. They'd see that I was being held against my will and would be able to get a message to my sister or to the cops or something?

Surely, there has to be a way out of being married to this…this… alphahole.. This…man who is gorgeous and hot as hell, and dominant, and such a fucking commanding presence that simply being near him makes my pussy clench on itself, makes me as horny as hell, makes my panties so wet, my core so empty, that I'll do anything for any part of him inside of me... Even his knife handle... Hell.

What the hell is wrong with me? Not that I am not aware of kinks and knife play, but really, I never thought I'd be into it. But then, I never thought I'd be so drawn to a man who is so completely wrong. Wrong side of the law, wrong attitude, wrong mindset, wrong fucking idea on what it means to be attracted to a woman. I mean, you do not first take your knife and use it to fuck her, just because you feel a connection to her.

Or maybe that's it. Maybe he doesn't feel anything, he just sees me as a possession—something he can own and possess and shag when the need overtakes him. But seriously, why would he do that? Use his knife like that? Not that it hadn't been hot as hell, not that I hadn't come all over his knife handle, and gah! What does it say about me, that I had found it such a turn on? Clearly, that darkness inside of me is more pervasive than I'd realized.

That's the only reason I am so freakin' attracted to the man who resembles the Lord of Darkness himself. And that voice of his? OMG, whatever happened to him must have been really painful, considering the scars on his throat, but hell, if it hadn't given him that hoarse burr that completely kills me every time he speaks.

I am screwed... I am way too attracted to him to marry him. Any more time spent in proximity to him is going to completely do my head in. As it is, when I close my eyes, I hear him, sense his touch on my skin, scent his dark, edgy, masculine scent, feel how it had been when he'd fucked me with his knife... My core clenches, my pussy flutters, and moisture laces my center. I am in so much trouble. I simply have to find a way to beat him at his own game.

But how?

I can't defy him... I can't obey him... But maybe I can pretend? I can find a way to win a modicum of his trust... Just until I find a way off of this island, at least.

The door opens and I turn to find Cassandra waiting for me.

"The Capo is waiting to have breakfast with you."

She beckons to me and I follow her down the stairs. She walks past the dining room where I had my last meal, past the door leading to the study, and past the main living room, to a small alcove that looks out onto the lawns, and beyond that, the sea. The small table is set for two and Michael is seated in a chair, reading something on his phone. He's, once again, dressed in a black suit, with a black tie. Does the man not have anything else in his wardrobe? He glances up and spots me, rising to his feet. He nods at Cassandra, who pauses, then comes around and pulls up a chair for me. I sit down and he eases the chair in, before going around to take his seat again.

He takes in my features, "How are you feeling?"

"Fine." I place my hands in my lap, "I am good."

"No lasting impact from the fall?"

"Told you, it was an accident," I murmur, "and you got to me in time…so…." I shuffle my feet, glance up at him to find him perusing my features.

A blush steals up my cheeks, "What?" I mutter, "You're beginning to creep me out with the way you're looking at me."

"And what about the other thing?" He seems to hesitate, and I stare. First, he actually seemed regretful yesterday that he'd fucked me with the knife handle. And this morning? He's being exceedingly polite and coming across as unsure? Wow.

"Karma?" he urges me. "You sure you're okay?"

"If you mean are there any aftereffects of being fucked by the blunt end of a knife handle, then no." I tip up my chin, "I am fine." My pussy clenches. *Except for that.* My stupid cunt wants more, and ideally, it would rather he replace the knife with the bigger blade… the one that he wields between his legs, I mean. Argh, I didn't just think that. My cheeks heat, and he arches an eyebrow. He stares into my face a while longer, then nods.

Just then, Cassandra arrives, this time with our breakfast. She places a large cup with what seems like a crunchy, frozen slushy in front of each of us. There is also a bowl of what looks like croissants between us, along with fresh fruit, muesli and a massive plate of fresh pastries. She places a small bowl of fresh-cut fruit before me, then adds the tiniest cups of espresso next to each of us. She leaves and I glance down at the frozen slushy in front of me.

"What's this?"

"A granita," he replies as he breaks off a piece of the croissant, dips it in the dark brown slushy, then brings it up to his mouth and closes his lips around it.

I can't stop myself from flicking my tongue as I watch him crunch down on the ice, swallow, then reach for another piece of croissant.

He glances up and I flush, look away, then back to his mouth. Watch as he repeats the action, making a slight humming sound. My clit instantly throbs. Shit. How would it be to feel those vibrations against the most sensitive part of me? Why is it that everything he does seems to have a one-way connection to my pussy?

He looks up at me, then at my plate. "Eat," he gestures.

"Can you pass me a croissant," I murmur.

"It's a brioche," he corrects me.

"Oh," I frown, "it looks like a croissant."

"It's similar, but different. This," he offers me the plate of brioches and I take one, "is a soft sweet bread made using Marsala wine and honey. It's uniquely Sicilian."

I break off a piece of the brioche, dip it in the slushy, then pop the entire thing into my mouth. The complementary flavors of coffee and chocolate burst on my tongue. I chew, crunch down on a few pieces of ice and swallow. "Wow," I breathe, then lick my lips, "what was that?"

He doesn't take his gaze off of my mouth. "That was a traditional Sicilian breakfast," he murmurs.

"I get that." I scowl, "But what did you say the slushy thingy is called?"

"A granita." He raises those deep blue eyes to mine, "The Arabs brought it with them. They called it *Sarbut*, the Brits call it *Sherbet*.... The Arabs left Sicily, but their influence in food and in architecture stayed on."

"It's yummy." The heat of his gaze sinks into my blood. The tension between us ratchets up. My heart begins to beat hard in my chest. I swallow, reach for a piece of fruit and pop it in my mouth. The juicy sweet flavors burst in my mouth. "This orange is delicious."

I pop another slice into my mouth, then jerk my chin in the direction of the fruit, "You're not having any of it?"

He chuckles, "I hope not, considering I am allergic to them."

I blink. "You're allergic to oranges?"

He tilts his head. "Surprised?"

"You mean the big, bad alphahole actually has a weakness?" I lower my chin, "Yeah, I am surprised."

"I am human, Beauty." He smirks, "Though you can be forgiven for thinking otherwise."

"Ha, ha." I laugh without humor, then reach for my espresso. "You really have a big opinion about yourself, don't you?"

"Nothing that's not warranted." His grin widens, "Eat up, Beauty, we have a packed day."

20

Karma

The packed day, as it turned out to be, was Michael taking me shopping in Palermo. We'd taken a motorboat across to the big island which Michael had piloted, then he had guided me to a gleaming red Maserati that had been parked not far from the pier. He'd told me to snap on my seatbelt before roaring out. A half hour later, we'd walked into this gorgeous boutique… Which had been closed off for the pleasure of the Capo, as the woman who ran the place had informed us.

She'd taken me inside, to a large changing room, complete with a sprawling couch, a large mirror that took up one wall, and next to it, a changing cubicle, where I now stand. I run my fingers down the pale green dress that dips modestly in the front, plunges at the back, and flows in an 'A' line to just below my knees. It's all right, I guess. The cut is awesome, the fabric is beautiful, but the color is all wrong. I blow out a breath.

How weird that he'd offered to take me shopping anyway, and

after I'd been so grumpy about the earlier pink dress I'd had to wear. There hadn't been many options in terms of color in the closet. It was either the cream-colored dress…or the beige skirt with the matching top, or the pink pant-suit—no seriously, it was a pink pantsuit—more suited to my sister Summer's tastes, really. I hunch my shoulders.

How is Summer, anyway? Is she enjoying her married life with her new husband? Has she missed me yet? Even if she does, I have no way of knowing, considering Alphahole had commandeered my phone. Most likely, he is putting up a good front with her, probably answering her text messages with enough alacrity that she doesn't suspect a thing.

Anyway, why would she miss me? I have always been the annoying, younger sibling who was critical of her innocent, trusting ways. She's older than me, but I've often felt more worldly-wise than her, more cynical… In many ways, I am darker than her. My tastes have always run to the extremes, while Summer is all pink roses and glittery unicorns and shit. I bow my head. A hot sensation stabs at my chest.

Shit, now I am feeling sorry for myself. I mean, things aren't that bad. I am standing here, trying on a dress that costs… I search for a price tag and realize there isn't one on the dress. Hmm, so it's that kind of a place. Not that I blame them. The dresses are exquisite and I am the first to not begrudge an artiste the value of their creations… It's just, this really is not my style. I take in the shimmering, silvery green of the dress. Guess the color's not too bad. I blow out a breath, then turn, just as Michael steps through the door that separates the changing cubicle from the rest of the room.

"What are you doing here?" I frown.

He drags his gaze down my face, my chest, the skirt of the dress, to my feet, still clad in the pink ballet flats—ugh!— that I had found in the closet at my room—I mean, the room at the place where he's holding me captive.

He raises his gaze to my face and those deep blue eyes gleam. "I came to check if you were okay."

"You mean, you came to check that your little captive hadn't escaped?"

"You couldn't escape me, even if you tried."

"Is that a challenge?" I set my jaw. "I could leave anytime I want."

He laughs, "The lies we tell ourselves."

"Better small lies than big ones."

The smile drops from his face. "I told you I am sorry for what I did yesterday."

"What did you do earlier?"

"You know what I mean," he says through gritted teeth, "I am trying to be nice."

"This is you being nice?" I scoff. "Please, save it for Clarissa—"

"Larissa."

"Whatever," I snap. "Like I care what her stupid name is."

"Jealous, Beauty?" He smirks and my traitorous pussy instantly throbs. Gah! Enough, already.

"I am not jealous." I draw myself up to my full height, which still means I have to tilt my head back, way back, to meet his indigo gaze. "In fact, I think you can fuck her day and night and I wouldn't care."

"Hmm." His grin widens, "I think you're lying."

"Oh, go to hell." I turn, face my reflection in the mirror, then gasp. He's right behind me.

He holds my gaze in the mirror, then runs his finger down my spine. I shiver and his lips curl. "Don't you like it?" he rumbles.

"It'll do, I suppose."

"What's that supposed to mean?"

"Well, firstly, I am not sure what I am doing here shopping for clothes. Secondly, even if I did decide to accept them from you, this is not my style."

"We are shopping for clothes because it was a chance for you to get out. And secondly, what do you mean it's not your style?"

"Don't do me any favors by planning an outing for me." I frown up at him, "And secondly, just that. This is not the style of clothing I wear."

"Surely, you must be able to find something in this shop that's to your taste?" He frowns.

"I suppose I might find a thing or two, if I look hard enough," I murmur.

"Hmm." He firms his lips, "So you don't like the one you are wearing now, either?"

I shake my head and his smile widens, "Then you won't mind if I do this?" He hooks his finger in the 'V' of the dress and tugs. The delicate fabric tears. I gasp as he rips the cloth all the way to the hem. The dress stays poised over my breasts, then with a whisper, it falls away. Leaving me clad only in my panties—I'd taken off my bra earlier to try on the dress—and in the stupid pink ballet flats.

His gaze eats me up as he slides it down to my breasts. My nipples pucker, and he lowers his gaze down to the shadowy cleft that can be seen through my panties.

"*Oddio,*" he growls, "you're fucking beautiful."

My thighs clench and moisture pools between my legs. More of this and he'll be able to make out the damp spot that I am sure is currently gracing the inside of my knickers.

Heat flushes my skin. I want to throw my arms around myself and hide from his gaze, but I don't. Instead, I tuck my elbows into my sides and watch as he drinks his fill of me.

He slides his palm around and flattens it against my belly. The dark skin on the back of his palm is a startling comparison to the ivory of my skin. He brings this other hand around to cup my pussy. Through the thin cloth of my panties the heat of his touch sinks right into my core. Without meaning to, I widen my legs. A low rumble of approval vibrates up his massive chest. He slips his finger under the gusset of my underwear. He brushes against my weeping slit and I can't stop the moan that bubbles up my throat. I lean back into that hard chest of his, thrust up my breasts, tip up my chin, and watch from under hooded eyelids as he slips his finger inside my opening.

Goosebumps pop on my skin. I bite down on my lower lip and his gaze instantly goes there. His lips part as if he's remembering how it'd been to eat me out. The thought sends a shiver down my spine. More moisture slides down from between my thighs. His breath catches. He slips in a second finger, then a third. A groan bleeds from me. I slide my arm up and around, hold onto his shoulder as he begins to finger fuck me. He doesn't take his gaze from mine in the mirror, and I swallow, watch as those darkening eyes grow blacker, more unfathomable. As if there is a fire deep inside that he's hiding from me. As he speeds ups and saws his fingers in and out of me, in and out, my breasts jiggle and my belly trembles. My entire body seems to be participating in this carnal exercise. I wind my fingers around his thick wrist, not so much to stop him as to hold on as he continues to weave his magic fingers in and out of me. The climax bursts upon me. I throw my head back and into his chest. My eyelids flutter down and he clicks his tongue. "Eyes on me, Beauty."

I raise my gaze to his again, and somehow, the intimacy of watching him jerking me off—of the very erotic picture we make, with me almost naked and him fully dressed, his fingers inside me, as he brings his other hand up to cup my breast, before he pinches my nipple with callous disregard—makes me throw my head back and scream as I fall apart. I black out for a few seconds, and when I open my eyes again, I am still in the same position, leaning into him, held up by his fingers in my cunt, that he pulls out.

"I screamed," I say in a dazed voice.

"Indeed." He smirks and my pussy clenches again. Argh. Stupid pussy.

"So, the rest of the people in the boutique would have heard too?" I frown.

"Since when did you start caring about what others think of you?" He tilts his head and something hot stabs at my chest. How the hell does this man know me so well? I really don't give a shit about what others think of me. But society dictates I should. And sometimes I give in to that pressure. And this man... My captor had cut through to the heart of my quandry with a few careless words.

He proceeds to lick his glistening fingers one by one, before he holds them to my mouth.

"Open," he commands and I part my lips. He thrusts his fingers in my mouth, and the sweet taste of my cum, the darker, edgier taste of him, crowds my sense. My core dampens all over again. Hell, I want him. I need him inside of me.

"Mika," I whisper, "please."

He curls his lips, removes his fingers from my mouth, then wipes them on my stomach. "Get dressed." He steps back, holding my shoulder for a few seconds while I regain my balance. "I'll be outside," he murmurs, not unkindly…just…without much emotion, as if he is simply attending to a chore. Is that all I am to him? A captive, a possession, an asset, someone he wants to wed out of some stupid sense of ownership.

"Michael, why—"

He shakes his head, "I'll see you outside."

21

Michael

What the hell is wrong with me? Why the hell can't I keep away from her? And after what I did to her yesterday, you'd think I'd have the decency to give her a wide berth? Apparently, not. Apparently, taking her virginity with a knife handle is not enough. Now, I have to jump her in a changing room cubicle and make her come all over my fingers.

I had planned this excursion with the purpose of trying to make up, somewhat, for what I had done. I'd thought a quick outing, doing what women seem to love most—shopping, buying new clothes—would take her mind off of what had happened, off of what a sick fuck I am. And maybe, in some way, I hoped to make amends for what I had done. Okay... I had been shamelessly trying to buy my way into her good books. The plan had been to leave her alone, to let her browse and choose the clothes she loved, but the situation had backfired on me.

I hadn't been able to wait while she changed her clothes. All I had been conscious of was that she was behind closed doors slipping out of what she had been wearing... She was probably naked and stepping into one of the new outfits. She'd pull it up and over her breasts, cover her flat belly with it, allow it to flow around her knees. I had tortured myself with visions of how the silent cloth would feel against her skin, as it caressed her nipples and slithered in between her legs, slipping across the newly-exposed and extra-sensitive skin there.

Before I'd realized it, I had made my way to the changing cubicle and stepped in. The thought of making her come in a public place had only added to the excitement. It had been hot and so damn sexy, seeing her respond to my ministrations. Clad in that green dress that had enhanced the emerald of her eyes... I had taken great pleasure in tearing it off of her body.

And she had shattered and wanted more. I had seen the need in her eyes, knew if I threw her down on the floor of the changing room, she'd have parted her legs and welcomed me into her weeping cunt. And I had wanted to take her right then and there. Make her mine, tie her to me, ensure I'd imprinted myself on every cell in her body. And it was precisely that overwhelming compulsion which had made me pull away.

This woman is like crack. Every time I see her, touch her, smell her fragrance, I want more. When I am with her, I lose sight of everything else… Everything except this need to bury myself between her legs and taste her, sniff her, absorb her essence into my body. It's crazy, the intensity with which I want her, and that urge only grows with every encounter.

When I am with her, I lose sight of everything that I have worked so hard to achieve. I am perilously close to throwing it all away for one more hour with her and that…is dangerous. For me, for my family, for my men who depend on me for survival. For the way of life that I chose a long time ago. How can I let one slip of a woman sweep in and displace all of that?

No, I have to keep my distance from her. I have to rush through this wedding, then ensure I use her to get to the Seven. Secure my empire and my position within the Cosa Nostra, and then I'll be free of her.

I thought I could, with a few more weeks, give her time to adjust to the idea of a wedding, but I guess I don't have that luxury. I need to get on with it. No more wasting time. She simply has to get on board with what is going to happen to her.

I watch from my position against my Maserati as she walks out wearing another dress. A dark blue, almost black colored, outfit that clings to her like a second skin. It stops just above her knees, and the neckline is high, except for the heart-shaped cut-out just above her breasts that shows off the shadowy valley between the mounds.

It is very different from the outfit she'd been trying on earlier, the one I destroyed. It is also much more her. More complex, more in keeping with the feisty personality that she has.

Have I bitten off more than I can chew with her? Did I make a mistake in taking her, in the first place? If I'd known just how much she'd turn my life upside down, would I have kidnapped her? Did I even have a choice in the matter?

As soon as I had seen her reciting Byron to herself in that moody voice as she gazed out over London... I knew that I had to have her. And here she is, within my grasp. So why am I still hesitating to make her mine? What is stopping me from taking what rightfully already belongs to me?

I track her progress as she walks over to the car, she holds a bag in each hand. I take them from her and she slides inside the car with a whisper of fabric and that luscious scent that is so very Beauty.

I shut the door, dropping the bags in the trunk—*Gesù Christo*, the woman's turning me into a chauffeur—before rounding the car to the driver's seat.

I fold my length inside. "Thought you didn't like anything you saw in there." I jerk my chin toward the shop.

"Guess I saw a few things which could suffice." She sniffs, "Besides, they are a step up from what's in the closet back at the house." She shudders.

"I take it the outfits in the closet back home are not to your liking?" I say dryly.

"Let's just say, they leave a lot to be desired, especially in terms of color."

I scowl. "What's wrong, in terms of their color?"

"They're all pink and beige and shit."

"So?"

"So?" She turns to me, "Hello, take a look at me." She waves a hand at herself, "Do I look like someone who wears those girlie colors? And their fitting..." She scoffs. "Not that they are not of good quality. That's their only redeeming factor, but seriously, they have this ladylike air about them—"

"And you're not a lady, are you, Beauty?" I lean in closer to her and her breath hitches. "You're someone who wants to be treated like a queen in real life and like a whore in bed, isn't that right, *Belleza*?"

Color reddens her cheeks and her pupils dilate. *Merda,* that turns her on, all right. Beauty has no idea just how depraved her tastes really are, does she? My cock tightens and my belly hardens. She opens her mouth, no doubt, to protest and I raise a hand. "Don't bother to deny it," I drawl, "we both know that's true."

She folds her hands over her chest. "You don't have a clue, what I like."

"And we both know that's a lie."

She scowls, then shifts in her seat. The pulse at her throat speeds up. *Porca miseria.* At this rate, I am going to pull her over, and have her riding my cock in no time. And I don't want to do that, not yet. Not until I have her married to me.

"So," I widen my legs, trying to make myself more comfortable, "what kinds of clothing would you rather wear?"

She firms her lips, "Doesn't matter."

I frown. "Tell me," I insist. "I want to know."

She blows out a breath, then shoots me a sideways glance, "I'd rather stitch my own clothing, if you really want to know."

"You would?" Then I nod, "Of course, you would, you are a tailor."

"A fashion designer."

"A seamstress."

"I'm a couturier, you ass."

"What-fucking-ever," I mutter. "You want to create your own clothing; I am sure we can arrange that."

Half an hour later, I watch from the comfort of yet another couch that I have draped myself on in a corner of a well-known fabric shop that also carries any tools she may need for stitching her wedding dress. I had my men talk to the owner, who was only too happy to shut down the shop to the rest of the public so my woman could shop in privacy.

Holdonasecond. Did I just think of her as my woman? I drag my fingers through my hair. Shit, shit, shit. When you start slipping up like that, and your subconscious mind insists on playing tricks on you, then you know you're really in trouble.

I follow her with my eyes as she literally vibrates with excitement as she examines the fabrics in front of her. Shades of black and gray, and a blue so dark that it could be mistaken for black in low light, a green so deep that it calls to mind the depths of the sea, a purple on the spectrum of—you guessed it, black. Doesn't the woman like any other color?

Her dark hair dances about her shoulders as she leans in closer to the man behind the counter. She says something to him and he nods. She lowers her head to examine the cloth, whispers something else and he bursts out laughing. He whispers something back to her, eliciting a smile, before he pivots, heads inside the shop, only to appear moments later with an armful of ribbons and fabrics in shades of—See if you can guess. Yes, black.

Together, they examine the cloth. The man glances at her bent head, a positively adoring look on his features.

Something hot stabs at my chest. Damn it, I knew it had been a bad idea to let her off the island.

It's only a matter of time before everyone else sees what I already know. She's special. She's different. Nothing, and no-one else, can hold a candle to her. She is unique, a magnificent creature who seems to breathe life into everything around her. There is something so luminescent about this girl, I wonder how has she survived this far without anyone else recognizing how unique she is?

I had, of course, from the moment I had spotted her. I haven't been able to let her go since, and look where that has gotten me. Skulking about in the periphery, stalking her like a creepy-ass motherfucker, while nursing a bad case of blue balls, and all because I can't bring myself to own up to just how drawn to her I am.

I had taken her with the intention of making her pay her father's debt. I had realized her links to the Seven make her a key asset. I should go through with my original plan of killing her… Instead, here I am, contemplating marrying her. Except, I can never allow for that to be real. If, for one second, I allow myself to think of how it would be to really be married to her… Hell… My groin hardens and my heart begins to race. I'd never be able to let go of her. I'd, forever, have handed over my power to her… And that, I cannot allow.

I am my own man. I built up the authority I wield with great effort and I cannot let anything or anyone get in the way of the empire I have envisioned for myself. It's all I have —the promise I made to myself that I will be the most powerful of all the Five Families—and I can't stop until I have achieved that.

I rise to my feet and stalk over to her. I loom behind her, and she glances up at me, "Hey, Michael," her face lights up, "this is incredible. The warp, the weft, the velvets and the chiffons... They are gorgeous. Look at the sheer variety of these decorative ribbons. And this lace—" She holds up a length of an antique, cream-colored mesh-like fabric, "It's incredible. It's so old, there are very few of this left anywhere in the world, and Roberto, here, is happy for me to have it."

I glance from her to the middle-aged man who watches her with stars in his eyes. Fucker. I can't stop the growl that rumbles from my chest.

Roberto pales; his throat moves as he swallows. He looks up at me, blinks rapidly. "Signor Capo," he mumbles, "I am more than happy for the Signorina to have whatever she so desires."

"The Signorina desires that you wrap up everything—" I rake my gaze across the heaps of fabric, and the various other sewing tools and other odds and ends that she's chosen. "—Everything that she has liked so far, and have them delivered to my place on the island." I jerk my chin toward the door, "Now, get out of the shop and leave us alone."

"But," he glances down at the heaps of fabric, then back up at me, "Signor, Capo…" He swallows, "Uh, the payment."

"Oh, for fuck's sake." I shove my hand in my pocket, pull out my credit card and hand it over. "Charge the whole damned thing, and anything else she'll need for creating her trousseau, to it."

"Yessir." The man grabs the card, turns to Beauty and smiles, as I fight the urge to bash his head in. He nods, "Signorina," then scampers off. The door shuts behind him as Beauty whirls on me.

"What the hell are you thinking? You gave him your credit card?"

"So?"

"And you're not going to check what he's charging to it."

"He won't dare pull a fast one on me. Besides," I smirk, "it's just money."

She scowls, "I can't accept all of this."

"You will."

"I don't want it." She all but stamps her foot.

Aww, how cute. "You do want it," I murmur. "You just don't know it."

"What will I do with so much fabric?" A line appears between her eyebrows. "It's more than I have bought in my entire life."

"Good," I bare my teeth, "you can use it to stitch your wedding gown."

"No." She shakes her head, "No, no, no."

"Yes." I allow my grin to widen, "You can and you will."

"I will not."

"Is that right?"

She folds her arms across her chest, "I refuse to participate in this sham of a wedding that you keep threatening me with. I refuse to give in and act all helpless."

"Pity, you'd make a great damsel in distress."

"But you are no knight in shining armor."

"I am glad you recognize that." I bend my knees, peer into her face, "You will do as I say."

"And if I don't?"

I glare into those bright green eyes. Eyes I can lose myself in, eyes that are angry and frustrated, and yet, so filled with life that they take my breath away. "If you don't, I will—"

The phone in my pocket buzzes. She glances down at my pocket just as I whip her phone out, stare at the message. "If you don't, I won't let you see the message that your sister sent you."

"My sister?" She cries, "Summer? That's a message from Summer?" She stretches out her hand for the phone and I hold it up and out of her reach.

"Give it to me," she huffs.

"First, agree that you will stitch your wedding dress."

"No."

"Then you won't see this message from your sister."

She hesitates and I glance at the screen. "Don't you want to find out how she is doing? How her husband is treating her after the wedding? Where they are going for their honeymoon—"

"Bastard," she snarls.

I arch an eyebrow, "Now, you are definitely not going to see her message."

I swipe the screen and she frowns.

"Hold on. My phone is profile protected. How the hell did you unlock it?"

I lower my chin, "Really, that's all you are concerned about? How I hacked your phone?"

"Jerk." She sets her jaw, "Guess you got someone to get around the security."

I tilt my head, and her color deepens. "Show me the message."

"Apologize first, for being so impolite."

"I won't."

"Fine."

I dance my finger across the screen, reach for the delete button, and she snaps, "Okay, fine, I apologize."

"That didn't seem like much of an apology."

"What the hell?" she snarls. "Do you want me to get on my knees?"

I arch an eyebrow and she pales.

"No," she says through gritted teeth. "Of all the annoying, stupid, humiliating things, you'd ask me to do that?"

I yawn and she snaps her teeth shut. Then she lowers herself to her knees, tips her chin up and purses her lips together, "Happy?"

"Not yet," I tilt my head, "open your mouth."

She pales.

I glare at her and she swallows, then parts her lips.

"Good girl." I slide my thumb inside her mouth, then lower my voice to a hush, "Suck on it." She doesn't take her gaze off of me as she curls her warm tongue around my digit.

The blood rushes to my groin. *Fuck.* I press down her tongue, as she parts her lips further. The thought of those lips wrapped around my cock… *Goddamn it to hell.* A surge of need races up my spine. To think, I'd thought I'd be able to stay away from her. I pull my fingers out, then jerk my chin, "Get up."

She rises to her feet and I flip the phone so she can peruse the screen. She reads the message, once, twice, then swallows. I lower the phone, frown down at her, "Well?"

"What?" She glowers back, "What do you want now?"

"What's your reply?"

"Oh," she blinks, "you're going to let me answer her message?"

"I am going to allow you to tell me what you want to say and I am going to type it out for you."

"Don't trust me, Capo?"

My vision tunnels and my balls harden. Shit, the sound of my title from her lips... It's so damn erotic. I toss the phone at her and she catches it.

"Go on, answer the message."

She blinks. "So, you do trust me?"

"I trust you…to say the right thing, Karma. If you don't, I know exactly where your sister and her new husband are right now, and trust me, they'll pay for your impertinence."

She scowls, "Fine, fine, you don't have to go all Godfather on my arse. I know you're too clever to simply hand the phone over to me to reply without having your own checks and balances in place."

She glances down and her fingers race across the screen. The sound of the message being sent fills the space. She straightens, then hands the phone over to me.

"That wasn't too bad, was it?"

"If you mean my having to beg to use the phone which, honestly, is as crucial as breathing...then yeah, it sucked balls."

"I need to wash out your mouth," I fix my gaze on her lips, "and it's not going to be with water."

"Whatever." She flips her hair over her shoulder, "You're all talk and no action, you know that?"

"Are you trying to get under my skin or are you trying to get under my skin?" I slide the phone into my pocket.

She tosses her head, "If that was a joke, I don't get it."

"Good," I widen my stance, "because by the time I am done with you, you won't be laughing."

"What's that supposed to mean?" She twists her fingers together, "I mean, seriously, you are worse than a B-grade Hollywood flick, Capo. Have you heard yourself lately?"

"How about we settle for hearing you as you come?"

"What?" She glances around the space, "Here?"

I twirl my finger in the air. She huffs. I glare at her and she pales.

"Do it, Beauty," I murmur. She spins around and faces the counter.

I press my palm into the small of her back and a shiver trembles down her spine. I push forward and she leans over beautifully. I glide my palm up her spine and fix my fingers around the nape of her neck. The length is so slender that my fingers meet around the front. She turns her head, and I urge her to press her cheek into the glass counter. Another trembling grips her. I increase the pressure around her neck and she subsides.

"Relax," I murmur, "I am not going to hurt you."

"No, you did that already."

I glance down at her face, at where she's staring up at me from the corner of her eyes, "And you enjoyed it."

She shakes her head, and I increase the pressure around her throat, "Don't lie to me." I lean in close enough for my breath to raise the tendrils of hair at her temple. "You loved every minute of riding my knife handle; you enjoyed coming on my fingers in the changing cubicle. Even now, bent over the counter with your arse up in the air and at my mercy, you can't stop your cunt from dripping for my touch, for my fingers to be crammed inside of you, for my mouth pushed up against your slit as you ride my tongue."

"N...no..." she stutters, "that's not true."

"It is." I close the distance between us so my pelvis is pushed up against her curvy rear end, so my dick nestles in the valley between her ass cheeks. So there is no doubt about just how turned on I am. How at my disposal she is. All I have to do is yank up the fabric of her dress, lower my zipper and—"

"If you're going to fuck me, why don't you simply do it and get it over with?" she huffs.

"Because that would be too easy?" I bend and place my mouth so close to hers that we share breath, "Because I am not going to put you out of your misery that easily. Because you can fool yourself all you want, Beauty, but the fact is, under that innocent exterior beats a heart that is every bit as perverted as mine, a soul that yearns for every depraved thing I can do to you, a mind that is, even now, racing ahead with the possibilities of exactly in what positions I can tie you down, how I can restrain you, how I can render you helpless and willing to take my cock in any position that I choose to give it to you...or not."

A low moan bleeds from her lips, and my dick instantly lengthens. I cup her ass cheek and her entire body grows rigid. I drag my finger down the fabric that clings to the cleft between her butt cheeks and her thighs clench.

"Shh!" I slip my hand under the slit that runs up the back of her dress, my fingers brush the back of her thigh, and a whine spills from her lips. I thrust my thigh between her legs, pry them apart as I slip my fingers in between them and freeze.

"You didn't wear panties?"

22

Karma

"The dress was too tight," I snap, even as a trembling begins in my core. I try to rise up but the grip on my neck holds my immobile. Also, his massive trunk-like thigh between mine has me pinned. Shit, how can this guy be so big? Not that I can forget his height, considering how he towers over me, but when he holds me down like this, exactly how much weaker than him I am is brought home to me. I am in his power. His to be played with. His to be used. His to own. His to…be brought to the edge of pleasure with the kind of sweet pain only he can bestow on me. I open my mouth to tell him just that, then snap my jaws shut.

No way, am I making that tactical error. If he knows how close I am to throwing caution to the wind, to forgetting who I am, and what my life used to look like, how the future I had envisaged for myself is slowly fading away… Poof... how it's all gone under the mesmerizing influence of his touch. Crushed under the overwhelming force of his dominance that demands that I lay here and watch him as he surveys my backside.

"Or maybe you wanted to tease me...?" He raises those unfathomable eyes to mine, "Tell me, Beauty, is this your way of telling me that you'd rather not wait for the holy union of our marriage, and that you'd rather that I fuck you right here and now?"

"Exactly," I murmur, "now you get it. The faster you shag me, the faster we can put this...chemistry we have, behind us. Then, you can send me back home and—"

"No."

"What?" I frown. "What do you mean, no?"

"No, I am not letting you go."

"But if you fuck me, you don't have to marry me, right?"

He laughs, "Whatever gave you that idea? This entire exercise is so I can make our arrangement official, remember?"

"But what benefit do you get out of it? I mean, sure you get a wife and someone to breed for you. But as we've already established, I am not the kind of woman you want."

"That's your conclusion, not mine."

"But seriously, Michael," I lift my head but he pushes me back down.

"Less talk, more action," he growls.

"You mean, more pretending to make me come without actual penetration?" I scoff.

His entire body goes solid. That's the only warning I get before he grips the sides of the slit in my dress and tugs. The fabric tears up the middle. He rips it all the way to the neckline and the dress falls apart around me. Cool air assails my skin and I shiver. "If you wanted to get me out of the dress, you only had to ask."

"And you'd have agreed?"

"Of course not, but maybe, I could have saved this dress. Not that I like the outfit or anything, but it was new, and someone had put time and effort into creating it, so... I just like to be respectful of other people's work. After all, I know what it takes to produce a design... And by the way, are you going to make this a habit?

Ripping apart the dresses I am wearing? Because when I wear my own creations, I promise you, I won't take lightly to that, I won't..."

"Shh." He puts a finger to his lips and I bite the inside of my cheek.

One word from him and I am ready to do his bidding. One glare from him and all I want to do is roll over and open my legs, my mouth, my arms, and accept him into my body, my soul...my mind.

Am I a feminist? I'd like to think so.

Would I ever let a man tell me what to do? Never.

But would I bow down to this man and let him disrespect and degrade me? Absolutely. A-n-d, that folks, is all you need to know. For I am hopelessly drawn to this alphahole, and hell, if I can understand why. Is it his dominance, his complete confidence that is so attractive? Is it his self-assured approach to most things that is a turn on?

All he's done since I've met him is hold a gun to my temple, then make me come on his knife's handle, then all over his fingers in a semi-public place, and now... He reaches around, yanks up a length of the decorative ribbon that I had been examining earlier.

He pulls my arm behind my back, then the other. He ties the swath around my wrists, once, twice, thrice, knots it, then tugs. The soft material rustles against my skin. A shiver slithers down my back

He brings the ribbon up until just below the elbows, then wraps it around. He puts one arm around both of my arms to hold them together while he wraps the length up until just below the elbows.

Then he wraps it under both of my hands, before pulling it back up to form a cinch. He uses the exact same process to create another band above the elbows.

He pulls the swath up over a shoulder, pulls me forward, then loops the ribbon down on the inside of one breast.

He takes the material beneath the other arm and up again on the inside of the other breast. Shit. He is, in effect, creating straps. Then he brings the ribbon back and around horizontally beneath the arm, wrapping between the two straps. I tug and realize he has, very effectively, tied me down in a matter of seconds.

"What are you doing?" I scowl.

"What does it look like?" He murmurs, "I am tying you down."

"You into Shibari, or something?"

"Or something," he agrees. "Let's just say, finding creative ways of restraining people happens to be one of my hobbies."

"Oh?" I wriggle around and find, while the fabric is loosely tied, it does a very good job of restraining my movement. He's pulled my shoulders back, so my breasts are thrust forward and into the glass counter and my arms are immobilized. All in all, while it's not uncomfortable, there's something very vulnerable in the position. It ensures that I feel exposed, laid out for his delectation.

"Michael," I frown, "undo me."

"Not yet." He steps back and I sense him surveying his handiwork.

"Hmm," he makes a sound of approval deep in his throat, and instantly, my nipples pucker. Hell, it's as if there's a direct line from his voice to all the erogenous zones in my body. He leans over me and heat surrounds me, pulls on me, swirls about me, and pins me down to the counter. I can't move and he isn't even holding me down any more.

"Look at you." His voice is low and melting. "All tied up and laid out like a buffet." His tone dips another octave and a pulse flares to life between my legs. I chafe my thighs together, clench my core in the hope of plugging the emptiness that yawns in my center.

"Michael," I groan, "what are you doing?"

"Admiring my handiwork, of course," he retorts at once.

Jerk.

"Please, Michael, please."

"What do you want, Beauty?"

"Fuck me, Michael."

"Not happening."

"What the—?" I try to rise up but he, once more, wraps his fingers around my neck to hold me in place. "What the hell are you playing at?" I snap. "Seriously, I am done with how you keep toying with me and then making me come—"

"So, you'd rather not come?"

"That's not what I said."

"So, you do want me to touch you."

"Argh, stop putting words in my mouth, asshole." I stare up at him from the corner of my eyes, "Honestly, what are you up to?"

"I think I need to stuff some of the fabric in your mouth."

"Don't you dare, you jerk."

"Then stay quiet, *Belleza*."

He slides his fingers between my legs, drags the edge of his hand against my pussy. My core clenches and my toes curl. Moisture pools in my center, slides down my inner thigh.

"*Dio cane,*" he growls, "you are soaking, Beauty."

"Oh, fuck off." I mutter. "How about this? Next time, I'll be the one to tie you down, and play with your balls, and then we'll see how you respond.

"You can play with my balls even without tying me down, baby."

I snort then quickly turn it into a gagging noise, "Seriously, that was a terrible attempt at banter."

"So why are you laughing?"

"I'm not."

"Yes, you are."

Her reaches for the curved ruler that I'd been examining earlier. He picks it up and I frown. "That's a French curve," I explain. "It's used to create the perfect curved line for pants and skirts."

"I can think of a perfect curved line I'd like to use it on."

I blink rapidly, "Wh...what do you mean?"

He releases his hold on me, steps back, no doubt, to admire his handiwork one more time. *Jerk!* Then he positions himself at right angles to my body, widens his stance, raises the ruler, much like the position of a golf player raising his club. My throat closes. My scalp tingles and a hot sensation coils in my belly. "Wh...what are you doing, Michael?" I gulp

"One guess." He smirks down at me, "Go on, surely you have an inkling by now."

"Are you..." I clear my throat, "going to use it on me?"

"Right on one." He brings it down and taps it against my naked backside. My breathing hitches. My core clenches. I lick my lips and his gaze drops to my mouth. His blue eyes blaze. His muscles uncoil.

He raises the French ruler again, swipes it against my arsecheek, and I yelp, "What the hell? Stop that!"

He chuckles. The asshole chuckles. "Come on, it didn't even hurt, Beauty."

"Fuck you," I snarl. "Why don't we exchange places and I'll spank your tight ass and then we'll—"

He brings the curved part of the ruler down on my other arsecheek and goosebumps pop on my skin. I huff, try to pull away, but of course, the bastard doesn't allow me to move. He places his free hand on the middle of my back, leans enough weight on me so I can't pull free, then he brings the ruler down on my other arsecheek. Fire sears my butt and I yell, "Goddam you, you...you jerk."

Whack! He brings down the ruler again and I howl. Again, and my entire body jerks. My nipples pebble, my toes curl, moisture laces my core and I squeeze my legs together. A groan bubbles up, and I bury my teeth in my lower lip to stop it from escaping. He pauses, and I glance up to find his gaze arrested by my expression.

His shoulders bunch; his chest rises and falls. I lower my gaze to the front of his pants, which is tented, showing just how much he is aroused. He drops the ruler on the counter, and the sound chafes across my already sensitized nerve-endings.

He massages my backside and pinpricks of pleasure crawl up my spine. He slides his fingers between my thighs, scoops up some of the cum from my core, then drags it up between my arsecheeks to my backhole.

"What the hell are you d…doing?" I stammer.

"What does it feel like?"

I hear the smirk in his voice. *Bastard.* He plays with my puckered hole and I tense.

"Shh." He brings his other hand up to massage the back of my neck. He digs his fingertips into the knotted muscles there and moves them in small circles. The tension instantly drains out of my flesh. My shoulders relax and a delicious warmth seeps into my blood. He slides his finger inside my backhole and I can't bring myself to protest. He pulls out his finger, slips it in again, works his way inside my channel. I wriggle around, dig my heels into the ground. He curves his finger inside and a trembling grips me. *Shit, shit, shit.* I shouldn't find what he's doing so much of a turn on.

He removes his hand from my neck. There's a whisper of fabric, the rasp of metal, then a thump. I snap my eyes open to find his knife laid out on the counter next to my face. Goosebumps pop on my skin. "Wh…what are you going to do with that?"

"Nothing you don't want me to."

I take in the handle of the knife and my heart begins to race. "Michael," I whisper, "you wouldn't…"

"No, I wouldn't."

"Huh?" I glance up from the side of my eyes, "So you agree that you are not going to…use it?"

"Is that what you want, Beauty?" His blue eyes are hard, all emotion wiped from his face. He seems cold and unreachable. Like he's putting me to the test. Like he's already decided about the outcome. Like he knows that I am going to refuse what he wants to do next.

I swallow, draw in a breath. I can't let him know just how afraid I am. How much I want what he can do to me, and yet, how scared I am that I will like it. What does that say about me? That dark side of me that I have always suspected I have. Which is the reason I had been down for becoming a goth… Which still hadn't satisfied that deep nothingness inside of me. The place where there is no judgment, where I can indulge my appetites, can allow myself to be used the way I want, for it seems to satisfy that need inside of me to become someone's fucktoy.

There, I said it. Well, in my head, anyway. Something I've known but which I've never admitted, even to myself. I know, it's me being judgmental about myself… Then, I'd met him and he'd ripped off my mask. He'd laid that kinky fucked-up part of himself out there and I had recognized it… Only, I have yet to come to terms with what that means… Still, I want to own it.

I want to be able to wear my smutty heart on my sleeve. I want to be free to be myself. No judgement. It's what he's offering me. A safe space in which to embrace my own fucked-up-ness. It took a beast to bring out the monster in me. I wonder what that means?

"No," I whisper, "that's not what I want."

His features seem to freeze. His gaze widens. Then, those blue eyes seem to catch fire. Cold fire that sweeps through my skin, heats my blood, and lodges somewhere deep in my gut. My heartbeat ratchets up and moistures slicks my core.

"Tell me," he rumbles, "tell me what you need."

23

Michael

"You," she whispers, "I want you, Michael. I want every depraved, dirty thing that you want to do to me."

My balls harden. Fuck me. How can she say that? How can she lay her innermost desires at my feet? How dare she trust me to do what I want with her? Doesn't she realize how dangerous that would be? How it would ensnare me, trap me into wanting her, feeling for her, tying her to my side and never letting her go? It would make me want to own her, to make her mine. Mine. And that, I can't afford. No distractions. Nothing that could touch my heart. That could infiltrate the walls I've built around myself.

The fact that she wants everything I can do to her… That she aches for my possession as much I want to own her. That she yearns to be at the receiving end of every filthy, fucked-up, obscene one of my actions… It shows just how well-matched she is for me.

It's why I must turn away from her. Why I must never be alone with her. Why I must kill her as soon as she's outlived her usefulness.

It's why I must walk away from her. Just...not yet. Not when she's tied up and laid out in front of me, asking me to fulfill the perverted fantasies I've had ever since I met her the first time.

And if I do, I am a goner. I'll never be able to leave her. It's why I need to stay away from her as I had originally planned. A promise I have broken many times over. It's why I am going to walk away from her right now, before I take that final step that will bind me to her irrevocably.

I grab the knife then slide it back in its sheath.

"What are you doing?" She frowns

I step back, reach for the ribbon that I knotted around her wrist. I tug on it, and it comes free. That's the beauty of knowing how to tie someone. The process of unbinding takes, maybe, one fourth of the time that it took to truss them up. If only it were that easy to loosen the ties she's already wrapped around me.

I tug on the fabric and it falls away. I step back and she straightens, then turns on me.

"What's wrong?" She glances between my eyes, "What happened, Michael?"

I school my features into a mask, "We're going to be late for our lunch. That's what happened."

"Lunch?"

I nod.

"But I thought that you—"

"Wanted to fuck your ass?"

She winces, "You had to put that out there, didn't you?"

"Just saying what's on your mind, sweetheart."

"If you think that's going to make me feel embarrassed, think again." She firms her lips, "You went to all that trouble of tying me up. You wouldn't have done that if you hadn't meant to...uh, fuck me."

"Told you, I enjoy tying people up. It's a skill of mine. Doesn't mean I fuck everyone I tie up."

"And those who you tie up and fuck, do you use your knife on them too?"

I draw myself up to my full height. "That's none of your business."

I turn and walk toward the exit.

"Michael," she calls out, "one of these days, you are going to have to tell me why you keep running away from me."

"You're mistaken." I glance over my shoulder and brush away a loose thread from the ribbon. "You need to care about someone enough to have any reaction to them, none of which pertains to this situation."

She pushes her shoulders back and glares at me. "You're an unfeeling asshole."

"Now that we have established that," I glance at her over my shoulder, "wait here while I get you an outfit from the car, so you can get dressed."

Half an hour later, I sit across from her as she glances around the space.

"Capo." Paolo walks up with his usual glower on his face. You'd expect a man of his girth, who runs the most popular restaurant in Palermo, to be the quintessential happy, jowly-faced proprietor who'd go out of his way to keep his clients happy. The reality couldn't be further from that. Paulo is the most ill-tempered man I know. He was just born that way, apparently. But his *Spaghetti alle vongole* is to die for.

He begins to talk to me in Italian and I gesture to Beauty. "English, please," I murmur.

He glances at Karma, then at me, "The usual, Capo?"

"For me, yes. For her…" I tilt my head, "She's allergic to seafood."

"Spaghetti *Aglio Olio e Pepperoncino* for the lady then," he states. "And a carafe of the house white?"

"Please." I nod as Karma opens her mouth, likely to protest. But Paulo has already turned to leave.

"Before you ask," I turn to her, "there is no menu here. You get whatever Paulo has made for the day."

"Huh?" She blinks, "So he decides what you are going to eat?"

"He's the expert, and whatever he cooks is the best you can find in the city on that day, so yeah, you get what he's cooked."

She takes in the tables and chairs in the small space, all packed to capacity. The dining hall opens onto the sea on one side. On the other is the kitchen, open to the guests, so you can see the chefs cooking while Paulo assembles the plates behind one of the counters.

"You come here often?" she asks with her head still turned away.

"Often enough."

"Is Paulo a friend?"

I chuckle. "That asshole is nobody's friend."

"So why do you come here, then?"

I tilt my head, "You still don't get it, do you?"

"What?"

"The food, Beauty, the food."

She scowls, "Still, you could have, at least, let me ask him what the options were."

I simply shake my head. "That's not how it works."

"What do you mean?"

"Firstly, you don't get a choice. You eat what he gets you. Secondly, even if there were a choice, I would have ordered for you."

She gapes. "Is that presumptuous, or what?"

"Be thankful I allowed you out of the house on this outing." I smirk.

"Big-fucking-deal," she murmurs under her breath.

"What did you say?"

"I meant," she clears her throat, "thank you." She coughs.

"That's what I'm talking about."

Just then, Giorgio arrives with our food. He places a plate of the Vongole in front of me and the *Aglio Olio* in front of Karma. He pours the wine into glasses, then sets out glasses of water, and fresh bread with a little receptacle containing olive oil. "*Buon Appetito*." He steps back, then leaves.

The scent of the pepper, parmigiana, and the intense fresh aroma of the vongole permeates the air. My mouth waters. I reach for my fork, twirl the pasta and take a bite. The plump, briny taste of the clams fills my mouth. The fresh pasta crowns the experience. I break off a piece of the fresh bread, dip it in the white wine sauce, and pop it inside my mouth. So fucking good. A groan rumbles from my chest. I glance up to find her staring at me. She hasn't touched her food.

"Eat," I gesture to her spaghetti.

She twirls some of the strands around her fork, just like I had taught her, and brings it up to her mouth. She wraps her tongue around the tines and wipes it clean. My dick twitches and blood drains to my groin. I watch as she closes her eyes, chews, then a moan bleeds from her lips. She snaps her eyelids open, stares down at her plate, "Wow… That was…"

"Almost as good as an orgasm?"

"Yep," she nods, "I have to say, on this occasion, I agree."

She scoops up more of the pasta, and I do the same. We eat in relative silence until our plates are wiped clean.

"That was incredible." She licks her lips, as she reaches for her wine glass and drains it. Warmth suffuses my chest. The sight of her content and radiating satisfaction does strange things to me. I want to always take care of her, feed her good food, take her to my other favorite restaurants… Be with her as she explores the culinary delights of my heritage…

Hold on, what the hell am I thinking about here? What the hell is wrong with me that I am suddenly envisioning a future with her?

Paolo ambles over to stand between us. He surveys our now empty plates, places his palms over his wide girth, "*Dolce*, Capo?"

"Yes," she says eagerly, "I'd love to eat whatever dessert you have made today."

"No," I snap, "we're done here."

He turns to me, a frown on his face, "You are leaving without having my dessert?"

Yeah, I know. Sacrilege. Not something I'd do on any other day. But right now, I need to get this scrumptious piece of temptation away from me and back in the cage I have created for her. Before I do anything else I am going to regret.

I rise to my feet. "*Grazi*e Paolo." I add in a conciliatory tone, "Maybe next time."

He glances between us, then turns to Beauty, "*Buongiorno, Principessa*." He half bows to her, "Did you enjoy your meal?"

"It was..." she searches for the right word, "incredible. The best pasta I have ever eaten. And such a simple dish... I can't believe you put all those ingredients together and came up with something so amazing."

Paolo's features light up. "I am so pleased that you liked it. You come back anytime." He turns to me, "Make sure you bring her back with you, Capo."

I stare. Paolo actually smiling, and being civil, and to someone he's never met before? That has to be a first. Clearly, I am not the only one who is falling under her spell. I scowl up at him, but he doesn't seem to notice. "You take good care of her, Capo." He holds my gaze.

I nod and he seems satisfied.

A young man scurries up to him with a paper packet which he hands to Karma. "Dolce for the dolce." He grins down at her and my jaw falls open. What the hell? Paolo actually allowed a take-away of his precious dolce? Unheard off. He treats his food with too much respect to do that. In fact, I can't recall a single instance before this when he's actually packed his food in a take-away container. But he did it for her?

Che cazzo!

I jerk my chin, dismissing Paolo, who glances between us again. A sly look comes into his eyes, but he doesn't say anything else. He nods once more to both of us, then turning, he saunters off.

"Well, that was rude." Karma scowls, "You all but told him to fuck off, and after he was being so nice to us."

"It's Paolo," I raise a shoulder, "he can handle it."

"What set you off now?" She glowers up at me. "Seriously, your moods are worse than a woman on her period."

"That was an incredibly sexist remark to make," I chide her.

She laughs. "You should talk. The most misogynistic, most toxic, meanest man I have ever encountered."

I tip an imaginary hat down at her.

"Only you would take it as a compliment."

I smirk, "Don't tell me you don't find it attractive?"

"Certainly, not." She scowls.

"Don't lie to me, Beauty." I widen my stance, "There's something inside of you that relishes the fact that I don't hide behind meaningless niceties. That you see me and you know what you get. That I don't conceal exactly how perverted I am." I lower my chin to my chest as I hold her gaze, "That you know exactly how sordid my thoughts are, and that my actions are even more debauched… And something within you is relieved that my warped tastes give you the permission to unlock all the lustful emotions you have kept to yourself. That—" I place my hands on the chair on either side of her and bracket her in, "the corrupt truth inside of you feeds off of my deviance, indeed wants to embrace my every obscene act… If I let you. Only, I won't."

"You won't?" She blinks.

"I won't," I reiterate. "For you see, you are an asset, first and foremost. A gorgeous one, one with the kind of baseness that I hadn't expected…but an asset, nevertheless. One I am in no mood to break in, regardless of how tempting that may be. No, you, Beauty, are my property, and I intend to ensure that I leverage you for the purpose for which I kidnapped you in the first place. You're my captive, nothing more, and it you would do well to remember that."

"As if you'll ever let me forget," she mutters.

"Good, we understand each other then." I jerk my chin, "You should know that it's time for you to fulfill your role, Beauty."

24

Karma

My role… My stupid role, as it turns out, is to play the part of his bride. Why the hell does he have to marry me, though? If I ask him again, he'll pull that line of the fact that my father owes him, blah, blah, blah. But surely, that's not the only reason he's marrying me? There has to be something more, something else, some other reason why he's going through with his wedding. It can't be because he finds me attractive, right? Though he does… I mean, he must, considering how he can't seem to keep his hands off of me every time we are together. And yet, he also pulls back before he can complete what he started. Like, at the fabric shop. It's as if there's an internal war he's waging with himself every time he sees me. He wants me, but he hates himself for wanting me…

And well, the feeling's mutual. I hate myself for how my body responds to him. For how I understand those dark desires inside of him. Everything that I have tried to lock up inside of myself, from the time I had first been aware of the edginess inside of me, seems to respond to his presence. It's as if I can't keep my innermost feelings hidden around him anymore. His corruption attracts the filth I'd thought I had buried deep inside of myself; which I had never dared to acknowledge, to be fair, before him.

That coarseness inside of me which had spurred me on to stitch the kind of wedding dress in which I had always hoped to be married. I run my fingers down the black silk dress that I crafted in just forty-eight hours. It's amazing what you can accomplish when you cannot access the internet or talk to any of your friends and family.

On our way back from the shopping trip, Michael had informed me that we were getting married in three days. He had told me that he would have a dress delivered to me if I didn't promise to stitch my own dress. He had seemed uncertain I'd have the time to do it myself, but I had assured him I could work quickly. After all, I already knew the design I wanted. Then, I had reminded him of all the fabric he had purchased for me and that it would be wrong to let that go waste. I had asked him for a sewing machine, and to my surprise, he had told me it was already on its way.

How strange that he hadn't refused me. If anything, he seemed more than happy to indulge me on this. Like he had in taking me to the fabric shop. He knows I am a designer, but has he guessed just how much I need to create? It's a passion so deeply embedded in my cells it's as vital as breathing. As intrinsic as that filth that resides in the core of me. Something I, in fact, channeled when I designed and stitched and gave shape to fabric.

Creating a dress, somehow, eases that heaviness that resides within me. Almost as much as getting myself off does. Well, okay, not quite, but the sensation is similar. It's like I am channeling all of those forbidden desires inside of me and giving shape to something concrete, something I can wear and feel and touch, something that, on some level, feels as real as the shadows that crawl inside of me.

I haven't made it out of the room in the last few days, pausing only long enough to eat. That's how it is for me. Once the muse takes over, I can't stop for anything. All I have to do is get out of the way and let the creativity pour through me.

So, I'd measured and pinned and cut and sewn, and adjusted, and hand-stitched the final embellishments. I'd tried on the dress earlier and known it was almost there... Almost... Something was missing. A last adornment, a final trimming... Something to just push it over the edge.

My brain feels too tired, my fingers begin to cramp from the amount of time I had held the needle between them. Not to mention, the headache that has been building up behind my eyes. Shit. I need a break. I stare at my reflection in the mirror and my knees threaten to buckle. I yawn so loudly that my jaw cracks. The cool night air blowing in through the open window makes me shiver. I peel the dress off, carefully lay it over a chair. Then, clad only in my panties, I crawl into bed and under the covers to close my eyes.

The next thing I know, something infiltrates my consciousness. I come awake, but don't open my eyes. There's someone in the room; I am sure of it. Someone who's not moving, but standing over me, watching me. The hair on my forearms rises. My heart begins to thud.

Ever since Michael brought me here, I've been unable to shake the sensation of being watched. I assume he has eyes on the room, that he's watching me... Hell, of course, he is.

I'm not naive enough to think he'd, for one second, take his attention off of his asset. But this is different. This is not the eye of a camera on me. This is someone watching me, in real time.

My left leg cramps. I want to shake it out, but resist the effort. I draw in a breath, force myself to stay silent. A gust of wind blows in from the open window. I smell the brine of the sea, before it fades away, leaving behind that unmistakable masculine scent of testosterone, musky like leather with a hint of woodsmoke, that fills my senses. My belly trembles and my thighs clench. Moisture laces my core and I know then, it is him. Fucking Michael. He's in my room. What the hell is he doing, creeping around here in the middle of the night... Or is it early morning?

Fucking stalker. I regulate my breathing, force myself to stay still. Force my muscles to unwind, one by one, as he remains motionless. The minutes stretch. My pulse rate ratchets up, as it always does when he's anywhere close to me.

He stands there watching me, not moving, not saying anything. Gah, what the hell is he up to? His breathing seems to deepen. I sense him shift closer, the heat of his body sears my arm, and I know he is leaning over me. I sense the warmth of his breath on my cheek, then the hair on my forehead rises. I sense him sniff at my throat…

What the—? Is he smelling me? The heat of his body recedes, I sense him straighten, then the unmistakable sound of flesh hitting flesh. Wait, what? Is he getting off? Is he actually masturbating here in my bedroom? Watching me?! Why the hell couldn't he do so when he was watching me via the cameras? Why did he have to come in and watch me in real time?

I sense his breathing grow ragged, and my heart slams against my rib cage. His actions seem to intensify, the sound of him pleasuring himself growing more frantic. My belly flip-flops and moisture laces my core. I resist the urge to squeeze my thighs together. To slide my fingers inside my panties and shove them inside my aching core. Damn it, I should not be turned on, should not find this—whatever it is he is indulging in—so much of a turn on. A low groan rumbles from him, then I hear his breathing catch, sense him shudder as he climaxes. Heat sluices my veins and my toes curl. My core clenches on itself. I want to come so badly, as well. Why the hell do I find this so much of a turn on?

Then heat envelops me, the scent of him grows deeper as he leans over me. Something wet touches my lips, such a whisper of a touch that if I hadn't been awake and attuned to him, I wouldn't have caught it. I resist the urge to flick my tongue out and sample it. I sense him hesitate, then he touches his lips to mine, but before I can react, he's moving away. I hear his footsteps recede, then the door softly closes.

I crack my eyes open, but of course, the room is empty. I flick my tongue out and the taste of him—musky, dark and salty—trickles over my tongue. Did he...is that…did he dab his cum onto my lips and then kiss me to rub it into my mouth? Oh, my god!

I run my tongue across my lips, and the salty, dark taste of him fills my palate. I swallow down every last drop of his arousal, then slide my fingers under my panties, inside my wet channel and proceed to work them in and out of me. In and out, I increase the intensity of my movements, add a third finger, then a fourth. Shit, it's no substitute for the thickness I really want between my legs… Or the closeness of his skin on mine, his breath on my cheek, his lips on mine, his tongue playing with mine... As he grinds his heel into my swollen clit and makes me come. Heat suffuses my skin. My toes curl, my thighs clench, as I continue to pleasure myself with my fingers, chasing that elusive climax. No way, can I go back to sleep when I feel so empty inside and yearning, and…strangely, very aroused after that bizarre performance from Michael.

Had he sensed that I was wake? Did he know just how much of a need that would kindle inside of me? Had he realized just how horny it would make me to sense him come by just watching me? The thought of his long fingers around his fat dick as he grasped his thick length and got himself off sends me over the edge. The trembling overwhelms me and I climax around my fingers. I collapse into the bed, rub my cheek into the pillow and blow out a breath. Then, I bring my fingers to my mouth and suck on them. If I pretend hard enough, I can taste the dark flavor of his mixed with the sweeter tang of my cum. A heaviness grips my limbs and my eyes flutter shut.

When I open them next, light is streaming in through the window.

I sit up, glance around the room. Had I imagined it all? Did he really come into my room last night? Had he actually jerked off watching me sleep? Shit. I drag my fingers through my hair. Why the hell am I not more shocked, more grossed out by what happened?

I swing my legs over the side of the bed, when there's a knock on the door. Cassandra walks in.

"*Buongiorno,*" she smiles at me, "it's such a beautiful day for a wedding."

I stare at her. Seriously, did she just say that? I brush past her and walk to the dressing table, sitting down. "I assume you are here to help me with my hair and make-up."

"I am here to help you get dressed for your wedding." She beams at me, her face all bright and happy, like this is actually some honest-to-god, real wedding, or some such shit.

"You and I both know, this wedding is a sham," I murmur, "so you can cut the act."

Some of the cheeriness fades from her face. Shit, now I feel bad for having burst her bubble, but c'mon. Why is she so happy? I don't feel cheerful or anything.

It feels weird, strange that I am going to get married to a man who is, not only my kidnapper, but is also, most likely, a criminal of the worst kind. Someone who may be achingly handsome, but is also so dangerous that you don't want to cross his path in the middle of the night. Or during the day, for that matter, considering that's when I met him.

I chuckle to myself and she frowns. I rise to my feet, head inside the bathroom, and take a quick shower, taking care not to wet my hair. When I walk out dressed in a bathrobe, she's standing by the dressing table.

I cross the room and seat myself at the stool in front of the mirror.

She comes over to stand behind me. "May I?" She gestures to my hair.

"Have at it," I murmur. "Only, I have to warn you that I have a certain look in mind."

"I am happy to help you."

"Good." I meet her gaze in the mirror, "I plan to wear my hair down so it flows around my shoulders."

"Keeping it simple." She nods. "That's good."

"After you dye it red."

"Red?" She blinks, "You want to dye your hair, red?"

"You heard me." I nod. "I need the color bright enough that it shows up against the black."

"Black?" She looks confused, then swallows. "May I suggest that—?"

"No." I slash my palm through the air. "I told you, I want to dress a certain way. And in fact, your Capo is on board with it."

"He is?"

"He bought me the fabric and did not refuse me when I told him that I wanted to wear my own creation."

"But.." she gulps, "it's your wedding."

"Is it, now?"

"It is, and the Capo would not appreciate it if you made a fool of him in front of everyone else."

"Well then, he should have picked someone else to be his bride."

"But he wants you." She frowns at my reflection in the mirror.

"Does he?" I snort, "He's only using me to further his plan, something he hasn't even revealed to me yet, by the way."

"Would it have made a difference if he had?"

I scowl, "I suppose not. Still, it might have helped me understand a little bit more about why he's gone to all this effort of bringing me here, and why he insists on going through with this charade."

"The Capo has his reasons."

"Yeah, yeah." I wave my hand in the air. "Whatever they may be." I raise a shoulder, "Not that it matters to me." I tie the bathrobe more securely around myself. "Now, are you going to help me or not?"

"How are you going to get hold of the hair dye?"

I can't stop my lips from curving. "I had Roberto deliver it to me, along with the materials for the wedding gown."

"Roberto?" She blinks, "You mean the man who runs the cloth shop in Palermo?"

"Fabric store," I correct her, "and yes, the same guy."

"The Capo won't be happy when he finds out about him."

"Then you'd better not tell him, huh?"

She firms her lips.

"Right, then," I rub my hands together, "are you going to help me or what?"

"Yes." She nods. "I'll help you." She reaches for the comb, runs it through my hair, "If you want to dye it, we'd better get started right away."

25

Michael

I stand facing forward, at the top of the aisle in the chapel. Aside from my residence, it's the only other building on this inland.

Next to me, Luca shuffles his feet.

Sebastian stands next to him, his dark blonde hair a contrast to the darker looks of the rest of my siblings bringing up the rear. Massimo, Christian and Xander are all clad in black tuxes and black ties…similar to mine. Hair combed back and gelled, and with their similar scowling visages, broad shoulders and towering height, the three resemble a American football team. Our parents certainly bequeathed their best features to them. Too bad, my father is a fucking *stronzo*.

Adrian brings up the rear of the group.

From the other side of the aisle, the Don folds his arms across his chest. I meet his gaze, hold it. I slide my fingers to my side, and my fingertips brush the knife in its sheath that I have tucked into my cross draw sheath; even as I play the fucking power game of who blinks first with my boss.

After a few seconds, he finally nods. "Good to see you finally settling down, son," he murmurs. His voice, low and deep, echoes in the empty church. Yeah... There are no other invitees. Just family. Which, sadly, includes the Don.

"I didn't invite you to hear your opinion on the matter, Father," I growl. "You are here simply because—"

"Of her." He nods. "I understand; you'll never forgive me for what happened to her."

"It's your fault she's dead." I scowl. "Because you couldn't control your temper," I say in a hard voice. Not one of us had been spared being beaten by him growing up. As the oldest, I had taken it on myself to shield my brothers and my mother whenever I could. More often than not, though, he took it out on her behind closed doors... And my mother never protested. It was her burden to bear, she'd say. She'd borne the almost daily beatings silently.

The day I had turned eighteen, she'd called me into the kitchen. Had fed me my favorite *lasagne al forno*. Then, she'd told me how I was now the man of the family and she made me promise to take care of my siblings, including my stepbrothers, when she was gone. A week after that, she had dropped dead of a heart attack. And with that, any gentleness in my life had gone out of the window...

Until I'd caught sight of *her*. Why is it that seeing Karma had awakened the kind of protectiveness I had felt for my mother? Not that there is anything similar between the two of them. My mother had been blonde, slim, so tiny that seeing her boys all grown up and standing here today, it's difficult to imagine them having come out of her.

The side door to the church opens, then an older woman steps inside the church. She wears her flowing mane of almost completely gray hair about her shoulders. She's barely five-feet four-inches, but her erect posture makes her seem larger than life. She's clad in a pale pink trouser suit and heels which, while fashionable, are also comfortable for walking. That's my grandmother, who, at almost eighty is still agile, independent and doesn't suffer nonsense from anyone. Not even my father.

I glance from her to him and my father raises his shoulder. "You know, I couldn't have stopped her from coming, even if I had tried."

I walk forward to meet her. "Nonna," I bend and kiss her cheek, "you needn't have come all the way here."

"My oldest grandson is getting married, and you thought I'd stay away?" She scowls up at me. "How could you, Michelangelo?" She scolds me, "I have been hoping for you to get married and have grandkids since you turned eighteen. You finally oblige me, twenty-one years later, and you think I wouldn't come to witness it with my own eyes?"

"I'd have brought my new bride to visit you," I murmur.

"And when would that have been?" She glowers at me, "If, indeed, you did get around to doing it. You think I don't how hard you work at building the business, that I am not aware of how ambitious you are, about succeeding," she jerks her head to the side, "him."

"I am still alive, Mother." The Don growls, "I'd thank you to remember that."

"What you haven't learned, Byron," she says without looking at him, "is that respect is earned, not demanded."

"Who cares, how you get it. Respect is respect, Mother." The Don folds his arms across his chest. "One way or the other, I'll get it, even from my own sons." He stares at me meaningfully.

I glare back at him. What a prick. How is it possible that he is my father? More to the point, how could he have come from someone as gracious and as caring as my Nonna?

She had been the one steady influence all through the turmoil of our growing years. And after our mother's passing, she had insisted on being a part of our lives. And yet, not even that had stopped him from beating us up. If anything, after mother's passing, his predilection to hit us had escalated. By then, I'd been strong enough to stop him. I'd managed to hold him back from hitting my younger brothers, though not even I could stop him fully.

When I had finally confessed to Nonna, she had been horrified.

She had immediately moved us in with her…and confessed that she'd suspected but had no idea it had been so bad. I hadn't been sure if I should forgive her, but she had intervened, and insisted that my father get help for his issues. Something my father had grudgingly agreed to do. I owed that much to her—that my siblings had been spared the torture of being around him. She had, at least, managed to salvage some of their growing up years.

Me, on the other hand… The damage had been done. Perhaps it's the reason I've turned out so twisted, in my own way. Perhaps blood is thicker than water… Perhaps his violent tendencies were imprinted on me more than I realized. It is the only reason I can think of to explain my twisted needs when it comes to sex. Something I'd hope to keep in check with Karma, except every time I see her, my base instincts seem to emerge. Something inside of me insists that I claim her, that I show her what it means to be possessed by that darkness inside of me. My cock instantly thickens. Shit. That's the last thing I need—sporting a hard-on while I am surrounded by family, and in church.

"Michelangelo," Nonna's voice intrudes in my thoughts. "I hope you'll forgive me," she says in a tone low enough that only I can hear.

I tip down my chin, gaze into her midnight-blue eyes, so like mine.

"If I had known, if I'd had even an inkling of how far he'd go with her, I would have stepped in," she adds.

I set my jaw.

"So you have told me before, Nonna," I say stiffly. "I understand you want to find a way of alleviating the guilt you are carrying inside, but you know, I can't forgive you."

She blanches.

"You had a ringside view of the marriage; you knew about your son's temper; you must have known that she was being abused; you must have guessed, when we turned up with bruises, that he was hitting us. Yet you never asked any questions. Not once."

A stricken look comes into her eyes before she wipes all emotion from her face. "I guess, much as I think I am moving with the times, perhaps in this, I am more old-fashioned than I realized." She swallows, "It was their marriage and I didn't want to interfere..." She glances away, then back at me, "Something I will never forgive myself for, Mika." Her voice softens, "But perhaps your father was preparing you for your future. Look how you turned out after all that—"

"Nonna," I say through gritted teeth, "is that what you think? That his abuse of me and my brothers was a way of building character? That just because his father beat him, he should also be allowed to hit us? Do you really think that this is the natural progression of things?"

She looks away

Silence stretches for a beat, then another.

"I.." she swallows, "I don't condone what he did." She looks in my eyes and says, "But you have to admit, it played a part in making you so driven to succeed."

I step back from her, and her hand falls away.

"Mika," she murmurs, "I was brought up never to question the man of the house. First, my husband, then," she glances at the Don, "my son." She folds her fingers together in front of herself, and I notice that they are trembling.

Nonna always comes across as so strong, I forget sometimes, what she has been through. My grandfather had not only abused my father, but also her. He had beaten her and she had borne it all without a complaint and emerged stronger. She had been through it first-hand—all the more reason that she could have done something to stop the abuse of my mother and us at the hands of our father. But she hadn't... And here we are. An emotionally broken, facsimile of a family, trying to project a strong, unified front, lest our rivals find out just how tenuous the bond between us really is.

"Perhaps, if I had been less traditional, things would have been different. I have been trying to change, but it's not easy." She swallows, "I know I have my faults, but you have to believe me when I say that I did what I thought was best in the situation."

"The scars he left on my skin may have healed, but there are others...more emotional ones that changed me in ways you can't even recognize."

"Mika—" Her chin wobbles, "Please, don't block me out of your life."

"I have never done so, Nonna, you know that." I draw myself up to my full height. "But you will also never have my complete trust, either." I hold my grandmother's gaze. She tips up her chin, and I recognize the stubborn set to her features. That iron resolve is something I share with her.

Once I want something, I go after it—like her. From the moment I saw her, I knew that she would turn my life upside down. All the more reason to get through this ceremony, then get on with the plan I have in place to consolidate my position with the Seven.

"I understand." Nonna, nods once, then steps back. She turns and walks slowly across the stone floor to the first pew. She sits down, and my father takes his place next to her.

The main church doors open just then.

I turn, watch her framed in the doorway.

"What the—" Luca exclaims next to me, "what the hell is she wearing?"

26

Karma

I stay there, poised at the threshold of the church. At the far end of the aisle, he turns to glance at me, then freezes. Even across the distance, there's no mistaking the tension that radiates off every inch of his powerful body.

Next to him, a man who is, clearly, his brother, and Seb, as well as several other men, who also look like brothers—I wonder how many he has—turn toward me, and a collective ripple of shock seems to run through them. I take a step forward, then another.

The cool interior of the church wraps around me like a shroud. I shiver, tighten my grasp around the bouquet of white zagara flowers from the orange trees, that Cassandra had managed to rustle up for me this morning.

My large train drags behind me, the weight of it tugging at my shoulders so it feels like I am physically dragging along at least three times my body weight as I place one foot in front of the other. My footsteps echo through the completely silent church. It seems I have struck my audience dumb. A giggle bubbles up and I swallow it back. It won't do to get hysterical. Not now, not after I've come this far.

With Cassandra's help, I'd managed to don my wedding gown... And when I had seen myself in the mirror... The contrast of my red hair with the black silk and lace and my pale creamy skin, all set off with the white roses...ah! Let's just say, I knew I had outdone myself.

I begin to move forward, when the church door snicks shut behind me. I resist the urge to turn, shove open the door and tear out of there.

Firstly, I am not going to drown myself... The last time really had been an accident, but either way, I am not going to risk running over the edge of a cliff again. Besides if I did that, it would show him that I am afraid. That I had lost my nerve. And no way, can I allow that.

My heart begins to race and my pulse pounds at my temples. A bead of sweat trickles down my back and another shiver grips me. Shit, I will not give in to my fear. Not now. I set my jaw, square my shoulders, then continue to walk down the aisle.

With every step, the rustle of my gown, the swish of my skirt against my skin, the susurration of the train against the stone floor... All of the sounds seem to grow louder, more amplified.

There's no music. Why the hell isn't there any music? Don't weddings typically play the wedding march, or whatever shit tune that accompanies a bride walking up the aisle to meet her end? I mean, her husband-to-be.

Maybe Sicilians do it differently? Bloody hell, maybe I should have specified that he play music for the ceremony. A chuckle bubbles up and I swallow it down. As if he would listen to anything I have to say, huh?

My blood begins to thud in my ears. My throat goes dry. All of their gazes are fixed on me, on my black wedding gown, that I had fashioned as an amalgamation of the most grotesque designs that I had come across. The sleeves are made of lace and encase my arms, so the cream of my skin is visible through the gaps. The actual gown is cut deep at the bosom, so the curves of my breasts are on display, almost until the nipples. The waist cinches in, before flowing into a full princess skirt, except it's ripped and hung with black pearls and hooks which jingle as I walk. My feet are clad in red velvet shoes, the only accessory that I had chosen from the clothes I had tried in the boutique the other day.

My nails are painted red, as are my lips, the color set off by the red of my hair. The overall effect, I know, is over-the-top, almost steam-punkish in presentation. I resemble a twisted goth princess… Exactly what I am inside. In many ways, this dress is also the truest I have been to myself. A no-holds-barred representation of the rebel that I truly am. It's the culmination of my emotions, my feelings, all the designs I had studied over the past many years… From the time I had realized that being a fashion designer was my calling. I have invested all of it into this dress. This is me. This is what I am. Outrageous, audacious, scandalous, and borderline offensive. This is what he gets for daring to seize me from my life and try to turn me into a pawn in his game.

He thinks I am simply going to turn the other cheek and allow him to walk over me? Well, he's wrong. This is me—unvarnished, unhidden, uncensored. This is me being truthful to myself, to what I truly am. A feisty girl on the cusp of womanhood, on the verge of making the world her bitch, who will never give in to anyone. Certainly not, to my captor, who thought he could make me pay for the sins of a parent I'd been sure was dead until not too long ago.

I square my shoulders, tip my chin up, then stride up the aisle. Closer, closer to the devil waiting at the end of my journey. With every step I take, I sense the tension that vibrates off of him. The way his shoulders bunch, how he widens his stance, how he tilts his head, stalking me as I draw nearer. His jaw flexes, a vein drums at his temple, yet his gaze is clear. Brooding, deep enough to lose myself in again.

I grab hold of that nothingness inside of him which seems to mirror the worry coiling in the pit of my stomach. Somehow, that lack of feeling in his eyes grounds me. What's the worst that he can do, eh? Kill me? I have already resigned myself to the fact that I may not get out of here alive. And somehow, that gives me the courage to close the distance between us. To pause in front of him. Even in my six-inch heels, I barely come up to his shoulder.

I tilt my head back, all the way back, making sure not to sever the connection between us. He drags his gaze down my face, to my mouth, to my breasts, down to where my skirt grazes the floor. When he lifts his chin and claps his gaze back on mine, his eyes are alight with an emotion I can't place. Anger? Hate? A combination of the two, maybe? Then his lips curl and I know it's neither. He's amused with me. Asshole, is laughing at me? I grit my teeth and his grin widens. He holds out his hand.

I stare at his proffered palm, then ignoring it, I step up to stand next to him.

I hear a slight gasp… Probably from the older woman I had spotted seated in the pew. Who is she? His grandmother? Like I care.

I stare straight ahead at the priest who begins to speak. His mouth moves, I am sure he is saying something, but I can't hear him. The blood thuds in my ears; my heart beats so loudly in my chest that I am sure it's going to break through my rib cage. Spots of back flicker at the corners of my eyes, and I must sway, for a grip on my arm brings me back into my body. I blink, become aware that the priest is staring at me.

I swallow and my throat is so dry that I can't form the words that tremble at the tip of my tongue.

The priest looks at me with a resigned air. He seems to be waiting for me to say something. What? What the hell am I supposed to say?

"Ask her again." Michael growls.

The priest draws in a breath, "Do you Karma West take Michael Byron Domenico Sovrano to be your husband, and promise to be faithful to him always, in joy and in pain, in health and in sickness, and to love him and honor him and obey him every day for the rest of your life?"

His voice slices through the nothingness in my head. Anger

thrums through my veins. Be faithful to him? Obey him? Love him? Are you freakin' kidding me?

I firm my lips as I stare back at him.

The priest glances from me to Michael who turns to me. He steps in front of me, then lowers his knees and thrusts his face into mine. "Answer the question," he growls.

"Fuck you," I say in a low voice, and his features brighten. His eyes gleam. Fuck, how sick is this man that when I insult him in front of everyone, he positively seems to relish it?

He places his big palms on my cheeks, and he squeezes down so my lips purse. He increases the pressure until a tear drop leaks from the corner of my eyes. "Say it," he snaps. "Tell me what I want to hear, Beauty."

Anger sluices a path through my veins. My vision tunnels and all my senses seem to pop. You want it, asshole? I am going to give you the answer you are looking for. "Yes," I force out the word. "Yes, I will."

"Good."

He straightens, steps back to stand next to me.

"Uh, do we have rings?" The priest blink rapidly.

Michael turns to me. "Her bouquet." He frowns. "Someone take the blasted thing from her."

Sebastian walks over, holds out his hand. When I don't move, he whispers in a soft voice, "Please, *principessa,* hand it over."

I glare up into his blue eyes. So similar to the alphahole standing next to me, yet so much warmer.

"*Principessa,*" he urges me and I extend the bouquet. He takes it, steps aside.

Michael grips my shoulder, applies enough pressure so I turn to face him. He slips a ring from his pocket and slides it over my left hand. A plain gold band, with a black diamond set in the center, surrounded by red sapphires. Huh. It fits… Of course, it does…

But the colors of the diamonds... They match my dress. How the hell had he guessed what colors I was going to wear? Of course, he may have seen me stitch the black dress on the closed-circuit cameras, but I'd only dyed my hair red this morning. How strange.

I glance up, in time to intercept an expression of... Possessiveness? Lust? A strange look filled with heat that he wipes off of his face instantly. I blink, captured by what I'd seen there for a second. Naked want... A yearning that struck me to my core. My pussy clenches and my fingers tremble as the priest asks, "What about the ring for the bridegroom?"

"Not for this bridegroom," Michael retorts.

I jerk my chin up, hold his once-more vacant gaze.

The priest clears his throat, "This...this is...ah...highly irregular, Capo."

No kidding. Like, of all the things that have happened so far, this particular aspect is the most shocking. A chuckle bubbles up and I stifle it.

Of course, the alphahole doesn't want to be constrained by a ring. While me... The bride must wear his mark of ownership at all times. Typical.

"Ah," the priest shuffles his feet, "in that case...you may now kiss the bride."

Michael steps forward. He notches a finger under my chin, angles it up as he lowers his face to mine. Closer, closer, the scent of him envelops me and a cloud of heat spools off of his body and crashes into me. I gasp, draw in a breath and the scent of him seems to infiltrate every cell in my body. His lips brush mine once. It's so soft, so unexpected, that I part my lips and he sweeps his tongue inside. He swipes his tongue across the seam of my lips, across my teeth, tangles with mine. His mouth closes over mine and he slurps from me like he's thirsty and I am his only sustenance. A moan bleeds from me and an answering groan rumbles up his chest. I step into him so my breasts are crushed into his chest. His entire body hardens, then a trembling grips him. He wraps his arm around my waist haul me to him as I slide my hand around his waist.

My fingers brush the dagger he wears at his waistband. I play with the sheath, then close my fingers around the handle of the knife. I draw it out as he winds his arm around my shoulder, the other slipping down over the curve of my hip. "Beauty," he breathes against my lips, "you're killing me—" He gasps. His eyelids snap open, his mouth parted slightly. He stares into my gaze. "You...you..." he growls, "you—"

I nod, "I stabbed you, and I am going to do it again." I pull back and he releases me. I raise the dagger, and this time, bring it down squarely in the middle of his chest.

27

Michael

I glance down at the dagger protruding from my chest, then up at her. The train of her black dress streams behind her. Her hair flows about her shoulders. She raises the dagger and the blood—my blood drips from her fingers. Her green eyes blaze at me, the look in them triumphant and stricken, at the same time. I hold her gaze, and in the depths of her eyes, I see myself reflected. I reach for her and she holds out her hand—the one without the dagger. Our fingers touch, cling together. Her lips part and my gaze drops to her mouth. The redness of her lipstick matches the scarlet that runs down the blade of the dagger.

"Beauty," I whisper, "what have you done?"

"I..." she swallows, "I didn't have a choice... I didn't mean to—" Her shoulders shudder. "I—"

Her beautiful features sway in front of my eyes. Black spots flicker at the sides of my vision. My knees seem to give way from under me.

I hear her scream and her fingers tighten around mine. The dagger slips from her fingers and clatters to the ground. The world tilts. Arms grab me from behind, and I shake them off. I steady myself, glance past her to find my brothers crowding in around us.

Sebastian reaches for her and I growl, "Don't fucking touch her."

I glance over their shocked faces until my gaze connects with Luca's. I glare at him, then lower my gaze to her face, then back to him. He nods. And a breath I hadn't been aware I was holding leaves me. I take in her pale features, her green eyes pooling with tears that run down her cheeks. I raise my palm, brush away the moisture on her delicate features.

"Shh," I bare my teeth at her, "you didn't think that I would die that easily did you?"

I tear at the front of the shirt and my buttons bounce to the floor. I glance down at the bleeding cut, then back at her. "You barely broke the skin," I drawl. "Seems I am going to not only discipline you but also instruct you on how to use weapons."

"Fuck you." Her chin wobbles, "I managed to hurt you. In my books, that's a win."

"You barely wounded me. You showed your cards too soon, Beauty."

Her breath heaves.

"I am afraid I am going to enjoy teaching you your place."

She stiffens. "You can go to hell," she snaps.

"Only if you'll come with me. Now that we are husband and wife, and all that."

"Fuck your sham of a marriage."

"It was very real, *mia cara,*" I smile at her broadly, "don't forget you still wear my ring."

She raises her left hand then begins to struggle with the ring on her finger. "Fuck, fuck, fuck," she snarls, "it won't come off."

"Of course, not." I smirk, "You didn't think I was going to leave anything to chance, did you?" I drum my fingers on my thigh, in part to distract from the pain in my chest. "It's half a size smaller, easy to push onto the finger, much more difficult to get off."

She stills, then raises her gaze to mine. "Bastard," she spits out, "how dare you?"

Behind me, the priest winces.

"Now you've shocked the Father."

Her cheeks tinge red. "The fuck I care?"

I click my tongue. "You're spirited, I give you that." I smirk, "I'll enjoy teaching you your place."

"Argh!" She makes a sound deep in her throat that seems to tug on my nerve-endings. The blood drains to my groin.

Then, Luca wraps his arm around her shoulders and urges her away from me. Her fingers drag against mine, as she pulls away. A shiver runs down my spine.

Nonna steps in front of her. I see her hand move, then the thud of a slap echoes around the church as her palm connects with Beauty's face.

"Stop," I call out. "She's my wife, mine to punish as I see fit."

Nonna's shoulders rise and fall. She turns, tips up her chin at me. Her features are flushed. She seems to compose herself, then nods at me, "See that you do." My grandmother pivots and walks out the way she came, through the side entrance of the church where, no doubt, her bodyguards are waiting for her.

"Take her to the basement." I jerk my chin at Luca.

Around me, my brothers stiffen, but none of them say anything. They wouldn't. They know better than to question my authority in front of the Don.

Beauty stares at me over her shoulder as Luca guides her away, Adrian in tow.

I don't take my attention off of her, until she's out of sight, out of the main door. My chest twinges, but I dismiss it. I glance down to find the front of my shirt sodden with blood.

I shrug off my jacket, then my tear off my shirt and press it into the wound.

"You need stitches." Christian murmurs, "I am calling for the doctor."

I am tempted to say I don't need to see a doctor, but I know better than taking foolish risks. I nod, as my father prowls over to me. "I hope you are not going to let this go unpunished." He looks me up and down, "She spilled the blood of a Capo; you know what that means."

I stiffen, "She's my wife. I decide how I am going to make her pay for what she did."

He chuckles, "No doubt, you can turn the consummation of the marriage into something that she will never forget."

I whip my chin up, glare at him. "Mind how you speak about her," I say through gritted teeth. "She's still mine."

"Not questioning that, son," he says in a soothing voice. "Just making sure you realize that this cannot be overlooked. When word of what happened gets out…" He shakes his head, "It will seriously undermine your position as being in the running as successor of the Don."

"And who will let news of this leak out?"

My father glances at the priest. I pull out the gun from the back of my waistband and shoot him in the forehead. The man collapses to the floor.

I turn to the Don, "That only leaves you as the weak point in this entire proceeding."

"You threatening me, son?" he asks in a mild tone. "Not even you would be foolish enough to do that."

"It was merely an observation." I tilt my head.

"As long as that's all it was." He bares his lips in the semblance of a smile, which is almost as sharklike as mine. Fuck! Apparently there is more of him in me than I'd like.

He glances around at the faces of my brothers, "I'll see the lot of you at our next meeting then."

Turning, he begins to walk away, then stops, "By the way, Michelangelo." He glances at me over his shoulder, "Congratulations."

He leaves by the side entrance. The door slams shut, the sound echoing around the space.

"Fucking fuck," I growl as I pull the shirt away from my chest. I glance down to where the blood flow seems to have lessened, then ball up my shirt and throw it on the floor. "What a fucking mess."

"Was that necessary?" Xander glances sideways at the priest's body, "Did you have to kill a man of god."

"I didn't have a choice."

"The man would have taken what happened here to the grave with him," he protests.

"And I made sure he did."

Xander grimaces, "And her... Did you have to send her to the basement?"

"It's where anyone who commits a crime against any of the *famiglia* is sent." I tilt my head.

"She's part of the *famiglia* now," Xander argues.

"She needs to prove herself first." Christian jerks his chin in my direction, "I agree with *fratellone,* here."

"You were very lucky," Massimo rumbles. "She missed your heart.

"She wasn't aiming for it," I retort.

Silence descends as the guys glance at me.

"You sure of that?" Sebastian drawls, "because from where I was standing, she sure seemed to be aiming to kill."

"To injure, at the very least," I agree, "but did she want to kill me?" I raise a shoulder, "I am not so sure."

"So why send her to the basement?" Christian frowns.

"Why not?"

"Because she's your wife?" Xander offers.

"And she stabbed me."

"As you said, she wasn't aiming for your heart," he retorts. "In fact, the wound isn't that deep; you've lost blood but you'll recover."

"She attacked me in front of the Don," I say steadily. "I don't need him seeing me as weak, no matter that it was my own wife who took a dagger to me."

"Bullshit." Xander scowls, "Since when do you let father steer your actions?" He prowls over to me, "No Mika, you are up to something else here."

I look him and down, "Are you going to tell me how I am supposed to treat my wife?"

Xander hesitates, "I don't presume to tell you anything, *fratellone*."

He murmurs, "I am merely pointing out that she is entitled to basic human rights."

"Is she though, after what she did?" I hold his gaze steadily and he glances away.

"I know you are angry, and I am not condoning what she did," he murmurs. "Still she is a woman, and she is the one you love..."

"Love?" I chuckle aloud, "You really think I am in love with her?"

"Why else would you marry her?"

I open my mouth to protest and Xander holds up his hand. "The way you look at her, Mika," his gaze softens, "it's the glance of a man obsessed."

"Obsessed with ensuring that I get the respect that is due to me from my own wife." I bare my teeth, "And that is the last I will entertain on this issue."

Xander hesitates, and Christian walks over to him. He claps a hand on Xander's shoulder, "Let the Capo handle this the way he thinks best."

Xander scowls at him, "You are a harsh man, but you are not heartless, Mika."

I tilt my head. "Not looking for a character reference." I glance around the assembled faces. "And that's the last I will entertain in this regard, do I make myself clear?"

The rest of them keep silent.

"Do I?"

They nod. "Yes, *fratel*—Capo," Sebastian replies.

"Yes, Capo." Christian adds.

"You got it, Capo." Massimo rumbles.

Xander draws in a breath. I hold his gaze and he nods. "As you wish," he says stiffly.

"Good." I walk over to where she had dropped the knife, then scoop it up. I wipe it on my shirt then slide it back into the sheath at my waist. "When does the doctor get here?" I glance at Christian.

"I sent the chopper for her; she won't be long."

"Good." I turn to Sebastian, "Take care of the body."

. . .

An hour and a half later, I've been stitched up by the doctor who had departed after administering an antibiotic shot. I change into a fresh pair of slacks and a shirt, then head down the stairs of my mansion. As I descend, it gets cooler. When I hit the lower ground level, it's at least ten degrees cooler than what I had left behind. That's the architecture of these old homes for you. The basements were always cool enough so you could use the space as a natural refrigerator to store food… Or temporarily keep dead bodies… As I have done in the past.

I head down the corridor to the door at the far end. I grab the handle, twist it and shove the door open. Step inside the gloom that's illuminated by the light streaming in from the lone window near the ceiling.

On the far side, there is a single bed and on it, Beauty is curled up. Her black dress slashes across the white of the mattress. The train flows behind her and trails on the floor. Her red hair flows about her shoulders and over the side of the bed. Her body is curved into the fetal position. Her slender fingers pillow her cheek.

I let the door slam shut behind me. The sound echoes through the cell and she visibly jolts. Her eyelids snap open. She spots me but doesn't move. I prowl over to stand over her. She tips her chin up, meets my gaze.

"What do you want?" she snarls, and a chuckle boils up. This woman... She, seriously, has some gumption. After stabbing me in the chest, at our wedding, she acts as if she's the injured party. Fuck, if that isn't hot. I swallow down my mirth, school all emotion from my face.

"On your knees."

28

Karma

"What the hell does that mean?" I scowl up at the man who towers over me. Michael's a tall guy, at least six-feet four-inches in height, but in this light, and with the angle at which he is poised over me, he looks positively massive. His shoulders block out my line of sight, his dark eyes seem to merge with the blackness around him. My heart beat ratchets up. Shit, this is not good. I am in a cell, on my own, with the man—okay, technically, with my husband—who is not in the least bit happy with me. I glance around the cell and he shakes his head.

"Don't even think about it." His lips curl, "If by some miracle, you get out of the cell, the only way out is up and my brothers are standing guard as we speak."

"So the entire family is on this?" I swallow. "Why am I not surprised? After all, torturing helpless women must be your family's past time."

"Hmm." He drums his fingers on his massive chest, then winces.

My stomach tightens. So, I had managed to wound him, after all, though you can't see it, with how he's standing with his spine straight, and dressed in clean clothes. You wouldn't guess I had had my dagger—okay, his dagger—buried in his chest less than a few hours ago. Again, that may be a gross exaggeration, considering he is nowhere near death's door. Bastard looks like he's ready for an evening out in those tailored pants and shirt.

He lowers his arm to his side, then jerks his chin. "You heard me," he drawls, "Get on your knees, Beauty."

"And if I refuse?"

"I'll make you," he props his massive hands on his lean waist, "and trust me, you don't want that to happen."

I glower back at him.

"Do it, Beauty." He lowers his tone to a hush, "Now."

His voice slices through the thoughts in my head. Only when the room rights do I realize that I am sitting up on the bed. Without taking my gaze off of his, I swing my legs up on the bed, then behind me as I push up to kneeling position.

"Happy?" I snap.

He shakes my head, "You know that's not what I meant." He stares down at the floor then back at me.

"What, you expect me to read your mind?" I huff.

"Don't try my patience," he murmurs.

"Or what?"

"Or." He moves so quickly, I blink. The next second, he's grabbed me by the back of my neck and hauled me up to my feet, on the bed. My heels, which I still hadn't removed, dig into the mattress and I totter. With his other hand, he grabs me at the apex of my thighs. His big palm closes around my pussy and he lifts me down to the floor

I totter on my heels and he holds me there for a few seconds until I've regained my balance. Then he releases his hold on me, only to clamp a heavy hand on my shoulder. He applies enough pressure that I have to sink down on my knees. Good thing the dress is so thick that it cushions them from the dirty floor. My poor dress, it's never going to recover from this assault… First, by the droplets of his blood which had splashed onto the bodice, and now, from the filth on the floor. Ugh! And this is so not the time to be thinking about the state of my dress. Not that I intend to wear this one again. No, it's served its purpose and it is expendable. Like me.

Stop it, stop it. Don't give up even before you've started fighting. After all you've only begun this… Whatever it is, for which he brought you down here. If he had thought that he would intimidate me… He is succeeding.

My heart slams into my ribcage as I kneel there, while he looms over me like some stupid medieval knight… Only, he's not a knight. He is a devil, a monster, a man with no remorse, no emotions, no feelings. A brute who takes what he wants, when he wants, and there is no reasoning with him.

I'd known all this when I had reached for his dagger. Call it impulsive; call it a sense of inevitability which had gripped me. When I'd realized that he was tracking my sister and her new husband; that he wouldn't hesitate to hurt them; that nothing I said or did would, ultimately, help me in any way; that once I was married to him, he'd take full advantage of me… And then kill me...

I'd known then, that this is a fight to the finish. My life is already in danger. Likely, I am never walking away from this. No way, am I also going to endanger Summer's life. No, I had to do something about it. I had seen my opportunity and seized it. I hadn't even realized what I intended to do; not until my fingers had brushed the handle of the dagger. I had pulled it out, and I had not hesitated. Had I meant to kill him? Honestly, I don't know. Had I, for one second, thought that I would actually succeed in hurting him? I'd hoped so.

At least, I had managed to cause him some pain… Had put a halt to the sham of the proceedings. My fingers brush the palm on my left ring finger. Yeah, except for the stupid wedding ring that refuses to come off, which insists the wedding ceremony was, unfortunately, very real. I swallow, tip up my chin at him. Damn, if I am going to let him break my spirit… At least, not that easily. "What are you going to do?" I demand.

"That's what I am trying to figure out." He stares down at me, an expression of something—curiosity, a certain interest even in his glance as if he's trying to figure me out. Shit, that's the last thing I want, to be seen as a challenge by him.

And yet.. I can't stand down, I can't. Something inside of me... That same darkness that has crawled at the edges of my consciousness all this while, insists that I stand up to him. That I confront him, defy him, make him realize that he can't just bend me to his will that easily.

I pretend to yawn, then pat my fingers to my lips. "Well whatever it is, you'd best get on with it." I look him up and down, "My knees are already beginning to ache."

"It's not only your knees which will be hurting by the time I'm through with you." His lips curl, "Unless that's your plan, hmm?" He circles around me and I sense him sizing me up... For what? What could he possibly have in mind that could be worse than anything he's done to me so far?

"Maybe you think that if you goad me enough, I'll lose my control, that I'll do something to slip up, something that you can take advantage of and try to escape, hmm?"

"You've already told me your family is guarding the entrance to the dungeon—"

"Basement," he corrects me.

"Funny, from where I am, it resembles a torture chamber."

He laughs, "You think this is a torture chamber?" His grin widens, "Wonder what you'll think when I take you into the real torture room."

"Oh," I swallow, "you're joking right?"

He arches an eyebrow. "Have I ever joked with you?"

Of course, he hasn't. The alphahole doesn't have a single funny bone in his entire body. Hell, even if I were to tickle him, he'd probably just respond with that glowering expression, before telling me that I bore him.

My pulse begins to race and sweat laces my palms. Shit, shit, shit. Had I actually thought that this man was going to let go of me that easily? Wait, actually, I hadn't thought much at all. But the fact that he has an honest-to-god torture chamber down here, one that he plans to use on me... Shit, I am not ready for that. Seriously, not.

"So what…" my voice cracks and I clear my throat, "what are you going to do next?"

"It's more about what you are going to do next, Beauty."

How I hate that nickname. I am going to find a way to get back at him for this. For making me feel so helpless, like I am completely at his mercy, which I am… But hell, does he have to rub it in this way? Of course, he holds the power here, doesn't mean he has to go all villainous on me and threaten me without saying anything. Argh!

I fold my fingers in front to stop them from trembling, then force myself to meet his gaze. *Don't say it, don't say it.* But there's no other way out. Best I pretend to play along… At least, for the time being. At least, until I have figured out a plan of action.

I set my jaw, "What…what do you want me to do?"

His pauses, taps a finger against his chin, then nods, "Strip."

"Excuse me?"

"You heard me. Take off your wedding dress, wife."

I grit my teeth, hating the fact that I can't tell him off for calling me that. Loathing the fact that he is, on this account, at least accurate. I am his wife…technically.

"Don't make me wait," he says in a casual voice, "and don't even think of disobeying me. You know I can strip you of this dress very easily, I am giving you a choice here."

"Oh, yeah?" I scoff, "What's that?"

"You can strip your dress on your own steam and then I can fuck you, or *I* can strip off your dress and then..." He bares his teeth, "I can fuck you."

29

Michael

A trembling grips her. A shudder runs down her spine. She squares her shoulders, then shoves her hair back from her face, with trembling fingers. Hmm, my Beauty is all sass, but deep down, she's scared. Good. She should be. Right now, I am not sure, exactly, what I am going to do to her, but anticipation is half the enjoyment, after all. Besides, I love it when I surprise myself... I relish it even more when my opponent surprises me. And make no mistake, Beauty here, is the deadliest enemy I have ever faced. I'd underestimated her once and she'd drawn my dagger on me... I am not gonna let her pull a fast one on me again.

I snap my fingers, "Don't keep me waiting." I fold my arms across my chest, stare down my nose at her.

She sets her jaw, then draws in a breath. Her chest rises and falls and the peaks of her breasts threaten to overflow the low neck of her gown. I widen my stance, watch as she tips her chin up.

"You'll have to help me." She scowls at me.

"What do you mean?"

"My zipper," she snaps. "I can't reach it; you'll have to help me with it."

Che cazzo! "Are you serious? You want me to help you with the zipper?"

"You want me out of this dress?" She arches an eyebrow, "Then you'll have to help me."

"If this is a joke of some kind..."

"It's not a joke, you asshole," she snaps. "I had help putting it on, and now I need help taking it off." Her cheeks heat. She glances away, then up at me. "Trust me, I don't feel like asking for your help on anything either, but it's not like I have a choice."

Perhaps it's the ring of truth I hear in her tone, or the fact that, clearly, she is uncomfortable asking me to help... Or the very feminine blush on her cheeks that, somehow, touches a place deep inside of me.

Either way, I find myself moving around to sink down behind her, and onto the train of her dress that is piled around her. She pulls her hair over one shoulder as I reach for the zipper and being to lower it. The rasp seems to echo around the empty space. The fabric parts, revealing the ivory of her skin. Goosebumps rise as the cool air touches her back. I lower the zipper all the way down to the small of her back.

The dress slides down one side, revealing the curve of her shoulder. I take in the graceful arch, the tendrils of hair that cling to the column of her neck, the ridges of her spine and ribcage under the ivory of her skin. Something hot stabs at my chest. My heart stutters. My groin hardens. I lean in, touch my lips to the exposed shoulder and she shivers. I press tiny kisses up the curve of her shoulder, push aside the ringlets on the nape of her neck and kiss the soft skin there. A moan bleeds from her and she lowers her chin, giving me further access. I push aside the dress, down her other shoulder. It slides down, then stops when it catches over her breast. I shove the dress and it falls to the crook of her elbows. I slide one hand around to cup her breast, and she shudders. I bring my forefinger and thumb to her nipple and squeeze. A soft cry falls from her lips and I am instantly hard. I slip my other hand around to squeeze her other breast. I massage them, pinch the nipples and she leans back into me.

"Michael," she pants, "oh, my god, Michael."

I continue to knead her breasts, pausing only to pinch her nipples, again and again. Her entire body trembles. She arches her spine, throws her head back and into my chest as she stares up at me from under heavy eyelids.

"Michael, please, please..." she cries, "please, Michael."

I release one breast, slide my hand down her belly to cup her pussy. "Part your legs," I command, and she instantly widens her stance. I pinch her clit ring and she shudders.

"Oh, fuck." She writhes in my arms, "Oh, my fucking god."

"Your mouth, Beauty," I murmur. "Your dirty mouth is a fucking turn on, you know that?"

I thrust two fingers inside her soaking channel and her pussy instantly clamps down on the intrusion. I push my fingers in and out of her, even as I continue to massage her breast. I pinch down on the nipple again and twist, and her entire body bucks. "Your breasts are so fucking sensitive." I lean into her as I slide a third finger inside of her. I continue to fuck her with my fingers as I twist her nipple. She screams and her shoulders shake.

She thrusts up her chin, opens her mouth. "Kiss me," she demands. "Fucking kiss me, already."

"*Gesù Cristo,*" I swear, "you're something else, you know that?" I lower my face, then close my mouth over hers. I tangle my tongue with hers, swipe it across her teeth, across the seam of her inner lips, as I bury my fingers deep inside her, then curve them.

A groan bleeds from her and her entire body quakes. The scent of her arousal surrounds me, sinks into my skin, coils around me, and threatens to bind me to her. My belly knots and my groin hardens. My dick lengthens and my balls draw up, and I know if I don't bury myself inside her sweet, hot center, I am going to come in my pants.

Fuck me. I did not mean for it to get this far, did not come here to lose control. I meant to punish her, to show her that she could not simply disregard my rules and do as she wants. That, no way, will she disobey me again, let alone pull a knife on me. The same dagger that I had held over a flame, and allowed to cool before sliding it into the sheath at my hip.

I release her breast, reach for the knife and pull it out, then hold the blade to her throat.

I sense her stiffen, even as she continues to kiss me back. I draw the blade down to her breast, circle her nipple with it. She shivers, tries to speak, but I absorb the sounds. I continue to finger fuck her, even as I thrust my tongue in and out of her mouth, drag the blade down the curve of her breast to rest it in the space between the mounds.

Her entire body trembles, her pussy clenches around my fingers, and I know she's close, so very close. She pushes down with her hips, chasing her release, and I pull my fingers out of her and release her mouth at the same time.

She blinks, stares up at me as I press the edge of my knife into her chest. A trickle of blood runs down her belly, streaking across the black of her dress. It's fucking arousing, watching that combination. So similar to the red of her hair.

"Why the hell did you stop?" She pants, "I was so close."

I smile and she flushes. "You better finish what you started, *stronzo.*"

I chuckle, "I see you've been brushing up on your Italian."

"I see you've been brushing up on your alphaholeness." She bares her teeth, and fuck me, but her anger is such a turn on.

I wrap my fingers about the nape of her neck, then rise to my feet and pull her up with me. The dress falls to the floor and she stands there, clad only in her lacy thong, surrounded by the yards of fabric that make up her dress.

She trembles and her eyes gleam. "How dare you?" she snarls. "How dare you withhold my orgasm?"

"Because I can?" I keep my fingers around the nape of her neck as I circle to stand in front of her, "Because I'd prefer to mark you first; because you need to earn every single orgasm, from now on."

"Fuck you." She tosses her head, "If you think I am going to do a single thing that you ask of me, then you are sadly mistaken."

"We'll see." I press the tip of the knife into the skin between her breasts, and she shivers. "You may deny it, but everything in you yearns for my touch, for me to etch my sign of ownership into your skin, for me to tattoo the symbol of my possession onto you, to own you, to dominate you, as only I can."

Her pupils dilate and her breathing grows more ragged. She wants everything I can do to her. I have no doubt about it. She wants my body, wants the pleasure I can wring from her, yet she resists me, resists submitting to me, resists allowing herself to trust me. Not that I have given her any reason to do so, but if she wants me to complete what I started then she is going to put herself in my hands completely. I step back, wipe the blade on my sleeve, then slip it into my sheath.

Turning I head for the exit, when she calls out, "Wait."

I keep walking.

"Damnit, Michael, stop."

I reach the door, and she draws in a breath. "Please," she whispers, "please stop."

"What's that?" I pause, but don't turn, "I don't think I heard you."

"Bastard," she bites out, and I push open the door.

"Please," she begs, "please stop, Michael."

I turn to glance at her over my shoulder.

"Are you going to leave me here?"

"It would seem that way."

"But...but...it's freezing."

"Those yards of fabric," I glance down at the dress strewn about her feet, "I am sure they can finally be put to good use."

She pales. "I hate you," she declares. "I fucking hate you."

I tilt my head, "Which doesn't matter to me one bit, you understand?"

"What do you want from me?" She folds her fingers at her sides, "Why are you doing this to me?"

"You brought this on yourself, Beauty, when you tried to kill me."

"You kidnapped me first."

"So?" I look her up and down, "I am the one who holds the power here."

"Like you'll ever let me forget that."

"No, but it's time you realize how serious I am about you acknowledging it too."

"And if I don't?"

I bare my teeth, "I am looking forward to convincing you otherwise."

Turning, I head out of the door, then stop. "There's one more thing," I stare at her over my shoulder, "you will not come until I give you permission."

30

Karma

I pull the train of my dress around my shoulders, and huddle into the mattress of the narrow single bed. Seriously, this entire thing sucks. Why the hell had he left me behind? I mean, who leaves their wife in the basement of his house on their wedding night? Michael fucking Byron does.

Yeah, yeah, I know what you are thinking. When it suits me, I am his wife, and when it doesn't, I am not. And isn't that the truth of it? I bring up my hand, stare at the ring on my finger. The black diamond in the center is smooth enough that I can see myself reflected in it. And the rubies surrounding it... Wow!

Honestly, if I had chosen a ring for myself, it would be this. Not that I had spent much time thinking about my wedding... Considering I had been too busy trying to focus on my fledgling career as a designer. And then there was that little issue that I had been in the foster care system until my sister Summer had turned eighteen and found a way to become my legal guardian.

So no, weddings and wedding dresses and wedding rings weren't exactly the kinds of dreams I went to sleep with every night. And yet, I had known exactly the kind of gown I'd wanted. I hadn't hesitated when I had stitched it. And the ring… OMG, the ring… Fact is, I love it. And I hate myself for it. And I hate that he knows exactly what I like. And the fact that he knows how to play my body, and that he knows that holding back my orgasms is a surefire way to break me down.

He had given me a taste of how good it could be between us, and yet, he hadn't yet fucked me. I squeeze my thighs together. The way it had felt to have his fingers in me as he had twisted my nipples… Goosebumps pop on my skin and it's not only because it's cold. The thick fabric of the train of my dress is actually quite a comfortable blanket… It's annoying how he'd been right about that as well.

Is there anything that over-the-top, control freak isn't right about? I turn on my back, pull up the skirts of my dress. I had worn it after he'd left because it had felt like the quickest way to stay warm, and to a certain extent, that was true too. Except, it's uncomfortable to sleep in it… Or wait, maybe I am uncomfortable because the bastard hadn't let me come. He hadn't let me orgasm, damn him. And he'd told me I can't climax until he tells me to, but hell, if I am not going to try.

I pull up the skirt of my dress, and making sure I am still covered by the train, I slide my fingers into my panties. I thrust a digit inside my sensitized channel and gasp when I find myself wet. Pinpricks of pleasure radiate out from my touch, and I add a second finger, then a third.

It's not enough, damn it. Nothing will be enough to plug that nothingness that yawns in my core, but this will have to do for now. I begin to fuck myself, weave my fingers in and out, as the tension begins to build at the base of my spine. I increase the intensity of my movements, and my entire body shakes. I squeeze my legs together, close my eyes as I shove my fingers in and out of my melting channel. And again. And again. The waves build up from my core, radiate out and up my spine, I don't stop, I keep going. Come on. Come on. I am so close now. The waves spiral upward, and just as the climax threatens to spill over, his command echoes in my ears, *You will not come until I give you permission.*

I yank the fingers from my core and the orgasm recedes. The emptiness inside of me seems to grow bigger, thicker, until it envelops all of me, consumes me. Sweat beads my upper lip, sticks to my palms. Heat flushes my skin and I throw off my cover… I mean, the goddamn train. I swing my legs over the side of the bed, glance about the space.

He must have cameras here…somewhere, right? I stare at the walls, glance up at the ceiling… There! Above the doorway is the unmistakable eye of a camera. Aha… So he does have eyes on me, after all… Had he just seen my performance? Had he taken in how I'd almost orgasmed?

Does he realize just how close I am to losing my freakin' mind? My stomach rumbles and my tongue sticks to the roof of my mouth. Bet my hair is a rat's nest, given how I had writhed on the goddamn bed earlier, too. Not that it is my most pressing concern, but a girl has a right to be concerned about her looks, right? So what, if I am his stupid prisoner? Surely, he won't deny me my basic rights… Like using a goddam, proper bathroom.

I stare at the bucket in the corner of the room. If he thinks I am going to be using that, he has another think coming. I have my dignity, goddamn it. I am not peeing in a stupid bucket, no bloody way.

I shuffle my weight from foot to foot. What the hell can I use to get his attention? Something that will ensure he comes back here…?

I take in the space, the light from the single bulb in the ceiling that came on earlier. At least, he hadn't switched that off. It would have been goddamn creepy if he had, not that I am afraid of the dark… But still, I prefer not to think about this space with the lights off. I shudder.

I glance about the space again… Nothing… There is no piece of wood, or a nail…or anything I can use… And the goddam bucket… I refuse to touch it. Ugh. No, he has to come for me. He has to get me out of here… And there is only way I can think of to force his hand.

I stare up at the unmistakable eye of the camera above the door, then I begin to undress.

31

Michael

"What the hell is she doing?" I glare at the screen which is linked to the camera that's trained on the cell. Karma stares into the lens—of course, she'd figured out where the camera is. Not that I had tried to hide it from her or anything. It had been an interesting experiment, on my part, to see how long it would take her to spot the camera… And clearly, she hadn't realized she was being watched when she had writhed under the train of her dress as she had tried to make herself come.

That had been hot, and so fucking erotic… I am not ashamed to say that I had grabbed my dick and jerked off in tandem. And when she had stopped just short of actually orgasming...that's when I had stopped too... And fuck, if that hadn't been a surprise. Why the hell hadn't I let myself come? Not out of some twisted sense of wanting to keep her company as she stayed unsatisfied, that's for damn sure.

Of course, I could have taken her earlier… I had had her in my arms, my dick nestled in the valley between her ass cheeks, and though I had been fully dressed, it hadn't stopped me from rubbing myself against her curves. Like the pervert that I am.

And I had opted to walk away from her. I had thought I was denying her… Turns out I was denying myself, as well. As she had worked her fingers in and out of her cunt—not that I had been able to see her sweet pussy, but my imagination had filled in the gaps—I had mirrored her rhythm. Speeding up when she had and pausing with her. I hadn't been able to take my eyes off of her; had watched as she had jumped out of bed, glanced around the space, then turned to face the camera, as if coming to a decision.

Then, she had begun to strip.

And *maledizione,* I can't stop myself from taking in every inch of exposed skin—as she pushes the dress down her shoulders, then down her flat stomach, as she wriggles her hips and eases the dress down her legs, letting it fall about her ankles, along with her panties. She straightens, kicks aside her clothes, and the breath whooshes out of me.

Fuck me, but she is naked. Absolutely, completely naked. Except for her gorgeous hair that flows about her shoulders and curtains her breasts so the pink nipples peek out from between the strands. Her hips are rounded, her belly flat, before it leans into the dip of her sweet slit, encased in the fleshy folds of her luscious pussy. I tap on the screen, zoom in to her core and spot the glint of metal—fuck me, it's that damn clit ring of hers, the one that drives me crazy. That makes me want to thrust my head between her legs and bite down on that ring and tug so she feels the pull all the way to her nipples—yeah, that ring. Except for that adornment, her skin is completely bare.

I had touched her there, so I knew she had done as instructed and shaved between her legs… Hell, I had instructed Cassandra to make sure that she did it. So, I knew that she had followed my instructions, but to see her like this—full frontal, fully nude, bared to my gaze as she props her palm on her hip, bends a knee and strikes a pose, as if daring me to take in her glorious nakedness.

And I do… I zoom out again, so I can see her in totality. Those high cheekbones, parted rosebud lips, her slender throat, those high pointed breasts, curvy hips, fleshy thighs that I want to mark with my blade, before I run the tip around her pussy, then trail it down her clit, down her inner thighs, to those narrow ankles and tapered feet. I want to suck on her toes as I draw lazy circles up her calves, until I reached her plump behind... Which I, absolutely, want to bite down on as I slide my fingers inside her forbidden back channel, opening her up, readying her for my intrusion. First with the handle of my knife, then with my dick. I drag my fingers up the handle of my knife and my dick lengthens.

Transferring the knife to my left hand, I reach down between my legs and grasp myself again. I pump myself once, twice. My cock elongates...but it's not enough. Fucker knows it's my hand that's doing the work and it wants more... So much more. It wants her cunt, her pussy, her tight, melting channel to sink into. Her pussy to clamp down on my cock, her cunt to milk me as I come inside her and fill her up and mark her as mine. Only mine.

The door behind me opens and I clench the knife more tightly. "Michael, what the hell is happening—?"

"Not now," I snap, without turning around. "Get the fuck out, Luca."

I sense him hesitate, then the door closes and his footsteps recede.

Yeah, so my brother had almost seen me jerking off... Something that hasn't happened since we were teenagers. Not that he had seen me... Not that it would have mattered if he had... As long as he didn't see my queen, naked and exposed to me on the screen.

I squeeze my dick, then drag my fingers up my cock, as she slides her fingers down between her pussy lips. She thrusts one finger, then another, inside her channel, then adds the third. She continues to push her fingers in and out of her cunt, in and out. Her breasts jiggle and her hair sways about her shoulders, as she tips up her chin and holds my gaze. Her mouth opens, and I can almost hear her moan of pleasure as she continues to fuck herself. She licks her lips and I swear I come right then.

The blood drains to my groin and my balls harden. She increases the pace of her movements and so do I, mirroring her rhythm as she thrusts out her chest, brings up a palm to cup one breast. She twists her nipple and lust roars in my veins. I reach forward, glare at the screen as she moves her hand to the other breast, gives it the same treatment.

Fucking fuck. My thigh muscles grow rock hard; the pressure at the base of my spine tightens. I am so fucking close, so on the edge. Heat suffuses my skin and my dick screams for release. I cup my balls and squeeze as, on screen, the witch smiles. Huh?

Her eyes gleam; she tosses her hair as she lowers her hand to her side. She pulls her fingers out of her cunt, holds her hand up. The moisture on it glistens and, fuck me, but my mouth waters. Maintaining eye contact, she licks each of her fingers, one by one, making a meal out of it, and my balls draw up. That's when she bends and draws her dress up over her shoulders. What the hell?

She turns her back on the camera, heads toward the bed. She pulls her train over her body, covering herself from neck to toe completely, then she turns her back on me, and the *strega* falls asleep. I swear, she switches off, just like that, for she doesn't move. Not a peep out of her. She sinks into slumber as I watch her prone figure.

I glance down at my raging hard-on, wanting to get myself off. And I could. I could continue pumping my shaft until I come. Only, it's not going to be anywhere near as satisfying as coming inside of her.

Damn woman had gone toe-to-toe with me, and had defeated me at my own game… I stare at the screen as a chuckle bursts out of me. *Well, well… Beauty, this round is yours. But you had better be prepared for what's coming next.*

I grab my handkerchief, wipe my cock, then tuck it away. I clean my fingers, shove the piece of cloth in my pocket, then rise to my feet.

32

Karma

I rub my cheek into the soft pillow and snuggle in. Warmth surrounds me, cocoons me, sinks into my body. I slide my hand across the mattress and the bed is so comfortable. My muscles are so relaxed, my entire body seems to be floating on some kind of cloud. Hmm. I try to turn and find something heavy around my waist holds me down. I try to pull away, and the weight around my middle intensifies. I crack open my eyes, glance down to find a thick arm about my waist. Huh? Thick fingers that lead to a wide wrist, which is attached to a sculpted forearm.

I manage to turn, enough to take in the tattoo of a knife on his tanned skin. It sports an intricate handle and the blade features a single eye. The blade points toward his fingers and the overall effect screams danger and caution. The corded muscles of his forearm wind up to massive biceps which are twice the size of my neck, at least, so it seems. I gulp, follow the arm to where it is attached to wide shoulders, a chest so broad that it blocks out everything else from my sight. A smattering of hair covers those sculpted pecs…which are demarcated by a white bandage that is taped vertically across his sternum. The contrast of the white against his darker skin is a shock. As is the fact that his chest is decorated with tattoos. Tattoos? Whoa, and there are so many of them.

I take in the design of a knife, the blade of which is painted with fire. Next to that is a design of a knife with the blade featuring roses. Then, another tattoo of a knife, with the blade featuring the sun; another one in which the blade is filled with stars; one in which a snake winds around the blade… Wow… And that's just on the skin I can see. How many more knives does this man have inked on his skin? Why is he so obsessed with them? And P.S. How the hell did I get here? In his bed, with him wrapped around me like a boa constrictor around its prey. Ugh, why the hell did I have to come up with that comparison in my mind?

I tip my chin up, take in that thick hair that falls over his forehead. Those dark eyelashes that fan over his cheekbones, the hooked nose, that thin upper lip, the pouty lower lip, that square jaw of his… And have I told you about his lips? Full, dreamy lips that look so hard but are so soft to kiss.

Again… How the hell did I end up here, anyway? Once more, I try to move out from under his arm, and this time, he hauls me to his chest. "Stop struggling," he rumbles, "I am trying to get some rest."

"*You* are trying to get some rest?"

I stare at his relaxed features. He looks almost content… Asshole. He'd spirited me away from that stupid cell—not that I miss it, by the way... And also, that reminds me, I need to pee… I really have to pee; I wriggle my hips and something stabs into the valley between my butt cheeks.

It can't be… Uh, it's not…uh, his dick? Of course, it is… Bastard's all aroused and I don't think it's only because of morning wood.

"Let go of me," I hiss. "Honestly, how dare you bring me here?"

"Would you rather I'd left you in that cell?"

I still.

"Thought not." His lips curl, "Best get your rest while you can, Beauty."

"I will not."

"Trust me, you are going to need it."

"Oh, yeah, and for what might that be?"

The next moment I squeak as the world tilts. I gasp, then glance up into those deep blue eyes of his. His arms bracket me on either side of my head, and he manages to keep most of his weight off of me, except for his hips, which are flush against mine. His thick length stabs into the soft valley between my thighs, and I almost moan aloud at how good it feels. Oh, yeah, he's naked under the covers. And so am I…for I can feel every thick, fat inch of his cock as it happily nestles against my core.

My belly quivers, my thighs clench, and my cunt…argh! My cunt seems to curl in on itself in anticipation. *Down, stupid pussy, you don't get to be this needy. He's the monster who kidnapped you for revenge, remember? He forced you to marry him. And now he's your husband. And I'm his wife, and uh…! Doesn't that mean I have to indulge in certain wifely duties?* My throat seems to dry up. I lick my lips and his gaze drops to my mouth.

Oh, my god, when he watches me with that single-minded intensity, I can forget that there is a world outside of this cocoon, which is composed of his body, his chest, his scent… His heat, that flows around me, pins me to the bed, the force of his dominance a low-pitched hum that sinks into my blood and coils straight down to my clit. I draw in a breath and he jerks his chin up. His gaze holds mine. Dark, deep, so many secrets and yet, underneath all that there is a vulnerability.

What the fuck? This man has no weaknesses. Besides, any possible empathy he had for me is probably gone, now that I took a knife to him. Gah, what had I been thinking, with that pathetic attempt at trying to wound him? I should have known he was much too strong to be disabled that way. But I had gone with my instinct... And see where that got me? Under him…in his bed, surrounded by him. OMG.

I swallow, then slap my palms against his chest, "Let me the hell go."

"No."

"How the hell did you bring me here?"

"How do you think?"

"How the hell did you bring me here without my even realizing it?"

"It's easy when you sleep like the dead."

My cheeks heat. That much is true. I sleep like the proverbial log… Once I fall asleep, a bomb could go off next to me and I wouldn't realize it. I purse my lips together, "Some of us sleep with a clear conscience, while others..." I scowl at him, "clearly, are haunted by the screams of those they have killed."

His gaze intensifies. For a second, the expression on his face is bleak, then he nods, "That much is true."

I blink. "It is?"

He nods. "I was twelve when I killed my first man. It was my father's idea."

"What do you mean?"

"He put a gun in my hands, told me it was time I became a man. He had his men drag out a traitor from among them, and—"

"It was your job to kill him?" I whisper.

He nods.

"And you did…kill him?"

He nods again, "One shot between the eyes." He forms his fingers into the shape of a gun, places his forefinger and middle finger in the center of my forehead. "Boom." He mimes pulling a trigger and I flinch.

He drags his fingers down my nose, across my lips, to the hollow at the base of my neck. My pulse rate speeds up as he swipes his fingers down to the already healing scratch between my breasts… The tiny wound that he had inflected on me with his knife.

"Does it hurt?"

I shake my head and he digs his fingers into the scratch, reopening it. A sliver of pain fires across my nerve-endings. I wince. He glances down and I follow his gaze to find the blood seeping down my belly. He removes his fingers, only to bend his head and slurp at the open wound. A shiver of something—lust, fear, maybe a mix of the two?—ladders up my spine. He licks the scratch again, then glances up at me, "Does that disgust you, Beauty?" He tilts his head, "Me drinking your blood."

"No." My voice cracks, and I clear my throat. "No." I shake my head, "Strangely, I find it reassuring."

"Reassuring?"

"It confirms to me that you are human, for some reason. It tells me that you don't hide your proclivities. It..." I swallow, "it affirms that you don't shy away from what your heart wants, and that... That is something."

"Is it?"

I nod. "Most people go through life trying to ignore what they really are deep inside, but not you." I peer into his face. "What you see is what you get with you. You wear your likes and dislikes on your sleeve; you don't hesitate to declare what you want and go after it. You are brutally honest about your intentions, and for that, I am grateful."

"You are, huh?" he says in a strange tone. "I kidnapped you, Beauty. Held you to the marriage that your father had promised me."

"And I stabbed you for it."

"I locked you up in a cell as punishment. I withheld orgasms from you—"

"It's called edging," I murmur.

"I'm aware." His eyebrows rise, "Though I am not sure how a nineteen-year-old fashion designer whose claim to fame is hawking her clothes—"

"Designs." I scowl, "Thought I corrected you on that already."

"—at a flea market—"

"Camden Market is a world-renowned space for artists," I counter.

"—knows the term for an S & M technique, is something I am keen to find out more about."

"It's just...stuff I picked up along the way."

"Is that right?"

I nod, "Just like you learned everything about knives… Let's just say, I read up a lot of informative literature about BDSM."

"You did, huh?"

I bite the inside of my lip. "For example, I know that you like to indulge in knife play."

"Oh?"

"And blood play."

"Hmm." He tilts his head, "Tell me more about my depraved, filthy tastes, Beauty."

"What if I told you that I have always wanted to know how it would feel to be at the receiving ends of both of those?"

"I wouldn't think you meant it."

"And what if I said I do?" I tip up my chin.

"Then I would call you a liar."

"Why would you say that?" I frown.

"Because you don't know what you are talking about. You don't know what you really want."

"And I won't know, either. Until I try it." I set my lips.

"And what if it's too painful for you?"

"What if it's exactly what I was waiting for? What if that's why you were attracted to me in the first place? Because you saw me and knew that I was the kind of woman who you wanted to tie up, and deny orgasms, and use your special talents to get me to submit?"

"What if all of this is just you trying to pull a fast one on me?

I blink. My heart begins to race. "Wh…why would you say that?" I flutter my eyelashes. "Haven't I fought you every step of the way? Am I not the one who stabbed you?"

"And then you decided to bring yourself to the brink of orgasm not once, but twice, in front of the cameras, knowing full-well I would be watching."

"Did you like it?" I breathe. *Shit, what the hell am I doing? Pretending to be all worldly-wise and knowing what I am doing, and trying to beard the lion in his den…or in this case, in his bed.* "Did you?" I hold his gaze.

"And if I say I did?"

"Then I'd reply that it doesn't matter what my motives are. I am here, aren't I? Willing and ready to do as you command."

"You think you can throw the right words at me and get me to do what you want?"

"Am I succeeding?"

"No."

"Oh..." I pretend to pout, "So then, why are we still talking?"

"My point exactly."

He pushes off from the bed, stands over to me, only to lean down, then swing me up and over his shoulder.

"Put me down."

He doesn't answer. He marches to the bathroom, shoulders his way past the door, then heads for the toilet and places me on the seat.

He stands above me and I blink. "What fuck are you up to?"

"You needed to pee."

"Says who?"

He raises an eyebrow and I flush.

"So, what if I do? I could have walked here on my own."

"I carried you instead; deal with it."

"And how did you know that I had to, you know—"

"Urinate?" He smirks. "You can say it. It's a bodily function, just like fucking. Or would you prefer if I said fornicating?"

I scowl, "If you think you can throw clinical words my way to fluster me, then you are sadly mistaken."

"Good." His grin widens. He widens his stance and I don't dare look straight ahead...because, uh! I am at the exact same height as his big, fat dick, that I know is standing to attention against his belly right now. Yeah, okay, I peeked. I couldn't help it. It's right there in front of me. Also, since we had woken up, he had pressed that monster shaft against me, so I am well familiar with its length and its —gulp—girth, which is bloody impressive, I'll have you know.

"What are you doing still standing here?" I murmur. "I need to *urinate*."

"So go."I gape at his smirking face. "Not in front of you."

He folds his arms across his chest, and his stance indicates...he's not moving. Okay, whatever, like I care if he sees me pee.

I close my eyes, try to relax...but hell, I can't go. Not when Mr. Monster Cock is standing over me like Satan himself.

"Turn your back," I say through gritted teeth, "else I won't be able to."

I sense him hesitate, then feel the slight breeze as he pivots around. To my surprise, I hear him move away. I open my eyes, and sure enough, the space is empty. I sigh as I settle into place, and almost instantly, my muscles relax enough so I can let go. I finish my business, flush, wash my hands and face, smooth my hair the best I can, then hesitate. I take in my naked body, so very pale, except for the thin streak of red in between my breasts.

In a way, we match, I suppose. Only, the wound I bestowed on him is much deeper. I raise my hand to touch the scratch and the ring on my finger catches my attention. It picks up the color from my dyed red hair, and damn it… It really does feel like it's already part of me.

Why does he have to be so…so perceptive. Speaking of… I spin around, head for the door. "How did you know that I had to pee?" I demand. "I never told you that I wanted to."

Alphahole finishes stepping into his gray sweatpants, then turns around. "I guessed."

"You guessed?" I scowl. "How could you just guess?"

"It's morning." He shrugs. "It's natural to want to use the facilities after a night's sleep." He grabs a bathrobe, then walks over to me and holds it out.

I stare at it, then up at him. "Shit," I blink, "you removed my clothes last night..."

"You only just realized that?"

"No, I mean, yes, I mean…" I shove my hair over my shoulder. I must have really been out of, it if I hadn't even stirred when he'd undressed me.

"Your dress is safe. I've asked for it to be cleaned."

"Oh?" I blink rapidly at him. That's thoughtful of him. Though why would he do that? Why is he being so nice to me?

"Relax," he laughs, "I know how much your creations mean to you and that dress was so *you*… That I figured you'd want to keep it, and maybe, modify it and wear it again."

My mouth drops open. That's exactly what I had planned to do, but how the hell is he able to read me so easily?

"Fine, fine," I grouse. "It's what most women do—adapt their wedding dresses so they can wear them again."

"Is it?" He frowns, then raises a shoulder, "Good guess, huh?" He jerks his chin toward the dressing gown, and I slide my arms through the sleeves. I knot the tie around the middle as he runs his palms down the shoulders, in a gesture that is both soothing and possessive. Huh. What the hell is this man up to? I turn around and scowl at him, "Out with it, Mister. What are you planning now?"

"Breakfast?" He smirks. "Do you like pancakes?"

33

Karma

I have been transported to some strange, alternate reality. That is the only reason I can imagine for why I am sitting here, at the breakfast counter of the kitchen of this manor on an island somewhere off the coast of Italy…watching a Mafia Capo, clad in only gray sweatpants and an apron, cooking at the stovetop.

OMG! That's so damn hot. His broad back is to me and I can't take my gaze off the play of muscle, the shift of those sculpted planes under his skin as he bustles around the space. He pours out the pancake batter onto one skillet, while in another, he cracks eggs. On a third pan, he's frying bacon and on the fourth burner, he has hash browns sizzling. OMG. My head spins as I watch him manage all four dishes at the same time, and not lose a step. He wipes his hand on the apron… Did I already mention? Yes, the man is wearing a freakin' apron… And honestly, he looks too damn sexy… Gah! My mouth waters, and it's not for the food.

I must have made a noise because he smirks at me over his shoulder, "You all right over there?"

I open my mouth to speak, but all that comes out is a gurgle. Damn! I reach for the glass of water on the table in front of me, and take a sip to clear my throat. Then scowl back at him, "Of course, I am."

A strand of hair falls across his forehead and he brushes it away. the gesture is so familiar...so very Mika. My heart stutters, and I can't take my gaze off of him.

"You sound like you have a lot on your mind." His grin widens. No doubt, the fact that I am staring at him is inflating his already inflated ego. Jerkass!

I carefully place the glass of water back on the table, then meet his gaze, "I was just wondering how you managed to get all of those clothes, and all in my size, in the closet before I first arrived? Did you order them on your way here, after you knocked me out?"

"I simply pressed down on the carotid artery on either side of your neck, and you lost consciousness."

"Thanks for the medical lesson." I scowl. "If you don't want to tell me about how you acquired the clothes for me—"

"Yes."

I frown. "What do you mean, yes?"

"Yes, I ordered them on the phone to have them delivered before we arrived at the island, while you were unconscious."

"You had all of those clothes, shoes, and underwear delivered in a few hours?" I blink. "How did you manage that?"

He stares at me and I huff, "Yeah, of course, money can solve anything." I hold his gaze, "And what about the shampoo and shower gel in the bathroom?" I tip up my chin, "Did you order that too? How did you know what fragrance I prefer?"

"Your scent, Beauty," his lips twist, "it's a combination of moonflowers and your essence. It's uniquely you... I found the most highly-rated sources and bought them for you."

Heat flushes my cheeks. Why the hell does that feel so intimate? After everything he's done to me, the fact that he accurately identified the fragrance of the shampoo I use should be the least of my worries. I shuffle my feet as another thought strikes me, "So, does this mean that you had already decided that you were going to— "

"Keep you? Play with you? Marry you?" He raises a shoulder, "Not consciously. All I knew was that I wasn't going to let go of you in a hurry."

I blink rapidly. What the hell does he mean by that? He isn't telling me anything I didn't already know and yet, these words seem very close to a confession of...something. Emotions? Feelings?

Nah, the Capo doesn't feel all that. All he means is that he isn't letting go of me until he gets what he wants from me. Yeah, I lean back in my seat. That's what it means.

My heart flutters and I rub at my chest. Please, please, don't tell me that my stupid heart condition is deciding now is the time to surface again. Not after I've been fine all these years, too. The sensation subsides and I blow out a breath.

He grabs a few slices of bread, pops them in the toaster, then turns to me, "I assume you like your eggs sunny side up."

I blink, then nod. I'm about to ask him how he guessed, but frankly, at this point, it doesn't matter. He's definitely going to have some dumbass explanation about it, and it's not like I want to know, anyway. I mean, the proof of the pudding is in the eating, and in this case, it's in the delicious breakfast that he serves up not ten minutes later. He places a plate piled with pancakes and drizzled with syrup, while on another plate, there are two eggs, sunny side up, with toast, hash browns, and bacon, which he sets down in front of me.

"Um, who is all this food for?"

"You?"

He grins and his face lights up. Oh, dear god, when he smiles like that, he's way too attractive. The bandage over his sternum is a stark contrast to the rest of his sculpted, tanned chest. And I can't take my gaze off it as he sits down in the chair opposite me.

"It doesn't hurt," he murmurs. "You didn't hurt me… Much."

"I don't know if that's good or bad." I fight the urge to apologize, then scowl back at him. "I did intend to cause you harm, you know?"

"No, you didn't." He reaches for the Moka—the Italian version of a coffee pot—and pours out the coffee he's freshly brewed, some into my espresso cup, then some for himself.

"What do you mean, I didn't?" I frown. "You a mind reader or something now?"

He raises his espresso cup to his lips, takes a sip, then sighs, "That's how coffee should be drunk—strong and intense and bitter."

"Just like you."

"What's that?" He smirks and I cough.

"Nothing, and don't change the subject."

"I wasn't."

"Yes, you were." I accuse him, "Here I am, trying to figure out what the hell you are up to, and you are extolling the properties of Italian coffee while making a combination of an all American/British breakfast...or a combination of breakfasts, that is."

"Don't you like it?" He eyes the food on the plates in front of me, "I figured you'd prefer this over a traditional Sicilian breakfast, but if you'd prefer something else..."

"It's not that." I drag my fingers through my hair. "I just wish you'd tell me why you decided to move me from the cell. And now, you are cooking me breakfast and..." I draw in a breath, "and this morning, even though you were, clearly, turned on, you didn't try to—"

"Fuck you?" The alphahole smirks as he reaches for his pancakes and begins to dig into them. As I watch, he inhales a quarter of the stack in seconds. Shit, and I haven't even started on mine.

"As you are well aware, your use of four-letter words doesn't bother me, in the least." I scoff as I cut into my own stack. "And yeah, that's what I mean." I pop the piece of pancake into my mouth and chew. "Whoa." I stare at him. "These are good."

"Surprised?"

"Well, yeah, I wasn't expecting you to cook." I frown, "Speaking of, where's the staff? Did you give them the day off?"

"The week off, actually."

"You did?" I dig into more of the pancakes and chew on them, "Is it some special occasion or something, that you allowed them time off?"

"It is." He nods, then pushes the plate with the eggs and bacon toward me, "You need to eat that too."

"After I finish the pancakes, if I have space, that is." I dig into the remainder of the food on my plate, then polish off the rest of the pancakes. I push my plate aside and he slides the other one in its place. "Eat," he commands, as he reaches for his second plate filled similarly to mine.

"Also," I say with my mouth full, "this is the first time I am seeing you dressed in sweats. Didn't think you owned a pair, considering you are always dressed in suits that seem to be from Saville Row."

He makes a sound deep in his throat, "Wouldn't touch those with a barge pole."

"Huh?" I frown. "Why's that?"

"I get my suits tailor-made by an artisan who has been stitching them for generations for the men in my family."

I resist the urge to roll my eyes. "Of course, you do."

He smirks. "You sassing me, Beauty?"

"Me?" I say crunching my way through the bacon, which is absolutely delicious, by the way, "Of course, not." I widen my gaze, "I wouldn't dare... My Lord." I flutter my eyelashes at him and his grin widens.

"Very good. Keep that up, and I may just be willing to give you your next orgasm."

"And there he is; the alphahole extraordinaire makes an appearance," I raise my eyes skyward, "just as we were getting along, too... Or at least, it seemed that way," I mutter under my breath.

"I heard that." He chuckles, "And to answer your earlier questions, one," he holds up a finger, "I learned to cook when I went to university in the US, and I enjoy American and British style breakfasts and didn't want to presume that the full English was the only kind of food you'd like to eat in the morning so I made both, and two," he holds up a second finger, "the reason I am wearing sweats is because there's no one else in the house."

"Oh." I set down my fork and glance around the space, "That's why the place seems empty. So, the staff is gone, and so are your brothers?"

"That's correct." He finishes off his bacon, then cuts up the eggs and scoops them up with a piece of toast. I watch as he chews his food, the tendons of his throat moving as he swallows. Fuck, but only Michael Byron Dominico Sovrano would make eating into an orgasm-inducing process. My throat goes dry. Somehow, I manage to chew and swallow my food, as he lowers his gaze to mine. He sets down his fork, then reaches for his napkin and dabs at his mouth. I lower my gaze to his lips and heat tugs at my belly. I squeeze my thighs together, mirror his actions and place my fork down.

"So, how come your brothers and the rest of your family and the staff are away?"

"Haven't you figured it out yet?" His eyes gleam, "Come on, Beauty, one guess, why there's no one else in the house..."

"Umm," I wipe my suddenly damp palms on my bathrobe, "because it's your birthday and you've given them all time off?"

"That doesn't explain why my family left the house."

"Because you fought with them and told them to leave?"

"It has happened on occasion, but no, it's not that."

My heart begins to pound in my chest. My pulse rate ratchets up. Moisture pools between my thighs and I slide my chair back... I try to be discreet but one of the legs catches on the stone floor and a screech fills the space.

I stiffen, but Michael doesn't move a muscle.

"You were saying?" He scratches the area of his chest around the bandage, and bloody hell, my gaze is instantly drawn to those gorgeous sculpted pecs again. What a pity that I had to hurt him. It feels like I have spoiled a work of art designed by God himself.

"Beauty?"

I hear the smirk in his voice and raise my gaze to his, "I was saying that...you gave your staff time off and probably sent your brothers on some Mafia-related job."

"Very good." He lowers his hand. "I knew you were smart."

I paste on a bright smile, even as my stomach flip-flops. This is not good. Not good at all. "So," I grip the edge of the table, "when will they be back?"

"Next week."

"Excuse me?"

"You heard me." His grin widens until he resembles one of those freakin' sharks in that stupid Jaws movie, the one that had made me laugh because the special effects, clearly, hadn't withstood the test of time, but right now there's nothing amusing about this situation, because Michael's shark-smile is infinitely more unnerving.

I gulp. "Wh… What do you mean?" I press the heels of my bare feet into the floor. Shit, why hadn't I thought to, at least, put on some shoes? Well, too late now. I'm just gonna have to face this situation head-on. "Well?" I scowl. "Tell me, Michael, what does it mean that they' re not coming back until next week?"

"It means," he yawns, "that this is our honeymoon, Beauty. You and me, husband and wife, darling." He smirks, "And this is when we consummate our wedding."

34

Michael

She blinks once, twice, I watch as the information sinks in, then color smears her cheeks. Her muscles tense and she draws in a breath, "You have got to be fucking kidding me."

She pushes back the chair and jumps to her feet. But I, too, am ready. I spring up, race around the table as she darts for the kitchen door. I grab her arm, turn her around and into me. "Let go of me, you oaf."

She struggles and I hold onto her, trying not to increase the pressure of my hands on her. I don't want to hurt her. And while I want to mark her, I want it to be intentional, not because I had done so by mistake. "Stop it," I growl.

"Oh, fuck off." I sense her raise her knee and move aside. I grab her around the waist, throw her over my shoulder and she screams, "Bloody hell, what do you think you are trying to do?"

"Only taking what's mine, by right." I pivot, walk around the breakfast bar and to the dining table. I shove the breakfast dishes aside, then lower her onto it. She tries to rise and I fold my body over hers, slam my hands on either side of her and bracket her in.

"I thought you wanted me to fuck you?"

"That was before."

"Before what?"

"Before we were married."

I blink, "So you were willing to shag me before we were married, and now that we legally can fuck, you don't want me?"

She tips up her chin, "That's right."

"Liar." I can't stop the smile that widens my lips. "You want me to overwhelm you. Want me to hold you down, take choice away from you. You want me to take you by force, isn't that right?"

She blinks, then glances away.

I freeze. "*Merda*," I glare at her, "that's what you want, isn't it? You want me to play with you before I bed you, Beauty?"

"No," she sets her jaw, "of course, not."

I take in her heightened breathing, her flushed features, the way she darts her gaze around the room then back at me. She may think that's not what she wants, but I know better. All the signs are there...

Seems this woman is more of my soulmate than I had realized. Every filthy need of mine is reciprocated within her. She wants me to chase her, hunt her down, capture her all over again; she wants me to establish, once and for all, just who is in charge here. The little minx wants me to leave her in no doubt of my dominance. Clearly, the fuckedupedness inside of me has found its match in her. How can she be so...very perfect?

I bare my teeth and she snarls back at me. Goosebumps pop on my skin. Fuck me, but she...is absolutely one-hundred percent in tune with me. She's mine to possess. Mine to own. Mine to claim. Mine to establish just how very much she belongs to me. Only me.

I push away from the table, only to reach for the tie of her bathrobe. I yank it open and she gasps. "What the hell do you think you are doing?"

"Nothing you are not going to enjoy, *piccola mia*."

"Go fuck yourself."

I laugh, "Can't wait to get started, hmm?"

"Buzz off, you ass."

"Gotta stuff that little mouth of yours, and this time it's not going to be with food." I jerk my chin at her, "Get up."

"What?"

"On your feet."

"First, you throw me down here. Now, you tell me to get on my feet. Can't you fucking make up your mind or—"

I hold out my hand and she squeaks. She stares at my proffered arm, then back up at me, "What are you doing?"

"Helping you up."

"Ah, hmm, okay." She grabs my hand, uses the leverage to haul herself up to sitting position. She lets go, then slides off the table.

"Take off your bathrobe."

She scowls and I fold my arms across my chest, "Don't defy me."

She huffs, then shoves the bathrobe off. "Happy?" She props a hand on her hip, thrusts out her chest as I look her up and down.

"Not yet, Beauty." I bend my knees, peer into her face. "Run."

"What?"

"Run, Beauty. I'll even give you a head start."

"What…what does that mean?"

"You heard me." I smirk. "Run now, *Belleza*. If I catch you… *When* I catch you, I intend to have my way with you…."

"And if I evade you."

"You won't."

"So sure of yourself?"

"I am sure of…" I glare into her eyes, "the fact that you want to be caught."

"No, I don't."

"Yes, you do."

"No."

"Yes." I snap my teeth and she jumps. I point my thumb toward the door, "Go, else I'll take this as your giving in without a fight."

She sets her jaw, "No fucking way."

"Good." A chuckle rolls up my throat and I swallow it down. "Go."

She blinks.

I reach for her and she squeals, then pivots and takes off for the door. I can't take my gaze off her pert, little butt as it twitches, as she bolts out the door. I amble over to the doorway, watch as she races down the corridor and up the steps. She flings the door open, bounds outside, and I follow.

I reach the doorway, leap down the steps. I glance around, and spot her running toward the back of the house. I take off in hot pursuit. I am not wearing any shoes…and neither is she. Only difference, I am used to running barefoot. It's how I grew up on the streets of Palermo. Sure, my father was the Don, but my mother was happy to let us boys run wild. She believed it would toughen us up if we went barefoot outside. And so, we had, until my father had found out and put an end to the practice. But that early experience now stands me in good stead as I run around the perimeter of the property. Where is she? Where the hell could she have gone?

Above me, the sun slides behind clouds. The temperature drops suddenly. It's late November, and while the weather is still pleasant, it's also more unpredictable. Sure enough a few drops of rain hit my arm as I pause, getting my bearings… Which way could she have gone? I close my eyes, attune my hearing, trying to catch any sound that would give away her presence… I tilt my head, wait…wait… A slight thud… The sound of bare feet on mud reaches me.

I turn, head across the clearing at the back of the house and toward the treeline. Step onto the muddy edge of the forest that borders the house. The dirt and stones bite into the soles of my feet. I push aside the discomfort, head toward where the sound had come from. Past the first set of trees, deeper into the forest, down the path that leads into a small clearing. I pause at the edge, wait…wait… A tiny sound… Almost an inhalation of surprise…reaches me and I turn. Lunge in the direction of the large oak tree that stands at the edge of the clearing.

Its branches spread out overhead, shielding me from the rain that is turning into a steady drizzle. I reach the massive tree trunk, throw myself around it, and she screams, then darts away from me. The pulse thuds at my temples and adrenaline laces my blood. A growl rips out of me as I lunge toward her, bridge the distance between us as I tackle her around the waist.

She screams as we both go down. I twist my body, make sure that she lands on top of me. She wriggles, yells out, and I throw my arms around her. I roll over so she is on her back on the grass and under me. She tips her chin-up and stares up into my face. I take in her flushed features, her hair flowing about her face, so fucking gorgeous. I lean in closer, wanting to sniff her, to lick her, to kiss those pouty pink lips of hers, then flinch when she lands her fist in my shoulder.

Pain shivers down my chest as the wound she'd inflicted on me protests at the impact.

She swipes out her fist again and this time I duck. "Stop that," I growl.

"No." She brings up her knee and I lean some of the weight of my lower body onto her, effectively arresting her in place. Which also means that my already swelling thickness lodges neatly in between her legs. She freezes; color smears her cheeks. Her chest rises and falls as she glowers back at me.

She throws her fist and I block it. I grab her arm and wrench it over her head. Then do the same with the other. I shackle her wrists together. "Gotcha." I bare my teeth, "I caught you fair and square, *piccola mia.*"

"The fuck I care?" She wriggles in my grasp, writhes under me as she tries to break free, and the friction of her soft core against the tent in my crotch sends shivers of anticipation up my spine. I plant my thigh, then the other between her legs, wrenching them apart. She strains in my grasp, scowls up at me.

"Let me the fuck go."

"No." I bare my teeth and she makes a sound at the back of her throat. "Tell me you want this," I growl. "Tell me you want my cock inside you; tell me you want me to fuck you; tell me you want your swollen hungry cunt clamped around my shaft as I plow into you."

Her pupils dilate until there's only a ring of green left around the black.

The scent of her arousal bleeds into the air, and fuck, if my cock doesn't leap forward right then. I transfer the hold on her wrist to my left hand, then shove the waistband of my pants down with my other hand.

"No," she snarls, "no, no, no."

"Yes, Beauty, yes."

I notch my swollen shaft against her entrance, then pause, "Say you want this." I tease her entrance with the head of my weeping cock and a moan bleeds out of her, even as she fixes me with a scowl.

"Say it," I insist. "Say you want me to own you, to punish you for trying to kill me, to fuck you so hard that my cum seeps out from your pores."

She sets her jaw, then scissors her legs around me. She thrusts her pelvis up so I slip inside her.

35

Karma

What are you doing? What the hell are you doing? Why are you taking him into your body? Why are you allowing him to do exactly what he's been threatening to do? Why do you have your legs wrapped around him as you hold his gaze, as you take in his gorgeous features, that thick corded neck, those broad shoulders that shield you from the rain that patters down from above?

He holds my gaze for a beat, then clucks his tongue. He pulls out of me and I scowl, "What the fuck? Thought you wanted to consummate our marriage?"

"You can't top from the bottom, Beauty."

"What the hell do you mean by that?"

"You know what I mean." He lowers his head until his eyelashes sweep over mine, "Say you want this, tell me you want me to fuck you."

"I want you to..." I swallow, "to nail me," I whisper.

"What's that?" He tilts his head, "Don't think I heard you."

"I want you to...to take me, you asshole."

"Say it like you mean it." He smirks. "Say you want me to fuck you."

"Fine, fine," I yell, "I want you to shag me, you bleeding idiot. I want you to fuck me, you—"

He propels his hips forward and impales me in one smooth move. I gasp and my breath catches in my chest. He's so damn big, so huge; I am so full. Oh, my fucking god. I swallow, open my mouth, but no sound comes out.

"Lost your ability to speak, hmm?" His smirk widens as he pulls out of me. He slides his free hand under my knee, heaves it up, so it's next to my chest, opening me up, then he thrusts forward with such force that my entire body jerks.

A moan bleeds from my lips. Oh, my god. Oh, my god. This is... fucking insane. It feels so fucking good, so right... I can't understand how every part of me feels ready and aching and wants more, so much. I make a sound deep in my throat and he nods.

"I know what you want, Beauty."

You do?

He holds my gaze as he begins to fuck me in earnest. In and out, in and out. I dig my heels into his back just above his tight butt as he plunges into me over and over again. Every time he rams into me, my body jolts. My breath shudders. Pinpricks of pleasure scream up my spine. The climax crashes over me and I scream, as he continues to fuck me through the aftermath that ripples through me in waves. He stares into my eyes, then releases my hand only to cup my cheek, "Fuck, you're beautiful when you come, you know that?"

I stare up into those cold, remorseless eyes of his. I watch myself watch him as he rams into me again and again. His features grow intense, his muscles coil and uncoil as he seems to put all of himself behind the movement. He releases my wrists, only to slide his thumb in between my lips and I suck on it. His gaze narrows as he pulls out, then propels his hips forward and buries himself to the hilt again. He hits that spot deep inside me, and to my shock, I find that shivers start at my feet again.

"No," I moan, "it's too soon. I can't come again."

"You can." He pounds me again, this time, with such force that his balls slap against my inner thighs. He pulls out, then tilts his hips, and nails me again, and I swear, I feel him in my throat.

"No," I whine, "no, no, no."

"We gotta work on your vocabulary, *piccola mia.*" He impales me again and again as the rain increases in intensity. The raindrops sting my legs as I lock my ankles around him, as he glares into my eyes, "Come," he commands. "Come all over my cock, wife."

"Oh, my fucking god." I throw my arms around his neck and scream as the orgasm sweeps up my spine to burst behind my eyes. I'm dimly aware of him picking up speed and ramming me over and over and over again. Then, his big body shudders and his dick swells inside me. I feel his butt tense as he comes deep inside me. He slumps down, and I sense him holding his weight off of me and on his arms as the aftershocks ripple over me. I open my eyes and flinch when I am faced with his intense gaze.

"What?" I murmur. "Why are you looking at me like that?"

"You okay?"

I nod, dimly aware that I still have my arms and legs locked around him. He slides his hand under my neck, the other under my waist. The next second, the world tilts as he flips our positions. He places me on his chest, then wraps those big arms around me.

"I need to get you out of the rain," he murmurs as he contemplates the rain that's pouring down on us. We are shielded somewhat by the branches of the tree overhead. Still, we are both completely drenched. And dirty and filthy.

Somehow, it feels right that he chased me down and took me in the open, exposed to the elements like we were animals. He's the most untamed man I have ever met. A beast who wears a tailor-made suit that only enhances that savage part of him that had attracted me from the moment I'd met him.

I raise my hand to his neck, trace the scar there. "How did you get this?" I murmur, "It seems painful."

He wraps his fingers around mine, guides my hand back to his chest. His fingers graze the ring and he freezes. Then he traces the diamond in a slow circle.

"We need to get out of here," he finally says, then pushes himself, and me, up to sitting position.

"Fine, fine," I huff, "if you don't want to tell me about the scar, I'll understand." I toss my hair over my shoulder, "You only have to say so. No need to brush off my question, you know."

He glances down at me, then sets me to the side before tucking himself inside his sweatpants. He rises to his feet, then holds out his hand, "Come," he murmurs, "let's get out of the rain."

Fifteen minutes later, I scoop up some of the hot water, then pour it over myself as I lean back into his broad chest. He'd carried me up and back into the house, pausing only to rinse the mud off both of us in the outdoor shower attached to the house, before he'd carried me into his bedroom. He'd filled up the bathtub in the ensuite, throwing in salts that had fizzed and bubbled before the space had filled with the scent of roses and lavender. When I had commented that it was a terribly feminine scent, he'd admitted that he'd bought the salts for me. Huh, okay. I hadn't expected to hear that.

I'd decided to keep the rest of my questions to myself for a little longer. Not that I don't want to find out more. It's just, after being freshly fucked, I want to revel in the pleasant buzz that grips my limbs, and the silence that seems to have taken the place of the thoughts that normally buzz around in my head. Apparently, the Capo fucked all thoughts out of my head. I snort, then swallow down the rest of the laugh that bubbles up. Either I am getting light-headed, or a little hysterical, or both…

He reaches for the shampoo, pours some of it out, then begins to work it into my hair. The complex scent of moonflowers fills the space. "I love this scent." I murmur, and I sense him smile above me.

"I know."

"It really is annoying how you always seem to have all of the answers."

"I don't, actually," he retorts. "For a long time, I had no idea what I was going to do with my life."

I turn my head and he increases the pressure on my hair so I have to glance forward again.

"Thought you were born into the Mafia, so you didn't have a choice but to join the family business?"

"You always have a choice, in everything you do, Beauty." He urges me to tilt my head back as he digs his fingertips into my scalp in slow circles.

A warmth envelops me and the muscles of my neck relax. "Hmm," I sigh, "you sure are good with your fingers, Mr. Capo."

A chuckle rumbles up his chest and the vibrations sink into my blood. The warmth of his body, combined with the heat from the hot water, envelops me fully. I close my eyes and give in to his attention as he begins to wash the suds out of my hair with the hand shower. Then he positions my head against his shoulder, and I sink into him further. He holds the hand shower over my breasts, then moves it down my belly. He dips the hand shower under water and holds it right over the entrance to my pussy.

"Ooh," I murmur, "that's…ah…nice."

"Nice, hmm?" His breath teases my temple a second before he runs his tongue around the shell of my ear. He bites down on my earlobe at the same time that he pushes the shower head right up against the entrance of my channel.

The pressure of the water is muted, yet it stimulates my clit. I wriggle around and he brings his big hand down onto my hip and holds me in place.

"Relax, Beauty," he murmurs, "I know what you need."

Do you? Do you know how much I love having your hands on me? How much I want you to debase me? How much I need you to degrade me? How I want you to humiliate me, to make me submit, to reach out to the darkness inside of me and bring it to the light so I can see myself through your eyes? Feel my desires as they ripple up your skin, sense how I break you apart, as you shatter me and put me back together in a design that mocks the girl I used to be.

Do you, my Capo, understand what it means that I met you this way? Even though the timing of our encounter is all wrong, even though the nature of our tryst is suspect... Even though you claim that I am your wife…though we both know this marriage is a sham. One that is a means of helping you get what you desire, that allows you to fulfill all of your ambitions... And me...what about me? What about what I want, what I need, what I want to do to you as you pleasure me?

I grip his wrist, applying enough pressure that he pauses. I turn my head, glance at him from the corner of my eye. I urge his hand back and he frowns. I turn around so I am kneeling between his legs, facing him, in the bathtub.

Then I bring his hand back between my legs and position the shower head back at the entrance of my channel. He arches his eyebrow at me and I raise a shoulder, "I can see you this way."

He moves the shower head closer to my clit and a shiver runs up my back. I reach down to grasp his erect cock, as he reaches behind him and increases the pressure of the water. The stream gushes up and against my already sensitive clit and I gasp. I tense my fingers around his cock, and damn it, my fingers don't meet around his girth. I mean, I'd felt him inside of me...as he'd stretched me, and filled me, as he'd pushed his way down my throat...but I hadn't realized just how big he is, in relation to my hand. I swipe my fingers down to the base of his shaft, and he grits his teeth.

A nerve throbs at his temple, as he grips my hip with his other hand, bracketing me in. I part my legs, allowing him to bring the spray even closer. The spray massages my pussy and I can't stop the moan that bleeds from my lips. I hold his gaze as I swipe my fingers up the length of his cock. I drag my thumb across his swollen head and he bares his teeth. I squeeze down his length again and his chest rises and falls. "You're fucking killing me," he growls as he reaches behind to turn off the water before letting the shower head sink to the bottom of the tub. He wraps his fingers about the nape of my neck, and the tips almost meet around the front of my throat. I swallow and I can feel him feel the action.

The skin around his eyes tightens. "Take me in your mouth," he orders.

I glance down, then back at his face. I take a breath, then lower my head to the water. The depth is just enough to cover my mouth, as I close my lips around his cock. A groan rumbles up his massive chest, as he increases the pressure on my throat. "Take me down your throat, I want to feel you swallow." He lowers his voice to a hush, and OMG, that dominance in his voice chafes across my nerve-endings. All of my pores seem to pop. My core clenches and moisture pools between my legs as I open my mouth wider, then drop my chin as I take him down my throat. And promptly gag. He holds me in place as my eyes water.

"Take it all in, Beauty," he growls, his voice hard, his gaze burning into me, a challenge in them, maybe? And fuck it, but I want to show him that I am not some stupid, virginal woman who can't keep up with him. So, I draw in another breath through my nose, hold it, then relax my throat as he pushes me down and I take him in as deep as I can. The water flows over my nose and I don't dare breathe as I lick my tongue up his swollen length.

He presses his thumb into the front of my throat and groans, "Fuck me, but you have no idea how hot that is, Beauty. To feel my cock as it slides down your throat." His breath catches, "It's fucking erotic." His tone deepens, "You're a fucking queen... My goddess."

Umm, okay, is that the blow job speaking, or does he really mean it?

I draw back, so my nose is above water, draw in a breath, then plunge down again. This time his cock slides down my throat easily as I lick down his length, then up again as I pull back. I wrap my lips around the head of his cock, give it a slurp, then again.

"*Dio cane*!" he growls as his fingers tighten around my nape. He urges me to lower my head, as I open my mouth as wide as possible. He applies enough pressure that I take him down my throat, then he pulls me back, allowing me to take a breath, before he once more pushes me down. His dick slides down my throat, and again. The next time he pulls me back, I take in a breath, and he pauses. "You good?" He tilts his head, "If you want me stop, Beauty, you only have to tap my thigh, and I'll release you."

I stare up at him, and he curls his lips. *Bastard*. No doubt, he expects me to tap out. He probably wants me to admit that he's too much for me. That I can't take his rough handling of me. That I am not able to keep pace with him. That I am too weak to bear his proclivities…and… I know, I know… It's stupid that I have to turn this into some kind of competition. I mean, ultimately this is about him manipulating my body to suit his needs. Not that I am not getting any pleasure out of it, but surely, he could be more...gentle on me…

Except, I don't want him to be gentle. I want him to take me as he would any common whore. I want him to use me as his personal fucktoy… Yeah… I know, I need therapy, surely. Who would want a man to debase her, demean her, use her mouth for his pleasure, use her cunt to bring him satisfaction, use her every hole as it would best suit him? Me… That's who. And no, I am not going to apologize for this anymore.

I have always known my tastes are warped, my preferences extreme, my needs different from what most women want. No pink roses, or candles or soft beds… Okay, maybe the third one is okay… But only so they bring out the contrast to the unyielding body that pushes me into said bed and masters me. So yeah… This is me… unapologetic, uncaring, not in denial for what I want. Not when I've met a man whose tastes, surely, run as much to the extreme as my own.

I wrap my fingers around the base of his dick and squeeze hard.

His breath catches. Color smears his cheeks. I bring my other palm down to cup his balls. I massage them and his chest rises and falls. His shoulders flex. He seems to grow bigger, darker, more dangerous, if that were possible. A cloud of heat spools off of him, and slams into my chest. I gasp and sweat beads my brow.

He bares his teeth, then pushes me down, watching as his cock disappears in my mouth. He pulls me back, then presses me down, again and again. His movements speed up. His gaze intensifies. I don't take my gaze off of him. I keep the connection alive as he fucks my mouth, as tears run down my cheeks, joining the rest of the bath water. Heat flushes my skin and my pulse rate speeds up. I am turned on by how he is using me, and fuck, if I'll do anything to stop myself from relishing how he uses me. How his body reacts to what he's doing to me.

His chest planes flex, his belly clenches. The skin around his mouth tightens as he squeezes my hip with enough pressure that I know I'll bear the imprint of his fingers for days. Hell, if he hasn't marked me already, in ways that may not be visible, but which I will carry inside of me. On my dark soul, which speaks to his. In my mind, which is racing to keep one step ahead of him. In my heart, which is already his... Fuck... No, no, no. No way... I can't allow myself to fall for this beast.

His nostrils flare, he grits his teeth, and I know then, he's coming. A groan rumbles from him as he pulls me back, then urges me down to take his cock all the way down my throat one last time. His entire body tenses, then he throws his head back and growls as he shoots his load down my throat.

36

Michael

Black spots flicker at the edges of my vision. I come with an intensity I have never experienced in all of my thirty-nine years. The orgasm seems to go on and on, then fades away as suddenly. My shoulders relax and I stare down at the witch who did this to me. The water laps over her mouth as she meets my gaze from under half-closed eyelids. I pull her up and off of my cock, watch as she licks her lips. There's no evidence of cum around her mouth, and it's not because the water wiped it clean. I had blown my load down her throat. She had taken me so deep inside that there was no chance of cum spilling from her lips.

I haul her toward me, then close my mouth over hers. The salty taste of my cum, the sweetness of her palate, that sexy feminine scent of her, tinged with moonflowers... All of it overpowers my senses. I pull her into my chest, wrap my arms around her as I ravish her mouth. As I suck on her tongue and drink from her. As I lose myself in her. Fucking only her. I tear my mouth from her, gaze into those green eyes. Pupils blown, color high on her cheeks, her lips are swollen from my attention. I glance down at her creamy breasts, cup one, then bend down and kiss the nipple. She shivers as I similarly anoint the other pebbled tip, then press small kisses back up her throat, to her mouth.

"Michael," she whispers as I brush her lips with mine. I lick her mouth, then rub my nose against hers, before kissing her one eyelid shut, then the other.

"Michael." She wriggles in my hold, and I pause.

"What is it?" I murmur as I press more kisses to her forehead, to her temples, lick the shell of her ears before sucking on the lobes of her ears.

"Michael," she pouts, and this time I lean back.

"What?"

She opens her eyes and scowls up at me, "I need to come."

I blink, then burst out laughing. "*You* need to come?"

"It's not funny." She slaps my shoulder, "You just had the most intense orgasm ever—'

"It was okay," I lie.

"Bullshit." She presses her forefinger into my chest, "You came like you were the last man on earth and this was your very last orgasm, ever, and you hadn't had sex in months before this."

"Days," I raise a shoulder, "but who's counting."

She opens and shuts her mouth. "You're a real piece of work, you know that?" she snarls, tries to pull away and I tighten my grip about her.

"You know I don't try to hide the kind of man I am. It's what you like about me, after all."

"Not." She leans back, trying to put space between us, as if I am going to let her.

"Liar," I murmur. "And you were right."

"I was?"

I nod. "That…" I rub my nose with hers, "was the best orgasm I have ever had."

Her eyes open wide before she schools her features, then sniffs, "You don't have to sound so surprised. When I set my mind to something, I don't back down; and I told myself that I was going to suck your soul through your dick."

"Is that right?"

She tips up her chin, "Are you denying that it was an out-of-body experience for you?"

"It was…" I scan her features, "more than that. It was like dying a little, and much as I am not a fan of the French, la petite mort—the little death, is the best way to summarize how it felt."

"Oh." She blinks, "Okay, that's good."

"It was more than good… It was *eccezionale,* Beauty." I smirk, "And now it's your turn."

I rise to my feet and lift her up with me. I step out of the bath tub, grab a towel and hold my hand out for her. She steps down from the tub, and I pat her shoulders, her breasts, her waist, her hips, the dip between her legs, her ankles, her pretty feet. By the time I straighten, she's staring at me with parted lips. I use the same towel to squeeze the excess water from her hair, then rub myself dry and toss it aside. I bend my knees and lift her up, and throw her over my shoulder.

"Hey," she protests, "what are you doing?"

"Making sure my wife gets the orgasms due to her."

She huffs against my back, "Wish you wouldn't call me that… It feels…too intimate."

I chuckle, "We are in my bedroom, after I came down your throat in my bath tub, and now I am about to put you down on my bed, and make you come all over my tongue, so this, *tesoro, is* intimate."

I slap her bottom and she protests.

I lower her onto the bed, and she sprawls on her back, her long, red hair still dripping and flowing around her shoulders.

She shoves the strands away from her face, then tips her chin up. She pushes up to her elbows, thrusts her chin out, then bends her knees and slides them apart. I rake my gaze down her flushed face, over her heaving breasts to the juicy flesh between her legs.

Fuck me, but she's a temptress, a gorgeous siren, an enchantress come to tempt me from my path.

And apparently, I am more than willing to let her distract me…

For now. I walk around the bed, then stretch out next to her with my head on the pillow.

She turns over, braces herself on her elbows. "I thought you owed me an orgasm?" She pouts.

"And you'll get it." I tap my chest, "Come 'ere."

"Huh?" She frowns, "What do you mean?"

"Ride my face, Beauty."

She blinks, then crawls over to me. Throwing a leg over my chest, she positions herself over my face. I stare up and into her most intimate place, the pink lips flushed and swollen, and glistening with evidence of her arousal. The opening of her channel that would be warm and wet and welcoming, and so fucking tight that I could lose myself there for days. The sweet, sugary scent of her arousal, and beneath that, the light trace of moonflowers. Always fucking moonflowers. I am going to have to plant a garden full of them, then roll about in them, so I can always carry her next to my skin.

Fuck, she's truly getting under my skin. I really do need to fuck her out of my system so I can get on with my life.

"This is bullshit," she mutters from above me. "Why are you staring at me like that; it's so embarrassing." She tries to move away and I grasp her hip. "Shh," I glance up at her, "I am studying the lay of the land."

"What?" She scowls, "I am not some stupid, rival gang that you need to plot against and figure out how to overpower."

"But you are as deadly, Beauty," I place my other palm on her hip, and hell, she is so tiny that I could easily span her waist with one palm. She seems fragile, but packs a punch. She looks like a gust of wind would blow her over, but she has a spine of steel. This woman has so much gumption, such strength, such resilience... And if I let her, she could wield so much power over me.

Nope, not happening. Never going to allow someone else to hold sway over me. I am going to fuck her, then use her to get to the Seven... And once I have the alliance locked down formally with them... Well...then I'll decide what to do with her.

I pull her close enough for my nose to nudge against her center. I draw in a lungful of Beauty and my cock instantly thickens.

"Oh, my god." She moans, "Why did you do that?"

"Don't you like it?"

"I... I..."

I sweep my tongue up her slit and she shudders. I slurp at her pussy lips and she shivers. I curl my tongue around the swollen bud of her clit. Her entire body trembles. She tries to close her thighs; I lean in, so the width of my shoulders is in between them. I plunge my tongue inside her sopping wet channel and she squeaks. Her pussy clenches down as she digs her fingers into my hair and tugs on it. My scalp tingles. Pinpricks of heat race down my spine, and my groin hardens. I push my face closer to her core, then begin to fuck her with my tongue. In and out of her, in and out. I lick the cum that dribbles from her channel and a whine bleeds from her lips, "Oh, my god, Mika." She warbles, "Oh, my fucking god."

A chuckle rumbles up my throat. I continue to thrust my tongue in and out of her as she yanks at the hair on my scalp, and holds on.

"Oh, Mika. Mika. Mika," she chants as she thrusts her hips forward, trying to encourage me to bury my tongue deeper inside of her. I curve my tongue inside her channel and she huffs. I hold her upright with one hand as I slip my fingers around and in between her ass cheeks, to play with her back entrance. She stiffens and I lick up and into her, again and again. Her entire body trembles. Her thighs clench. I pull my tongue out of her channel, then slide my thumb inside her backhole, even as I bite down on her pussy, and she screams as she comes. Moisture drips out of her, down her inner thighs, and I lap it up.

I lick up her slit, between her pussy lips as she slumps over me. I lower her to the bed, push her onto her front, then arrange her on her hands and knees. I press my palm into her upper back and she pushes her cheek into the pillow. She thrusts out her hips, and fuck me, but her heart-shaped derrière sends the blood racing to my shaft. I grab my cock, position it between her pussy lips. Then grab her hips, and in one smooth thrust, I impale myself to the hilt. Her entire body jolts and a moan bleeds from her lips as her pussy clamps down on my cock.

All of my sense focus in on her and I begin to fuck her. I slam into her with such force that the headboard slams into the wall. My balls slap against her clit as I set a punishing pace. Sweat beads my shoulders, as I pump into her wet, soft, tight channel. She grabs hold of the headboard, holds on as I plunge into her, over and over again. The pulse beats at my temples, my heartbeat ratchets up, and my muscles tense as the pressure at the base of my spine builds up on itself, and becomes bigger and bigger, until it seems to consume my entire body.

"Fuck," I growl, "f-u-c-k, Beauty." I grip her hips, as she pushes up. She widens her stance, reaches down and between our legs to grip my balls. She squeezes and heat sears my spine. All of my pores pop, and with a growl, I pull out of her, then ram into her once more, so she has no choice but to release me. This time she grips the headboard with both of her hands. "Come with me, Beauty. Come the fuck with me, right now."

I thrust into her and she throws her head back and screams. Her entire body shudders as the orgasm grips her. Moisture floods her channel and I continue to thrust into her over and over again as she collapses. Only then, do I allow myself to come.

37

Karma

When I wake up next, I am alone. I glance around the large bed, at the crumpled sheets, at the darkness gathering outside. Shit, did I sleep the day away? The last I remember, he'd carried me to the bed, and proceeded to fuck me... I mean he hadn't been kidding when he'd said that he'd pump me with so much cum that it'd overflow from my pores. I bring my hand to my nose and sniff. That dark, edgy scent of his, laced with the lighter notes of moonflowers, fills my senses. I smell like a combination of me and him. A combination of me and him.

I sit up so suddenly that the blood drains from my head. Shit. I lean back against the headboard, until the world stops spinning. A combination of me and him.

Fuck, fuck, fuck. I allowed him to fuck me without protection. What had I been thinking? Or rather, I had not been thinking at all. I had been swept away on a sex cloud; lust had addled my brain and turned my thoughts into mush. And he… He hadn't said a word. Fuck, fuck, fuck.

I throw the covers back and begin to pace. The is what he wants…for me to fall pregnant. To fuck me nonstop until I am carrying his child… And then, I'll have no choice, but to obey him.

As if he doesn't have me under his thumb enough, as if he doesn't control me enough, as if he doesn't already own me, body and soul… And to think, I had thought that I was falling for him. Jeez, give a slut some big dick energy and she instantly thinks she's in love.

Jesus fucking Christ, I am pathetic. No doubt about it… And it's not about the fact that I wanted him to fuck my brains out, which I now suspect he actually did, or that I wanted him to do every filthy possible thing that a man could do to a woman, and things I haven't even read about yet. No, it's the fear that I had been so careless. I had gotten so carried away by everything that had happened, so taken in by his personality, so complete consumed by his charisma, so absolutely owned by his dominance—

And there it is—he had successfully made me submit without my even realizing it. I had not only given him my virginity, but I had also sacrificed my free will at the altar of his arrogance. I had simply rolled over and allowed myself to be taken in by his…cock, his sexual proficiency, his…his…larger-than-life presence. I had thrown caution to the winds… Hell, I hadn't even thought about the fact that I could fall pregnant.

As someone who grew up in the foster system, I am well aware of the risks of having a child when you are unable to care for it. And while Summer and I had been lucky in that we had had decent foster parents, still, we had learned very early on to protect ourselves. And I had forgotten all about it. A few days in his presence and I am losing myself, losing my independence and my pride. He's bringing the woman I am deep inside to the surface… And I don't want to deny who I am. I don't want shame to prevent me from being myself. … But, here I am, facing the very real possibility that I might have conceived a child by my captor already, and that is not a part of my life plan right now.

Fucking hell. I grip my hair and tug on it. Think, Karma, think.

You have to do something about this. But what? I glance around the bedroom…his bedroom… Shit, I am standing here naked, and he could walk in at any moment. I'll take one look at his delicious body and all other thoughts will leave me. I'll probably throw myself at his feet and ask him to fuck me again.

And would that be so bad? To let him have me, to assuage this hunger deep inside of me. So what, if I fall pregnant? It would mean that he'd have to keep me, he'd have to protect me, he couldn't harm me then, right? And this…this is exactly what he wants. For me to give up my will, and my ability to make decisions, my prerogative to choose… He wants me to lay it all at his feet so he can dominate me absolutely. And that…that I cannot bear.

I want children…eventually. And if I am pregnant, I will keep this kid too… Only, no way, am I going to let his presence taint his or her life.

Either way, I need to get the fuck out of here. Surely, there has to be a way off the island? A boat somewhere…? No way, would his staff and his brothers and the rest of his team leave him without, at least, some way to get off this place. If there is a way off, then I am going to find it.

I pivot, run out of his room, down the corridor into what had been my bedroom. I race across the floor to the closet. Pull out underwear, scrounge around until I find a pair of pink jeans and a white sweater. I pull on the clothes, along with a pair of beige-colored ballet pumps. Ugh! Hate the colors, but they'll have to do. At least, they are comfortable and I can run in these ballet pumps. Too bad the asshole had taken the clothes I'd been wearing when he'd kidnapped me. Guess he'd only wanted me to wear the clothes he bought for me.

My stomach flip-flops. *Oh, hell no, I do not like that gesture of ownership; I do not. Totally, not.*

I glance around the room. Anything else I can take from here? Anything to protect myself? Anything I can defend myself with? His knife. Of course.

I retrace my steps down the corridor, back into his room. As soon as I enter, the scent of sex hits me. My belly quivers. I only have to scent his smell and my entire body seems to go into overdrive. Fuck that. Don't look at the bed. Pretend he didn't just fuck you on those sheets.

I scan the room, spot his knife on the side table. No way. Did he actually leave it behind? He must have been more distracted than usual to do that. Or…he's not far off. Shit, maybe he went to get some food to eat or something? I run over to the side-table, grab the sheathed knife and tuck it into my waistband at the small of my back. Then I race out of the room, to the staircase, down the steps.

I hit the ground floor and hear the sound of his voice from the kitchen. Guess he's speaking to someone. The sound of pots and pans being thunked around reaches me.

Is he cooking again? For me? For us? I pause. I could just walk over to him, hug him and join him for a late lunch… Or an early dinner… Or—I shake my head. Fuck no, this is exactly why I need to leave. All of these thoughts of domesticity and cozy meals and hot, steamy fucking between the sheets… *OMG! Stop it, right now.*

I walk away from the kitchen, across the big main living room, to the front door. I yank it open, slip through, then close it softly behind me. I race down the steps, down the driveway, toward the main jetty, then stop. I can't see any boats there. There has to be another jetty, another boathouse. Another way to get off this island.

I retrace my steps, then run around the perimeter of the house. When I reach the kitchen windows, I duck low, straightening only when I reach the end of the house. I break into a sprint, taking the path that runs through the forest, past the clearing where he had tackled me not too long ago.

The rain has eased off, and while the ground is slushy, it doesn't pose a problem. I run through the trees, emerge on the other side, and spot a boathouse. Yes! I take the steps that lead down to the structure. When I reach the shed, I push the door and it opens. Huh. Okay, I wasn't expecting that.

I step inside the gloom, take in the boat tethered on the water between the two ramps on either side of it. The far side of the boathouse is open, and beyond it, I can see the inlet of water that leads out to the open sea. Shit, how the hell am I going to navigate that? I don't know how to navigate a boat, but I know how to drive. I mean, it can't be that different, right?

I step in, close the door behind me, when a hand clamps down on my mouth.

No, no, no. I begin to struggle, and someone hisses in my ear, "Stop it, I am trying to help you."

It's not his voice. Michael's voice is darker, more...gravelly, deep enough to send a shiver down my back. This man, whoever it is, also has a strong voice. It's just not intense enough to be Michael's.

"I know you are trying to get away from him, and I can help you."

I freeze.

"I am going to take my hand away from your mouth now," he murmurs. "Promise me you won't scream?"

I hesitate and he whispers with more urgency, "Nod your head if you agree."

I comply, and he removes his hand.

I draw in a breath, turn and blink up at him. His features are familiar—that height, the width of his shoulders. He's taller than Michael and more leanly built. Where Michael is all raw power and blatant dominance, this man wears his sophistication like a veneer. His muscles coil and his gaze sweeps over my features…

No, underneath the mask he wears to the world, he is all ruthlessness and authority. Shit, this man is as dangerous. Maybe more so, because he conceals his savagery with refined elegance.

"I… I saw you at the wedding." I murmur. "You're Michael's brother?"

"Younger to him by only a year." His jaw hardens. "Funny how fate determines exactly where you land in life, isn't it? Take birth at the wrong time within a powerful family, and you'll find yourself always in sight of the seat of power but never close enough to grab it."

"Ah," I nod. This man is bitter, maybe aggrieved about the fact that he isn't the eldest in the family. He wants revenge for that? Perhaps he's even upset for something that Michael did to him? No wonder he saw his opportunity and moved in now. "I don't intend to become a pawn in whatever twisted games you and Michael are playing."

"And what about the games he is playing with you?" He tilts his head, "What about the fact that he kidnapped you, then married you to pay your father's debt, then threw you into a cell."

I stiffen. "What are you trying to say?"

"That we can help each other."

I frown, and he chuckles. "Not like that." He steps back, putting space between us. "Not that you are not attractive, but you are married. The two of you exchanged vows in front of a priest, so you are morally his. Also, Michael has filed the marriage papers signed by both of you with the local municipality. So legally, as well, you belong to him."

"Hold on," I scowl, "I didn't sign anything."

He stares at me and I throw up my hands, "Jesus, he forged my signature, didn't he?"

"Do you blame him?" He raises a shoulder. "Even I can see that you'd have never agreed to sign it of your own free will, and seems, he wanted you for his wife, at any cost."

"Which is why you want to help me get away from him," I firm my lips, "because you know it will hurt his ego more than anything to lose his most prized possession."

His gaze widens and he takes in my features with something akin to...respect? Maybe wariness, even. "I can see why he is so taken by you." His lips curl. "Perhaps you are more intelligent than you look."

I scowl. "Perhaps we need to get out of here, before he comes?"

I tip up my chin and he chuckles.

"He really has no idea what he's in for, does he?"

"Oh, I think he must be getting an idea about now." I brush past him, step onto one of the ramps, when I hear the sound of Michael calling my name.

"*Che cazzo,*" Luca growls. "He'll find us. Come." He brushes past me, up the ramp, and begins to undo the tether to the boat. I walk toward him, then clamber onto the boat. He finishes untying the craft, then jumps onto the vessel, which rocks from side to side. I grasp the edge of the boat, hold on as he brushes past me. He reaches the driver's seat, then presses his finger to the ignition button. The engine fires up, then stops.

"Fuck," he growls as he presses down on the ignition again. The engine coughs, roars to life, then dies away again.

"Oh, god," I squeeze my fingers together, "come on, come on, please, start."

He pauses and I shot him a glance, "Why aren't you trying to start it again?"

"Can't flood the engine," he explains. "Just need to give it a few seconds."

"It's time we don't have." I hiss, glance around the boat as the door behind us is flung open. I don't need to glance around to know he's entered the space. Anger thrums off of him, crashes into my back as I gasp. The hair on the back of my neck rises.

"Beauty," his familiar growl rumbles through the space, "what the hell are you doing?"

38

Karma

"What do you think?" I turn toward him. "I am leaving you."

"Not having much success, are you?" He prowls over to me, pauses on the ramp near the motorboat which has begun to drift away from the ramp. "Come back to me," he orders. "Now."

"No." I shake my head, "No, I will not."

"And you?" He glares at Luca. "I trusted you," his jaw hardens, "my brother, my second in command... The man I believed in all these years."

"Excuse me while I play the violin for your woes." Luca laughs.

"Who got to you, Luca?" Michael tilts his head, "This is not you. This bitter, cynical man, who is betraying me... This is not the brother I know."

"You don't know me very well then, do you?" Luca's lips turn down in a sad smile, "You only ever saw what you wanted; you always believed that you knew what was best for all of us."

"What are you talking about?" Michael frowns, "My entire life, to date, has been devoted to protecting all of you."

"If only that were true," Luca says in a low voice, "and you accuse Nonna of turning a blind eye when he beat up mother."

Michael stiffens, "What are you talking about?" He leans forward on the balls of his feet, "What did he do to you, Luca? Tell me what happened."

"Don't worry about it, *fratellone,*" Luca's lips twist. "You just worry about how you're going to explain how you let your wife run away from you."

Michael's shoulders stiffen. The skin around his eyes tightens. He glares at Luca a second longer, seems about to say something, then changes his mind.

"Why are you doing this?" He widens his stance, "Turn back, and I'll forget any of this happened."

"I think not." Luca's lips curve, "Not when I am enjoying the sight of the powerful Capo, reduced to begging his woman to stay. If you're not able to keep her, how are you going to take charge as the Don? Clearly, you are not fit to succeed him."

"So that's what this is about? Power?" Michael folds his fingers into fists at his side.

"When is it not about power?" Luca chuckles, then glances toward me. "Oh, I forgot, you think yourself in love, don't you? You think she is the woman who came to redeem you? Too bad, she doesn't feel the same way."

I stiffen, wanting to tell him to shut the hell up, but I don't. He's wrong, though. Michael isn't in love with me. All he wants is to possess me, own me, use me, then discard me. But I'm not going to correct him. Not when he's doing a damn good job of keeping Michael occupied while we wait to re-start the goddamn engine again.

"I would have done anything for you, my brother." Michael lowers his chin, "I would have given up anything for you."

"So, if I had asked you to hand over the title of Capo to me, would you have done so?"

Michael stiffens. A nerve pops at his temple, but he stays silent.

"Thought not," Luca murmurs. "Don't kid yourself, *fratellone.* All these years, you've kept me close just to keep track of my movements." Luca, shakes his head, "No brother, if I had told you how I truly felt, if I'd even breathed a word of the fact that I wanted to be Capo, you'd have killed me— "

"Or not," Michael folds his arms across his chest, "and now we'll never know. Either way," he nods toward me, "let her go. She isn't part of whatever power games you want to indulge in."

"I beg to differ," Luca smirks. He wraps his arm around me and I shoot him a confused glance. What the hell is he up to? And after he told me that he's not interested in me in that way.

On the ramp, I sense Michael tense. "Get the fuck away from her," he says in a voice so hard, so cold, that a shudder runs down my spine. My thighs clench and my belly flutters. Shit, I should not find his anger such a turn on. I should not find the possessiveness that laces his voice so damn sexy. I should not allow myself to turn to him, fix my gaze on his as I lean into Luca and murmur, "I don't want you, Michael. I want him."

Michael's nostrils flare.

Next to me, Luca's muscles bunch. But he must understand that I am playing along with him, for he hauls me closer. "You heard her." I can hear the smirk in his voice as he addresses Michael over my head, "She's not with you anymore."

"She's. My. Wife." Michael's voice whips through the space. The pores on my skin pop. My toes curl. Oh, my god. Michael Byron Domenico Sovrano in a rage...is, surely, one of the most erotic spectacles I have ever seen. It's definitely one of the scariest.

Why the hell does everything about this man turn me on...even as I am trying my best to leave him? I squeeze my thighs together, lift up my chin, "Your wife?" I snarl. "Is that what you call kidnapping me and forcing me to marry you?"

"It's what I call what happened over the last 24 hours between you and me," he snaps and my heart stutters. It bloody stutters. I draw in a breath and Luca's grasp about my shoulder tightens.

I try to pull away from him and he whispers, "Don't let him get to you. Remember, you're doing this because you want to escape him."

I stiffen, then firm my lips. "What happened between us was a mistake." I look Michael up and down, "If you think, for one second, you fooled me by what you did, you're wrong. I hate you." I swallow, "I loathe what you did to me, and if I had the chance, I'd turn back the clock and ensure I was never in the park where you first encountered me."

He pales, then sets his jaw. "We'll talk about that later," he says in a tone that is so soft that there is no mistaking the menace that laces it. Jesus H Christ, I've done it. He's so bloody pissed at me, that the moment we are alone next he is going to... Fuck me? Spank me? Both of the above, and maybe not in that order.

I gulp, even as wetness laces my core. Oh, my god, what's wrong with me that, even now, I can't get rid of the images that crowd my mind? Of him cramming his dick inside me, his touch on my skin, his scent in my nostrils, the heat of his gaze as he takes in my features, as he glares at Luca's arm about my shoulders.

"Take your hands off of her or—"

"Or what?" Luca smirks, "From where I am, there's not much you can do."

Michael's jaw tics. He squeezes his massive hands into fists at his sides, then takes a step forward. Luca tries the ignition again. The engine fires up, the boat leaps forward, then the engine dies down.

"Fuck," he swears, takes his arm off of me, then begins to play with the buttons on the dashboard.

"Couldn't you have thought of this before?" I hiss.

"It's a last-ditch resort." He bends, pulls out a panel, then yanks at some wires.

There's a flash of movement to the side. I turn, then scream when Michael dives into the water. He swims toward us and panic squeezes my chest. *Shit, shit, shit.* I need to do something about this, but what?

If he reaches the boat, if he gets on, no way, can we escape. Worse, if he gets his hands on me again... If he takes me captive again... He'll never forgive me. He'll make me regret trying to escape him. *And you'll love every minute of it.* No. I shake my head...

It's this addiction to him that got me into this situation, in the first place. It's because I couldn't stay away from him, that I let my guard down enough to, perhaps, even trust him, that I may now be pregnant with his child and... *No*... If that's the case, I definitely need to get away from him. He reaches the boat, grabs the edge and the craft rocks. I scream again, grab the back of the seat to steady myself. I need to do something, anything, but what?

"The oars," Luca jerks his chin to a corner of the boat. "Grab an oar and fight him off."

"No," I cry, "I don't want to hurt him."

"If you don't, he'll hurt you," he retorts. "You don't want that, do you?"

Do I? How can I tell him that I like it when Michael puts his hands on me? How it turns me on when he treats me like his plaything. How... I lose sight of everything when he's near me.

Oh, my god, I have no choice. I am going to have to do this. If I let him near me again... I am never escaping him... And my child... If I am pregnant, he or she will never know a normal life.

I scramble around the seat, totter toward the end of the boat, where one end of the oar pops out from under the cover of the tarpaulin.

Michael grabs the edge of the boat, begins to haul himself over the side. That's when I spring forward. I grab the oar and raise it. My muscles scream in protest. The oar is heavy enough that my knees almost give way under me. I manage to find my balance, and the oar slips from my hands. The edge slams into the side of his head. I tighten my hold on it, pull back as his gaze widens. Those blue irises flare with... Surprise... No, something else... Hate? No... Love? Not possible. It's lust. It has to be lust. And maybe possession. And anger that I've beat him at his own game.

Blood blooms at his temple and I fight the urge to run to his side and help him. He bares his teeth, swings one leg over the side and I scream. I bring the oar down on him again, just as the boat's engine roars to life. Michael's gaze holds mine. A beat, another. Then his grip loosens, and he falls back into the water. The oar falls from my fingers and hits the bottom of the boat.

I lean over the side, scan the surface of the water, then scream when he surfaces. He thrusts out an arm, and I reach for his hand, only the boat leaps forward as Luca shifts into gear. My fingers brush his, then he's gone, under the water. The wake of the boat fills the space where he'd been.

"No," I scream, "No, no, no."

To find out what happens next read Mafia Queen here

FREE BOOKS

Claim your FREE copy of Mafia Heir the prequel to Mafia King

Claim your FREE billionaire romance

Claim your FREE paranormal romance book HERE

More books by L. STEELE

More Books by Laxmi

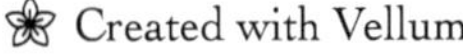

Created with Vellum

ABOUT THE AUTHOR

Hello, I'm L. Steele. I love to take down alphaholes. I write romance stories with douche canoes who meet their match in sassy, curvy, spitfire women :) I also write dark sexy paranormal romance as NY Times bestseller Laxmi Hariharan.

Married to a man who cooks as well as he talks :) I live in London.

Claim your FREE book => https://BookHip.com/ZMLZLG

Follow me on BookBub: https://www.bookbub.com/profile/l-steele

Follow on Goodreads: https://www.goodreads.com/authorlsteele

PPS: I am dying to meet YOU! Join my secret Facebook Reader Group and say HI => http://smarturl.it/TeamLaxmi

Spotify: https://open.spottily.com/user/q3x3wn4pjyk7d6ntq4oqplgdo

All my audiobooks => https://www.subscribepage.com/laxmiaudiobooks

Follow my Pinterest boards => https://www.pinterest.co.uk/AuthorLSteele/boards/

Read my books=> https://readerlinks.com/mybooks/950

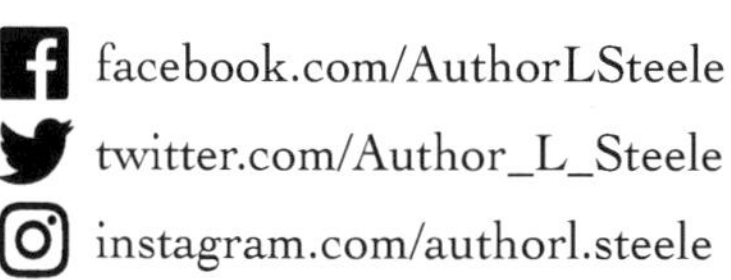